NIGHT KILLER

A. S. FRENCH

NEONOIR BOOKS

Bette Davis Eyes: Detective Flowers Short Story

Writing as Andrew. S. French

Science Fiction

The Time Traveller's Murder

The Mercy Sleep

Bodies

The Arcane Supernatural Thriller Series

Book one: The Arcane

Book two: The Arcane Identity

Book three: The Arcane Quest

Book four: The Arcane Ultimatum

The Ella Finn Fantasy Novella Series

Ella and the Elementals

Ella and the Multiverse

Ella and the Monsters

Ella and the Dreamers

Supernatural Short Stories

Dead Souls

The Shadow

Go to www.andrewsfrench.com for more information.

1 RUN

It started in her toes before surging through her body. Thousands of tiny bubbles of anticipation and anxiety flowed into her veins, so she was like a shaken-up bottle of Lucozade. She had to keep moving. If she stood still, the tension would explode from her. And they would catch her.

Big Ben struck ten times as she stumbled up Westminster Bridge Road, the concrete cutting into her skin as her fingers pressed into the wall. She glanced at the crowd gathered around the statue of Boadicea and Her Daughters, tourists taking snapshots and videos. Nobody noticed her; no cameras caught the tension in her eyes and the trembling of her lips.

The noise of mobile phones clicking away brought back a vivid flash of the last photo taken with her parents, the sound of her father's voice clamped inside her head. It was liquid Valium, calming to the point of comatose, each word more meaningless than the one before. By the end of each sentence, the girl was far less informed than if he'd said nothing.

Someone shouted behind her as her feet bounced off

the pavement, making her stumble and fall. Her breathing was heavy, the thump of her heart clawing at her ribs so intensely she thought it would rip its way from her body; all the time she was waiting for the hand on her shoulder, for the drag away from the tourists. The sculpted horses reared up, and she imagined their voices braying in her head. But it was her voice telling her what to do.

Get up. Get up. Keep running. You can escape.

She pushed upwards, forcing the adrenaline down inside her. She'd faced dread before, had handled pain daily, both physical and emotional.

Get over the river and slip between the shadows, into the warm, comforting, familiar darkness.

Traffic was busy on the road; it was the beginning of the week and hot for the night, but she'd expected more people and to hide inside a crowd. The continuous pulse in her ankle hampered her as she ran. She pushed everything from her mind and focused on moving, of running over the bridge, the smell of the river drifting up and washing across her face. The pounding in her legs was nothing to the muscle memory buzzing through the scar below her knee: a cut from a piece of glass when she was six. Twelve years later, the pain hadn't left her.

Fireworks exploded above as she glanced back for the shadow searching for her. Strangers were heading the other way, but she never considered asking them for help.

A giant sculpted lion peered at her as she turned onto the Queen's Walk. Birds swooped past as the breeze resurrected memories of the family she'd abandoned. She swept the sweat from her eyes, the liquid stinging at her. She kept on running, never looking back, trying to ignore the sights of the capital. The perspiration returned as the image of her mother clawed at her brain, scolding her daughter for not understanding the fundamentals of human existence.

There was a telephone box on her right, a blaze of memory obscuring her parents as she remembered her first night in London and sleeping inside a similar contraption. She'd kept her feet pressed against the glass to stop people forcing their way inside. How she wished she could return to that time.

She believed living on the streets that year had toughened her up and given her the skills to spot peril when it was near, but when her reason for existing was to seek danger, maybe she only had herself to blame for this. She'd skirted around the crime, the drug abuse, the violence, and the prostitution; had grown more confident with every risky escapade she survived: survived and thrived. She'd done it so many times before.

Which is why she knew she'd do it again, no matter this was the greatest challenge she'd faced so far in the city.

This is why I came here.

A smile leapt across her face as her feet pounded over the pavement, the adrenalin flowing through her legs to match the new-found confidence in her head. There was no sound behind her, only the noise of the blood pumping through her body.

A sleuth of furry bears gazed at her from a shop window as she turned right. The girl dodged between buildings, and jumped over discarded pizza boxes, broken bottles, and squashed cans; every time her feet hit the concrete, an electric buzz shot through her. Her heart tore at her ribs as she kept going, falling around the corner and into the shadows she hoped would hide her. The burger and fries from earlier clawed at her throat, forcing their way from her mouth and all over the wall, a technicolour yawn which left her dizzy.

She wiped at her face, knowing this was more than fleeing from certain capture; this was trying to run from her mother's fate again. She pushed her shoulder into the brick, pressing at the graffiti, her mind clawing at the haunting images of her mother.

The girl squirmed into the blanket of darkness, her breath erupting in short bursts as she paused for her pursuer to pass. She waited and waited, one eternity turning into another until fifteen minutes had flown by when she removed the fingers from her beating chest, and stared at them in the moonlight, surprised to see what was under her nails. She was about to remove the debris when different digits clutched at her throat and pulled her further into the gloom.

2 SOUND OF MUSIC

The Brood was an old converted church, stained-glass windows and pews included, sandwiched between an art gallery and a trendy restaurant, modelled as part Bukowski and part Chelsea Hotel. Along both sides of the street were pubs, dive bars and craft and art shops. The outside was timeworn and magnificent: three storeys high, with walls and ledges adorned with menacing gargoyles of all shapes and sizes. The entrance was a splendid arch which intensified the building's beauty; it was the last place I expected to be on a Monday night. And I couldn't remember the last time I'd been to a gig.

My father had been a compulsive concert goer; he loved folk music and jazz, and it gave him the chance to get away from my mother: she hit the bottle while he danced himself dizzy. I stayed in my room, happy in the fact he was out. I wasn't sure if my lifelong hatred of jazz was down to him or not. Once he got past his forties, he kept obsessive records of every gig he attended, including photos and plenty of video clips. Sometimes, when one of his favourite tunes came on the radio or TV, or I heard it in a shop or bar, the sound overwhelmed my brain and transported me back to the family home. I didn't expect tonight's entertainment to resurrect any childhood memories, so I pushed him from my head and led the girls inside, imaging him scowling at me for taking my teenage daughter and her friends to a rock show. Sometimes his voice lingered not only in my head, but in other places as well.

The venue smelt of stale booze and yesterday's sweat, with the stage at the rear and the bar opposite. Posters advertising future gigs covered the walls. A gigantic mural filled the ceiling: a ferocious-looking wildcat baring its teeth, the name of the club written inside its blood-red mouth. The Brood reminded me of a low-budget horror movie Abbey nagged me to watch only a few months back, with Oliver Reed at his maniacal best, while the main actress eats her afterbirth and little people clones beat grandparents and young schoolteachers to death with mallets. Was I a good mother for letting her see stuff like that? And here I was with her at a rock gig.

Still, the excitement in Abbey's eyes made me feel good. We hadn't been getting along for a bit, and I hoped this could bring us together. The last twelve months had been trying for both of us, and Abbey appeared to be drifting from me.

'You grab a spot down the front, and I'll get the drinks.'

She laughed with her friends as they pushed their way through the crowd. There were fifty or sixty in the venue, and I was one of the oldest. Most were women and girls, which surprised me.

'The Hex Pistols are at the Brood on Monday night.' Abbey had shouted this at me when I'd got in from work on Saturday, my head full of details most people would have nightmares about: the paedophile ring and their victims discovered in North London; the bloke with his ear bitten off in a café; the couple posing as social workers around Westminster duping pensioners out of money; and the gruesome sight of a body found in a Camden flat which had lain there undiscovered for weeks. The image of that was terrible and the smell even worse. These things spiralled through my mind like chapters on a warped DVD.

I'd grabbed a beer from the fridge, noticing one missing, and stared at Abbey.

'The Sex Pistols broke up years ago, love.' Abbey scowled at me, hating me using terms of endearment for her. She narrowed her gaze and pouted.

'It's the Hex Pistols, a four-piece feminist group protesting about patriarchy and inequality.'

The beer warmed and chilled my throat.

'That sounds fantastic, Abbey.'

I don't think she got the sarcasm, her eyes sparkling and growing wider.

'We can go then?'

Her happiness wiped the grime from my thoughts. I couldn't disappoint her again, and perhaps I'd enjoy the gig. And it would be an opportunity to spend quality time with my daughter. That's why I was now standing amongst the gloom and the sweat on Monday night.

What she hadn't mentioned was her friends joining us. I didn't know the lofty girl with the ruby hair, Bella, but Francine West was Abigail's latest best mate and wouldn't have looked out of place in a Dickens novel. She sported a red coat, possibly stolen from a Chelsea pensioner, and carried a silver cane. She was five foot tall, but the hat added to her height, wearing it not for effect, but to hide something. I'd met her in our kitchen two weeks ago, and the poor kid was quick to tell me she had alopecia.

The three of them strode to the front of the stage while I headed to the bar. I got the drinks, cokes for the girls and a bottle of Desperado for me. The barman poured the tequila fuelled beer into a plastic glass. I glared at him.

'No glass allowed on the dance floor,' he said through broken teeth.

'I'm not going to dance with it.'

'No glass allowed on the dance floor,' he repeated.

Around me, people drank cocktails through paper straws. The dullness behind his eyes told me it was pointless trying to explain the irony to him, but how would I carry four soft plastic glasses down to the girls?

Francine came to my rescue.

'Do you need some help, Ms Flowers?'

I smiled at her. 'Thanks, Francine.' I handed her two of the cokes. 'But you can call me Jennifer tonight.' I already felt like a dinosaur.

We made it down the front as the first band arrived on stage. I didn't catch their names, twin girls who looked a little older than Abbey and her friends. Each of them sat behind a set of drums - there were no other instruments - and belted out tunes blending modern rap with what must have been their African heritage. The teenagers loved it, and so did I. They played for thirty minutes and then left with a flurry of appreciation from the crowd.

'We need more drinks, Mum.' Abbey grinned at me. The girls had finished their cokes, but I hadn't touched my drink. I gave her some money and kept a careful eye on them as they strode to the bar.

It wasn't long before the next band arrived on stage, three young women playing keyboards, no guitars or drums. Most of the crowd swayed to the music, with no pause between songs as each tune merged into another. People swung around like hyperactive bumblebees, with their arms and legs going everywhere. I stood and watched Abbey and the girls joining in, letting their enjoyment wash away any thoughts I had of being a detective inspector in the Metropolitan Police.

Before the band finished, I downed my drink and slipped to the toilet. The teenagers were already on their third plastic glass of coke when I returned, and I wondered what damage I was doing to their health. When the Hex Pistols appeared, Abbey and her friends downed their drinks, content to dance the night away.

The Pistols were a four-piece, older than the other groups, brimming with confidence and energy even before they started. Then they made an unusual announcement.

'All the ladies to the front,' the lead singer said. Women and girls around me cheered, smiles beaming across the faces of Abbey and her mates, while the few blokes near us looked confused.

Abbey leant into me, raising her voice so I heard her above the din.

'They do this at every gig, so all the women and girls can mosh together without getting punched and groped.'

It sounded like a magnificent idea, but one bloke next to us instantly switched from confused to angry.

'I'm not moving,' he shouted while his companions headed to the back. The singer tried her best to explain to him what the aim was, but he either didn't get it or didn't care. 'You've got my dosh so I can stand where I want.'

I clenched my fist and considered whether I should intervene and put Abbey and her friends at risk. I didn't have to think about it for too long: the boos started instantly, coming from the rest of the men in the venue before every-one, except me, joined in. It energised Abbey and the girls, who lifted their arms and pointed at the guy shrinking into his skin. He was close enough for me to see his eyes darken and his lips curl into his teeth.

The band stared at him, and I assumed this wasn't the first time they'd encountered this, but they didn't shame him. I wondered if he understood such a thing, but he knew they'd beaten him with no person raising a finger. Well, apart from Abbey and her mates pointing at him. He scowled at them, and me, before scuttling away. I didn't know if he slunk to the back or left, but a mighty cheer erupted when the band began.

The music was noisy, angry, sensitive, sentimental, and nostalgic in a way I guessed most of the kids wouldn't recognise. I slipped to the side to find support from the wall since I'd stood around for more than an hour. I watched the girls, observing the pure, expansive joy spread across their faces; had I ever seen Abbey as happy as this before?

Memories of my first gig flooded back, with me squeezed between a sweaty, beery bunch of blokes and gazing at Goldfrapp when I was fifteen. My parents didn't know I'd left the house since I'd climbed through the bedroom window earlier that night. I went to the show on my own, and it was exhilarating. Now, watching Abbey and her friends, I wondered where my youth had gone.

The band was energetic, the three guitarists bouncing across the stage in perpetual motion, while the drummer beat the skins to within an inch of their lives. The music was raucous and groovy, and I recognised one tune, a cover of Blondie's *One Way or Another*, which brought the house down at the end. There was no encore.

After they'd finished, and the crowd had wiped the sweat from their bodies, Abbey burst towards me.

'Wasn't that fantastic, Mum!'

Whatever energy the band had, they'd transmitted some of it into my daughter as if they'd plugged her into the wall and their vitality flowed directly into her veins. Francine and Bella were in a daze, their eyes gaping and mouths wide in enormous smiles.

'Yes, Abbey.'

Before I added anything, she grabbed my hand and dragged me to the back of the room where a small section of the audience loitered around the merchandise stand.

'Can I have a shirt, Mum?'

How could I refuse? I glanced at her mates, who were still smiling, but with hands stuffed into pockets and tiny bits of disappointment behind their eyes.

'Do you all want one, girls?'

I made friends for life then. Francine and Bella swamped me with thanks as Abbey's face lit up like a crashed UFO. Was it this easy to be a proper parent?

The teenagers moved to the table to gaze at the shirts. They spoke to the band, who had made a swift journey from the stage to the merchandise. I handed the money over for three tops with the band's name and logo on them, the words with a blazing pair of eyes behind the letters.

While the girls picked their tops, the phone vibrated in my pocket. It was eleven o'clock, and I knew it wouldn't be good news. I accepted the call.

'You better not ruin my night, Jack.'

'You needn't come, Jen, but you have to be informed.'

I glanced at Abbey as she removed her jacket and put her fresh shirt over the one she was wearing; Francine and Bella did the same with their purchases. My daughter kept the change for herself.

'I'm listening.'

'There's a body of a young girl, found near the river.'

I didn't have to ask him if it involved foul play; we wouldn't be talking about it otherwise. His words lingered in my head as I stared at Abbey and her friends.

'Text me the location, Jack, and I'll be there in twenty minutes.'

I put the phone away and smiled at three happy teenagers, all of them wearing the same Hex Pistols shirt.

Francine grinned at me. 'What do you think, Ms Flowers?'

I stopped myself from swearing at her.

'Get your things together, girls, we're going on a trip.'

3 DUNGEONS AND DRAGONS

Abbey had begged me to take her to the London Dungeon for her twelfth birthday, and even though I didn't fancy being crammed inside tight hallways with tourists and teenagers for two hours, I gave in. Her favourite part was the Tyrant Boat ride, an excursion down the Thames to the Tower for execution. This wasn't because she had some morbid fascination with death or capital punishment, but because I got drenched that day. Now, the liquid bothering me as I returned to the Dungeon was the pool of blood I strode towards.

The London Eye stood to the side of me, Big Ben on the other, and a small boat trundled over the river as I approached Jack. The summer heat lay heavy in the air and on my shoulders, my partner wiping sweat from his forehead. Surprise filled his eyes.

'Is Abbey in the car with you?'

I told him about the concert. 'I've left Constable Sutton monitoring them.' I'd avoided looking at the body yet. 'If this takes too long, I'll get an officer to take them home.'

Athena Temple, the Head of Forensic Science for the

Met Police, waved at me from behind Jack. She wore a full dinner suit and had a cane in her hand, strangely similar to the one Francine had with her in the car. She turned to her team and handed the stick to one of them. Further back was the entrance to the London Dungeon.

'Enter at your peril,' Athena said as Jack and I joined her. At her feet was what I presumed to be a covered body. I ignored her little joke and spoke to my partner.

'Who discovered the victim?'

He pointed at a bloke on a bike a few yards away. The man was speaking to a uniformed officer, his eyes wide and hands trembling. Other constables cordoned off the area, keeping back the growing multitude. It was only Monday, but plenty of Londoners were littering the streets and enjoying a drink as the sirens blurted down the road. I watched them, my fellow citizens in this city, wondering how many looked upon my colleagues and me as the enemy and viewed us as a necessary evil: policing by consent and not imposition. As I scanned the crowd, there was a mixture of curiosity and anger in them. Was the killer standing there? I stared at the mass, their mood swirling underneath the frozen surface of their faces. I witnessed no flicker of emotion in them, no evidence of shock or horror. Perhaps the public had become so immune to violent death, it meant little to them anymore, even when they got as close to it as this.

'He was cycling home when he saw that.' Jack nodded at the Dungeon wall. We strode over together, and Athena Temple joined us.

'It's needed a lick of paint for a while, but not like this.'

Beyond the statue of a grim-looking robed man, at the left of the entrance was a large red stain running down the concrete and onto the floor. It led to a covered body. I turned to the Head of Forensics.

'Have you looked at the body?'

Her eyes sparkled as she peered at me; strands of molten gold tumbled from her scalp, cascading down her back as she pushed out her shoulders and wiped something from her lips. She was close to me now, and I smelt the aroma of mustard drifting from her coat. She must have caught me searching for stains on her clothes.

'I was on my second course when I got the call, and yes, I've examined the poor girl.' Athena Temple's tastes in everything from food to relationships were expensive, and she never relished being interrupted when enjoying the pleasures of life. 'Do you want to see under the cover, Jennifer?'

'That's what I'm here for.'

We returned to the victim; Jack knelt and did the honours. He removed the plastic sheet and, no matter how many times I'd seen this before, I clutched onto my chest. Some coppers get hardened to murder scenes, but not me.

Jack stood as Athena spoke.

'It looks like someone grabbed the girl near the Dungeon entrance or dragged her there. Then they repeatedly smashed her head against the wall.' The face was missing, replaced with a bloody pulp. 'Then they hauled the body here.'

Her words stuck in my mind, creating a terrible image of those events. I scanned the area, looking past the gathering crowd and towards the river.

'There are no witnesses?'

'None so far,' Jack said.

I focused on the girl. She wore jeans, a dark shirt, and a light jacket. From her physique, she appeared to be no older than a teenager, and my thoughts went to Abbey and her friends in the car. I reached down for the cover and pulled it over the body. I looked at my partner.

'Do we know who she is?' I should have asked who she was, but I wasn't ready to think of her in the past tense; it would come soon, but not yet.

Jack shook his head. 'She had nothing on her, no ID, or cards, or phone.'

I couldn't imagine a teenager in the modern world without a mobile. Perhaps whoever killed her stole it. We peered at the spot where her face should have been under the cover.

'Her fingerprints might be on file.' I spoke more in hope than expectation.

'The forensic dentist may have more luck,' Athena said.

Her words surprised me. 'You think there's enough for a match?'

She shrugged. 'It looks to be our best bet at the moment. Plus, teeth are incredibly durable. They can withstand heat to 1,200 degrees, so there should be something for one of our colleagues to work their magic.'

We moved from the body. Athena re-joined her team and coordinated the gathering of the rest of the forensic evidence. Jack and I stared at the crowd as they peered at us. He nodded at my car down the road.

'Are you taking the girls home now?'

'I'll get Constable Sutton to drop them off, and then head to the morgue for the autopsy.'

'This can wait until the morning, Jen.'

'How many cases are we working?'

He paused for a second as if pondering the question, but he already had the answer.

'There's the gangland shooting, the domestic violence

incident which escalated to murder, and the body found in the Thames two days ago.'

He was right on all accounts. 'This means we won't have a lot of time tomorrow, so since we're both wide awake, we might as well get a head start tonight.'

Jack squinted at me. 'Was that a joke?'

'Nope.' The late-night summer warmth disappeared in an instant, and a chill breeze leapt from the river and pounced at my flesh.

'If that's the case, you'll still need a pathologist to be working this late.'

'I've already texted Dr Cooper. She'll meet us there once Athena gets the body to the morgue.'

Jack pulled at the top of his shirt, and I recognised it was nothing to do with the sudden drop in temperature. Ever since his wife had kicked him out for having a non-physical relationship with a serial killer, he'd been like a lost puppy when around women of a certain age. And Dr Samantha Cooper, forty to his thirty-six, had been getting him hot under the collar for a few months. I assumed she knew of his infatuation and did everything she could to wind him up. She'd taken to dropping into the station unannounced once or twice a week, allegedly to pass on autopsy reports, but I guessed these visits were to mess with Jack's head. I hadn't worked out yet whether she did it to punish him or because she liked him.

He tried to hide it, but his eyes lit up when I mentioned her name.

'You're right. That makes sense, Jen.'

Behind us, the forensic team loaded the body into a vehicle.

'You can go home, Jack. I'll take care of this.' It was my turn to mess with his head.

He rubbed his hands before putting one on my shoulder.

'I can't let you do all the work, partner.' He glanced over at my car. 'Are you going to tell Abbey you're off to the morgue?'

'Of course. Give me two minutes, and then we'll go in your car.'

I left him with a smile on his face; no doubt he was already imagining Samantha Cooper with her arms fiddling around in blood and guts. Constable Sutton was speaking to the girls when I got there as if she was one of their long-lost friends. Abbey seemed excited.

'Mum, did you know Sarah's going to see Bella Boo next week?'

I had no idea who that was. 'Is that Betty's sister?'

My daughter, her mates, and the constable stared at me as if I was a relic. The teenagers pulled faces while Sutton replied.

'Bella Boo is a Stockholm-via LA DJ who weaves a comfortable ambience to escape from heartbreak and loneliness using atmospheric and techno sounds to create a safe space of ambient drone and quietly groovy jazz-flecked compositions.'

I glared at her as if she was speaking a foreign language. 'Is that so, Sarah?'

Heat spread across her face as her lips trembled. 'Yes, ma'am.'

Francine leant over Bella in the car and poked her head through the open window. 'Has there been a murder, Ms Flowers?' The excitement I'd observed at the gig had returned.

I ignored the question.

'Girls, Constable Sutton will take you home.' I turned to

Sutton. 'And then she'll pick me up when I text her where I am.' I didn't want Abbey to know I'd be at the morgue. There'd been a few instances lately where I'd caught her watching morbid programmes on TV about how famous pop stars had died, and I was reluctant to give her any strange ideas.

'Where are you going, Mum?'

The excitement had left her voice, and she sounded tired; I guessed she must have burnt up all her energy earlier in the night. At least the summer holidays had started, with no school tomorrow and for another six weeks.

I nudged Constable Sutton to one side, giving her a look which meant I'd be having a word with her later about what she'd said to my daughter.

'There are a few things I need to finish with Jack, love, and then I'll be home.'

I waited for her to squirm at the term of endearment, especially in front of her friends. Instead, she jumped out and threw her arms around me. Shock ran through every inch of my body. I couldn't remember the last time we'd touched, never mind hugged. I was speechless when she pulled away.

'Thanks for tonight, Mum. It was fantastic.' She grabbed at her brand new Hex Pistols top as she got into the car.

'Yeah, Ms Flowers, thanks for a great night, and the shirt,' Francine and Bella shouted as I returned to Jack. The uniformed officers had dispersed the crowd with no commotion. I reached inside my jacket for cigarettes, which hadn't been there for at least three years.

Jack waved at the girls as Sutton drove away.

'They seemed happy. Is everything okay between you and Abbey?'

Even though he had his fair share of personal problems to deal with, Jack was the only person I talked to about the Flowers household's growing tension. My fingers slipped from the invisible past in my pocket as we headed to his car. I watched the last of the light disappear into the Thames.

'Tonight could be a fresh start for us.'

First, I had to peer at the dead.

4 BODY OF EVIDENCE

Welcome to a world of tile, stainless steel, and porcelain.

Morgues in hospitals are usually in the basement or lowest floor. Often they're close to the kitchens, which I've always thought unfortunate, having food next door to the dead. They'll have access from the loading dock area, so the funeral homes can pick up the deceased. We were at the Iain West Forensic Suite, an extension to the Westminster Public Mortuary. Jack drove us, but we could have walked there from the London Dungeon in twenty minutes.

It was my first time there, and it impressed me. Most morgues have two areas: the coolers where the bodies are stored, and the autopsy suite for the examinations. Some will also have an office. This facility had a CCTV viewing area with a live link to the post-mortem room to witness forensic pathologists at work. With DNA and fabric transfer issues, the fewer people present, the less chance of contamination and the more reliable the evidence.

Jack appeared pleased not to go anywhere near the autopsy table, but I wasn't one of those officers who needed to isolate themselves from the bodies; being near the victim helped me remember my responsibilities. As long as I wore the right protective clothing, and kept a reasonable distance, there would be no problems regarding contamination of evidence. And Dr Samantha Cooper liked to keep her coppers close at hand; especially Detective Inspector Jack Monroe.

She marched into the viewing area flanked by two assistants. Cooper was a tall woman who wouldn't have looked out-of-place lying on one of the autopsy tables where she worked. Her skin appeared to have only a passing acquaintance with sunlight, and her dark hair might have been borrowed from the cover of a gothic horror novel. Her gaze was like Medusa's, with deep brown eyes ready to freeze you on the spot. Fortunately, she had a sense of humour which could fell a herd of elephants at ten paces.

'Well, if it isn't my favourite pair of detectives, Flowers and Monroe. No box that Pandora ever opened could bring so much trouble as you two.' She dismissed her assistants with a wave of the hand, and I watched them on the viewing screen enter the autopsy room. Cooper grinned at Jack. 'That's a fetching jacket you're wearing, Inspector, but you must slip into one of these to join me at the table.'

She opened a locker and grabbed two pairs of hospital gowns, plastic gloves and hats. Jack's face shimmered an intense shade of pink as he struggled with his words.

'No, we don't need to be inside, do we?' He turned to me. 'You can go, Jen.'

I took the garments from Cooper, removed my jacket, and got ready.

'I think Sam wants you there, Jack.' She stared at me. 'Don't you, Dr Cooper?'

She rolled her eyes and put on her protective equipment. 'It sounds like the perfect ménage à trois, Inspector.'

Jack sighed as he scrambled into his gear, and we followed her into the autopsy room. I watched him watching her, his gaze drifting from her face and down to her hands. I wondered if he considered how many entrails those gloved fingers had rummaged through over the years; and if he imagined entwining his with hers sometime soon.

The initial thing to hit you when you go inside is the smell: an aroma of strong cleansers and preservative chemicals. I noticed the signs dotted around the walls: ALL BODY AND BODY PARTS, INCLUDING FOETUSES, MUST BE SIGNED OUT; NO EATING OR DRINKING IN THE EXAMINING ROOM; and my favourite - PLEASE PLACE BODIES IN COOLER FEET FIRST. Someone had even typed THANK YOU underneath the request.

An assistant wheeled a stainless steel autopsy table over, while the other brought the body across on a gurney; then the two of them lifted her onto the table. A plastic sheet covered her. Cooper whipped it away like a magician at a show.

'Here's one I prepared earlier.'

Nobody laughed, but we all understood why she did it; if you didn't gain a sense of humour while doing this job, no matter how macabre, you'd soon lose most of your sanity.

'You've been busy.' They'd cleaned the remains of the face of blood and flesh, peeling back the skin to reveal the skull and quite a lot of the teeth and jaw considering the damage done to her head.

Dr Cooper's eyes glittered like burnt cigarettes. 'I was on a date when I got your text, Jennifer.'

Jack's shoulders shrank, but I was curious and a little apologetic.

'I'm sorry, Sam, but I guess even romance has to wait for murder.'

Cooper instructed her assistants to remove the clothing from the body.

'Oh, there was no romance involved, believe me.' They placed the items into separate, clear plastic bags. 'He was dim and duller than a wet afternoon in Leeds.' She knew that's where I was from. 'If he didn't exist, no one would miss him. A man so forgettable even his shadow ignored him.'

The assistants finished their work, leaving the body naked.

'Was this another of your famous blind dates?'

She picked up a marker pen as she considered the question.

'You'd think I'd have learnt by now about dating lawyers, wouldn't you?'

She turned to scribble on the whiteboard behind her. There are boards to write information on while doing the autopsy because the pathologist's hands are too bloody to use paper. Even if you're recording it, it's handy to see the info.

'Perhaps you should widen your scope of romantic partners, Sam?'

She rolled the pen between her fingers.

'You mean dip my wick into the gene pool which makes up the Metropolitan Police Department?'

The glint in her eye shined so much I didn't know if she was having another dig at Jack or flirting with me.

'I doubt even you would become that desperate, Doc.'

She laughed out loud, an ominous sound which made her assistants wince.

'Nobody would be as bad as the bloke tonight.' There was no point in stopping her talking about it; this was one of her coping mechanisms. I knew from experience it helped her focus. 'He wore a suit which appeared to have shrunk in the wash, the sleeves a quarter away up his arms, the jacket tight around his chest, the trousers so high on his legs you could see he had no socks on. Everything was the wrong size for him: his clothes, this world, and his personality.' A fire burned in her eyes. 'And when he opened his mouth, my God.' If she hadn't been wearing gloves and holding the pen, she might have slapped herself in the forehead.

'Not the brightest, then?'

'Lawyers, lawyers, lawyers. They spend so much time twisting lies into their version of the truth, they don't understand what's right or wrong anymore.' The bitterness of her divorce had never left her. 'A group of people yet to find a principal they wouldn't trade to advance their careers. And this one; if he was a meal at a restaurant, you'd send him back.'

Cooper let out a long breath, her assistants a safe distance from her, while Jack gazed at her as if desperate to be the next specimen for examination or her opprobrium. She wrote on the board as I spoke.

'How old is she?'

'The victim appears to be a teenage girl, maybe no older than eighteen. Caucasian.' She put down the pen. 'Apart from the obvious damage to the face, we might get this finished in record quick time tonight.' I assumed that information was more for her assistants than Jack and me. 'Much easier than the case we had yesterday.'

My partner found his voice. 'What case?'

Cooper gave him her widest smile, and I wondered how weak his knees were.

'We brought a woman in last night in forty pieces. Her husband, a cane farmer, had chopped her up after he killed her. He was about to make sausages from her when some of your colleagues arrived. She's in the refrigerated unit.' She nodded to our right. 'At least we identified her, but not this poor girl.'

She examined the victim's front, weighing and measuring and making notes on the board, and using a small recording device with her team. An assistant took instructions from Cooper to record everything on a body diagram. There wasn't much to record, apart from the head's damage, until they turned her over.

'Damn!' Jack said.

There were long red marks along the back of the arms, the legs, and down her spine. They appeared fresh. One assistant took photographs, while the other measured the length of the scars. I spoke to Cooper while she recorded her notes.

'Are those recent?'

'Made within the last week, I'd say. Inspect them, Jennifer, and tell me what you see.'

I leant towards the victim, peering at the back of the girl's arms without touching them. Then I scrutinised her legs and spine; there were four vertical lines identical in length on five different parts of the rear of her body.

'They look like barcodes.'

Cooper nodded at me. 'It's as if she was a commodity bought and used.'

The assistants took more photos and video while Cooper described the marks into the recorder. Jack sidled up to me while they toiled.

'Perhaps she worked the streets, and this was a rendezvous which went wrong?'

I looked at the girl's back, and those scars burned indelible images into my mind.

'It's hard to tell, Jack, but her clothes don't look like something a sex worker would wear. The violence used to batter her against that wall is more than an assignation turned nasty. This was personal.' I observed Cooper and her team do their work and thought of Abbey and her mates. 'Hopefully, we'll know more when we learn her identity.' Would there be parents and siblings to inform, friends and colleagues who'd been wondering what had happened to her?

Cooper picked up the right hand and examined the fingernails.

'There's something else.' She looked over at her assistants. 'Is there any mention in the scene of crime report about anything under the girl's nails?'

The taller assistant went to the laptop on the opposite bench and scrolled through the screen.

'There's nothing here, Dr Cooper.'

I returned to the body. 'What is it, Sam?'

She had a pair of tweezers in her hand, ready to pull out the trapped foreign object, only waiting for the assistant with the camera to come and video the motion. When they did, Cooper placed the thin metal under the nail and removed the item.

'What's that?' Jack said.

Cooper put it inside a small plastic bag. 'No need to put this under a microscope since I recognise it.' She laid the tweezers on the bench and held the bag up, so Jack and I saw its contents. 'It's a piece of audiotape, from an old cassette, used to record sound.' She handed it to me.

'Why would a teenage girl have this under her fingernails?'

Cooper took it back from me. 'That, Jennifer, is why you're the detective and I'm just a lowly pathologist.'

Jack was the closest he'd been to the body since we'd entered the room. 'Is there any more of it?'

Cooper shook her head. 'Nope. I've checked the other nails. Of course, there are her toenails.' She did a quick inspection and found nothing unusual. Cooper rubbed her hands. 'Are you staying for the internal examination?'

As she spoke, I received a text; Constable Sutton was waiting outside with my car.

'We'd better go back, Sam. I'll read your report in the morning.'

The clock on the wall behind her told me we were already into Tuesday. I had no desire to hang around and watch her cutting through this girl's rib cage, and then digging out the remains of her brain. I assumed Jack would be happy to miss that.

Dr Cooper had a saw in her hand as we made our goodbyes.

'Your colleagues took her fingerprints earlier, Jennifer. One of my staff sent X-rays of the teeth and jaw to the Missing Persons department. Hopefully, we'll have her identity for you soon.'

We dropped our protective clothing into a bin. Sutton was sitting in the car when we got outside. I reached for those non-existent cigarettes again as I spoke to Jack.

'You better ask her out before some dapper lawyer snaps her up, partner.' The chill of the wind nipped at my throat. He ignored my jab.

'How do we prioritise this with the gangland shooting,

the domestic violence incident turned to murder and the body in the river?'

It was a good question, but easy to answer.

'We know who the culprits are for all three, even if we're still adding evidence for convictions to the case files.' I twisted the collar up on my jacket, but it was little protection against the relentless wind coming off the Thames. 'Successful delegation is part of the job, Jack, and I'm sure we can find some willing constables to pound the streets while we focus on this girl.'

I smiled at Constable Sutton as I got into the back of the car and allowed myself to be chauffeured home for once.

5 TOWER OF STRENGTH

Abbey was asleep when I rose at seven. I'd popped my head around the door in the early hours of the morning, and she was slumbering on her bed, still wearing the Hex Pistols shirt. She'd looked so content, and I'd left her to rest. Now I was in the Murder Investigation Room, and Constable Jackie Grealish was pinning the crime scene photos to a board. Jack was speaking to Detective Chief Inspector Sandra Merson, the Senior Investigating Officer, while Constable Sarah Sutton brought me a cup of coffee I hadn't asked for. I took it from her.

'Is this you trying to get into my good books?'

She was ashen-faced as if she'd had little sleep, the lines around her eyes darker and thicker than they should have been at her age. I was thirty-six years old, but fifteen years on the force made me feel a decade older, and God knows how old other people imagined I looked. When I reluctantly peered into a mirror, I assumed it was my mother in her fifties gazing back at me. And that wasn't a pleasant image or thought.

'No, ma'am.' She glanced over at Jack and the DCI. 'I guessed you might need some extra sugar, considering.'

I didn't ask her, *considering what*. 'How long has the DCI been here?'

'She arrived before everyone else, ma'am. Constable Grealish and I got here just after eight, Inspector Monroe a few minutes later. They've been talking for a while.'

The coffee warmed my lips. 'Do we have the autopsy report and forensics from the scene?'

'Printed and on your desk, ma'am, and copies emailed to you.'

'Have you read them?' She nodded. 'Summarise them for me.'

'The blood and DNA are the victim's. There are no witnesses. Grealish and I are going out to check for any CCTV footage. Dr Cooper states the scars on the body are five days old. She was still waiting on a response from the Missing Persons Bureau when she sent her report over. That was at two o'clock this morning.'

'We have a name.' DCI Merson strode towards me with Jack in tow like a sick puppy; I wondered if she'd been giving him a telling off when I arrived. Her teeth were whiter than a hospital wall and smelt not too dissimilar. For a woman who should have taken early retirement six months ago, she was hanging around like an unwanted guest at a funeral. She was like cocaine, always getting up someone's nose; usually mine.

I inhaled coffee to clear my nostrils. 'Is this from the dental x-rays?'

'It is, Inspector Flowers. Our victim is Mary Witney, eighteen years old, originally from St Albans but moved to London last year.' She stared at my partner. 'I gave Jack all the details.'

I continued to stare at her. 'What about the other cases we're working on?'

She waved her hand in the air. 'I'm sure you'll cope, Inspector, you are our star detective, are you not?' She left the room without another word. Just being next to her had chilled my drink; I put it onto a desk and turned to my partner.

'You two seemed pally there.'

He shrugged. 'I think she dislikes me less than you, that's all.'

He was correct. 'Do we have an address for Mary Witney?'

Jack grabbed his phone. 'We do. And it's my turn to drive.'

He was right again, and it annoyed me.

TOWER HAMLETS WAS ONCE London's hipster hub, but now the cool kids had moved South and left fresh-faced bankers, sightseers and full-bearded freelancers behind. But the tourists still came: Brick Lane and Bethnal Green pulled in crowds of Friday night revellers, while Broadway Market and Columbia Road Flower Market were packed out with well-to-do thirty-somethings every weekend. I'd never enjoyed the area's social attractions, but Abbey spent plenty of time on Instagram to show me what I was missing.

Jack parked outside a Salvation Army church advertising a food bank. It wasn't nine-thirty, and there was already a queue waiting around the block; hunched-over women clutched small children who rubbed at their arms even though it was warm. Mixed between them were the old, and the dispossessed, the homeless and the desperate.

But if I glanced the other way, I had a clear view of Canary Wharf and the headquarters of some of the world's biggest banks. Volunteers brought boxes of donated foodstuff as we stood there and, I guessed, the chief executives in their ivory towers stretching into the London sky counted out their bonuses.

'It's by the church.' Jack pointed in the direction. 'It's a one-bedroomed flat.'

We were in the heart of London's East End and I wondered if the living conditions could be any worse in the country, never mind the city. Luxury apartments sold for millions; estate agents armed with shiny new catalogues described the area as "vibrant" and "edgy". This was estate-agent speak for "visible signs of poverty nearby" and the implicit assumption that some innovative property developers would gentrify the space in a few years. For now, we strode through a rundown neighbourhood with rubbish piled on the streets and dogs ready to snap at your ankles.

A large bloke with a face like a pufferfish waved at us near the flats. Sweat dripped from him like fat in a hot frying pan and the street stank of dried pizza and unwashed clothes. Jack approached him while I observed the twitching curtains and nervous eyes on the other side of the road. All the world's a stage, and we were walking straight across it; a real-life murder investigation for those addicted to true crime shows and detective fiction.

'Are you Arkwright, the landlord?'

He stuck out what I thought was a gloved hand until I got closer and saw it covered in thick hair.

'Are you the police?'

Jack ignored the hand and showed him his ID badge.

'Do you have the keys to Mary Witney's flat?'

He nodded. 'I'm not the landlord; I look after the

building for the owners.' He took us up the steps and opened up. 'You're lucky because they'll be knocking it down soon.'

The address we had for Mary Witney was on the fourth floor, so I walked towards the lift while speaking to him.

'Who's knocking it down, and why?'

He pointed at the metal door. 'That doesn't work. We'll take the stairs.' We followed him through the exit as Jack stifled a groan. Being kicked out of his house had done nothing positive for his lifestyle, and he'd put a few pounds on over the last six months. 'The building is owned by some corporate investment company. They want to replace it with luxury flats.'

'What will happen to all the residents?' Jack said through puffy breaths.

'They must be out by the end of the month.' The big man appeared to be in better condition than my partner. There was no need to ask what would happen to the tenants if they hadn't vacated the property by then.

We reached the fourth floor. 'Did you know Mary Witney?'

He shrugged. 'I met her when she moved in. The council paid her rent. If that was on time, I never saw her.'

Or any of the other tenants, I guessed. He opened the door and went to step inside before Jack stopped him.

'Best if you wait outside, Mr Arkwright.'

He didn't argue and stood to one side. We stepped in, and I closed the door behind me; then we put on protective covers for our hands and feet. The curtains were open, and a shaft of brilliant light cut the room in half. If I'd painted the walls black, the place couldn't have been any grimmer. The once frilly net drapes at the window were thick with grunge. The carpet stuck to my shoes as I moved forward, stepping over the upturned and damaged furniture. Books and magazines lay scattered over the floor, while someone had taken a sharp object to the two-seater sofa and chair and ripped them apart, spreading their insides across the carpet like vomited fabric.

The place stank of ammonia and bleach, with broken glass surrounding a smashed TV. I nodded to Jack, and then towards the bedroom. We'd expected nobody to be here, Mary Witney's name was the only one on the lease, but you never knew.

He placed his fingers on the door before pulling them away to show me the dirt on his gloves. Then he pushed it open with his foot. I followed him inside, discovering just as much mess: the bed ripped to shreds, the covers slashed and tossed over the floor. A small cupboard lay face down amongst the debris. We lifted it together, finding nothing but more grime. Had Mary Witney only had the clothes she wore when she died?

I flicked dust from my plastic covered fingers. 'Someone had a good time here.'

'There's just the bathroom to check.'

'Be my guest, Jack.'

I left him to it and strode to the window. If I opened it and stretched my neck out far enough, I would see the gilded towers of Canary Wharf. Instead, I glimpsed below and saw the crowd for the food bank growing longer. I glanced through the bedroom, wondering who had ransacked this place and if there was a connection to Mary Witney's murder.

That thought was lingering in my head when I caught my foot in one of the abandoned bedsheets, twisted my ankle and tumbled down. My fingers pushed into the floor as I banged my knee into the side of the bed. A stab of electricity rushed through my leg and into my gut.

The sound of my crashing brought Jack rushing into the room.

'Are you all right, Jen?' He held his hand out to me.

'It's only my wounded pride.'

I didn't mention the throb in my calf and took his offer of help. He was lifting me when I stopped halfway, attracted by the sight of the bottom of the bed, where I'd crashed into it, hanging off. There was something inside. As I got up, he noticed my hesitation.

'What's wrong?'

I brushed the filth from my trousers and pulled the broken wood away to reach in and retrieve a shoebox. It was heavy and I started to remove the lid.

'I wonder if this is what someone searched here for.'

Jack put his hand on my arm. 'It could be a bomb.'

I stopped the laughter in my throat. 'What makes you say that?'

'You never know with terrorists these days.'

I thought he was joking, but the startled gaze in his eyes told me he was serious.

But I wasn't taking him seriously. 'Do you want to leave?'

He shook his head. 'Go on, then.'

I placed the shoebox on the bed and removed the lid; inside was a cassette tape and recorder, one of those ancient ones from the eighties before recorded sound got smaller and digital. I picked up the tape.

'Why would a teenage girl have this hidden in her bed?'

'She had tape under her fingernails, remember.'

I did. I turned it over in my hand and checked either side. It didn't appear to be damaged, but someone had handwritten TAPE 1 on the back. I placed it on the bed and removed the cassette player/recorder from the box; the power cable was also there.

'My father had one of these at home and a collection of things he'd recorded from the radio.'

Jack peered at me through curious eyes. In all the years we'd known each other, I'd rarely spoken about my parents or childhood.

'Was the music any good?'

'He collected every jazz show he could find. I never listened to them.'

I took the cable and plugged one end into the socket near the bed and the other into the player. He seemed concerned.

'Shouldn't we wait until we get back to the station in case we damage it?'

'It's only a cassette, Jack, not a bomb.' I opened the lid and placed the tape into the machine. Then I hit play.

6 NOBODY'S DIARY

y name is Mary Witney. If you're listening to this tape, then I'm probably dead. This is my story, but I won't start at the beginning. I've always hated stories that follow a straight chronological order of I was born, then lived, and then died. I might be only eighteen, but I know that's not how life works. Some people are already dead when they crawl out of the womb; their circumstances prevent them from having a life worth living, usually because of their parents or family or their environment and lack of opportunities. And even if they have a decent childhood, avoiding the predators and the manipulators, they soon discover the promise of adulthood is all based on building blocks of falsehood and fantasy. There'll be none of that here.

I'll start with the memories of the man I cut up earlier. Two parts of his face lay in front of me, the nose sticking out at a strange angle, while the lips appeared transplanted from Mick Jagger. One of his arms seemed longer than the other, a cloud of freckles running from the elbow to his palm. He had a mark reminiscent of stigmata, and it reminded me of my younger days inside the cold and dank churches my mother dragged me to. He wore a Victorian waistcoat decorated with a gold pocket watch, the material comprising an eye-catching tartan. There was a stain on his trousers, a vibrant ruby red which could have been blood or wine.

The room stank of wet cardboard, and I pushed the jigsaw to the side. It was time to grow up.

The brutality of childhood and the indifference of parents; does this happen to us all? My father was six feet two and permanently angry; it meant his face existed in a constant flux where it was all eyes, mouth and nose blown up to twice their normal size. He looked like a cartoon character, minus the fun, constantly ready to explode.

When I was a kid, I'd collect bits of old bikes and make a proper bicycle. They were never sleek and stylish. And sometimes things fell off. There was always an element of danger. So it was for my old man's personality. He'd collected bits of ideas and thoughts over the years, and then stuck them together to form his mission in life, but what he'd gathered never fitted properly, and parts of his thinking fell away, so nothing made much sense to him. He was a living, walking jigsaw man, continually searching for that last piece to make him whole.

Mother avoided him wherever she could, his many frustrations taken out on her, while hers transferred to me. She was a complicated woman: someone who believed emotions a hindrance to a successful life and did her utmost to hammer home that message to me. When I was five or six, I found an injured bird in the back garden. I took it into our shed, put it into a box and looked after it for the next few days. I fed it, gave it drinks, and kept it warm. It was on the mend. And then she drowned it in the sink. She told me it wouldn't have survived in the wild and so she'd done it, and me, a favour. When she pulled it out, she used the same water to wash the cutlery and pots.

She believed a specific hierarchy to civilisation was built on three levels: at the bottom existed the disenfranchised scraping by on nothing and living in places cockroaches wouldn't go to die. Above them were the average middle-of-the-road Joes and Josephines who performed essential jobs like working in health care, or the shops, delivering food, or cleaning. At the top were the minority of the population, useless people contributing zero to society; exaggerated snake oil sellers making money off those doing the hard work.

I asked her where we as a family fitted into this structure, but her answer was for each of us to live only to be agents of change; according to her, existence was futile unless we made it better. It sounded good in theory, but her definition of better seemed unlikely to find its way into a standard dictionary.

They're both gone now, my parents, to their different places, but they have never left me. The memories bounce through my head as I rush from the flat and dodge the rats outside, and they aren't only of the four-legged kind. That creep Arkwright always lurks nearby, the smell of him making even the vermin sick. His excuses change every time: he's come to fix a leak or check the gas, or the neighbours have complained about me, or he promises me an extension on the lease, with less rent, if I do some favours for him.

'What favours?' I said. His grin was a snake crawling across his twisted face.

'You're too smart for your own good,' he's spit at me when I turn down his advances with a cutting quote from

Nietzsche or Louise Brooks. It's my fault I like to read, my fault I excelled at school, no matter how much it annoyed my father and humoured my mother. He told me I wasn't like other girls, the other kids, and he was right.

But that's enough about them. Time I focused on the two people I had to meet in the park. This was another of my risky encounters; that's what my therapist would have said to me: the one who recommended the jigsaws as therapy. However, I doubt she would have approved of the ones I'd bought from the internet of scenes from infamous horror movies.

My journey was uneventful; Mother would have hated it, Father would have raged at it. Her impatience and boredom would have forced her into action, driven her compulsion to do something extraordinary which would worry those around her; he would have drunk and ranted and spread his invective everywhere. They were in my head, and I needed to get them out, desperate to be free of their influence. But they would never leave, no matter how many times I used the pain to force them out.

So there I waited, fuelling my desperation again.

I sat in the park for an hour waiting for my new friends, my knuckles turning red from the strain. Why would they keep their promise to come for me, these people who I'd only seen behind masks, in those rooms and buildings where blood and pain strode hand in hand? Why was I anything to them when I was nothing to myself?

My fingers fiddled with my jacket. What if they decided they didn't need me when they arrived? What's the worst thing they could do to me? Blacklist me on the circuit? Then I'd have to move to another city, or maybe one of those small English villages where people keep their dirty secrets well hidden. I knew all about those.

Warm air wafted over me, the beams of sunlight glowing on my skin. Daffodils and roses bloomed everywhere, slicing through the freshly cut grass. Children played while adults idled away their time. I gazed at them, these seemingly happy families, and imagined a different me in a parallel universe.

Just when I'd given up, a hand fell on my shoulder. The shock of it consumed my breath, a surge of electricity exploding through every inch of me.

'Don't turn around,' a gruff male voice said.

'We can trust her,' this from a girl sounding younger than me.

'I know who you are,' I replied. 'You're Mr X and Missy.'

Their names were a facade and stupid, but an essential part of the world the three of us moved in.

'Put this on,' Missy said as her delicate fingers slipped over my shoulder to hand me a mask from a fancy dress party. The scars on her wrist were fresh and familiar. I took it and slid it over my face, the material sticking to my skin in the heat. How many masks had I worn in my life? One more wouldn't make any difference.

Mr X and Missy didn't speak again, so I turned to look at them; she was small and thin like me, while he was the opposite, over six feet tall with a powerful physique frantic to burst from his suit. It seemed out of place there. Both of them wore the same masks as me. The day was hot and the sweat trickled down our faces.

'Follow us,' Mr X said as the two of them marched away. I stayed glued to the bench, my brain and body knowing this was my last chance of avoiding the inevitable. But I welcomed the new world they were about to lead me to; this was what I'd waited for all my life.

I stood, glancing at the families enjoying their summer sun. No one stared at us, nobody appearing to wonder why three people wore fancy masks for an afternoon in the middle of London. Everything happened in slow motion, and terrible things existed just beyond the twilight of my vision.

We strode from the park and into a waiting car, the two of them in the front, with me in the back. He drove. We didn't speak. I pushed the memories into the shadows of my head and anticipated what awaited me. After a thirty-minute journey, Mr X parked outside the entrance of an abandoned building. I shivered with expectation, wondering if more of his group would be there. There's one of them for each letter of the alphabet, he'd told me the first time I met him in the club, but I think he was trying to intimidate me by creating some ridiculous secret society.

The three of us stepped over broken glass and disused needles. Missy moved forward and pushed the heavy door open, and we went inside. I'd seen her twice before this, never without her mask on, but I guessed she was the same age as me. How does anyone so young get involved in this world? And I've seen far too much in my eighteen years. I'm a few months away from starting at one of the most prestigious universities in the country, but it meant nothing compared to that trudge through the gloom and stink of the building with two virtual strangers.

My head throbbed as we headed towards the noise down the corridor, a low, groaning wail heralding the end of the world. I wondered what this place used to house as we continued, moving past empty offices and discarded filing cabinets; there were large industrial sewing machines stacked in three rows down the middle of the building, with bits of material and clothes scattered across the floor.

When we reached the end, someone was waiting for us: a young man strapped to a chair. The sounds were coming from his lips. He was shirtless, a muscular torso crisscrossed with cuts and whiplash. It was colder inside, but sweat continued to slide down my cheeks.

'You started without me,' I said.

'He wanted it,' Missy replied. 'He's been waiting for you.'

Her laugh stripped me to the bone. Then she handed me the knife. My face reflected in the blade, the light catching the darkness behind my eyes. For one brilliant, terrible instant, my mother gazed at me, confirming what I'd always suspected regarding my genetic predisposition for things normal society frowned upon.

I'd waited eighteen years for this, but would I go ahead with it? The young man's eyes sparkled ocean blue and swept over me. He wanted me to do it, begged me with his gaze. That's what I keep telling myself.

'Just be careful,' Mr X said. 'You must push him to the edge, but not beyond it.'

But someone did, and I'm not sure who. I left in a haze, a mental fog still possessing me now as I dictate this. All I remember are the words Missy said to me as we departed.

'We are the night killers.'

7 NOISE ANNOYS

The hissing sound at the end of the tape cut through the silence. Jack and I gazed at each other, struggling for the right words. I removed it from the player and put that and the tape in the box. He stared at me.

'That was unusual. How much do you think was the truth?'

I held the shoebox under my arm. 'The marks on her back imply involvement in something painful, perhaps criminal. That tape claims at least two others were with her, and it sounded like they enjoyed torturing people.'

'If what she said is true, it's more than that, Jen. She might have killed someone.'

'Or it's all the fantasy of a troubled teenage girl. You heard what she said about her parents. If her childhood were as she claims, it would have a terrible effect on most kids. God knows what it would have done to her mental health. And that's before she even hits the streets of London.'

He looked at me, appearing unconvinced. 'There was something else on the tape. Could you hear it?'

I nodded. 'There were background noises. Perhaps she recorded it here, and they're sounds from outside.' I glanced around the room again, seeing if we'd missed anything; if there was something here to show the type of activities she'd described.

'She might have had others with her when she made it.'

'That's a possibility. We have to get this to the station and let one of the Digital Forensic Technicians in the Audio Laboratory listen to it.'

We left the apartment, finding Arkwright loitering in the corridor.

'Have you finished, Inspectors?' He pulled something from his teeth as I peered into his eyes.

'You must come with us, Mr Arkwright.'

His shoulders trembled as his gaze switched between Jack and me. 'Why, what have I done?' His lips shivered, the words jittering out of him.

'We need a statement about your relationship with Ms Witney.'

He scratched at his hand and flakes of hair drifted onto the dirty floor. 'Relationship? There is no relationship. I only met her once.'

Jack took him by the elbow. 'That's not what she claims.'

I didn't feel like informing him she was dead; there was something about him which led me to believe he knew more than he'd let on. We exited the building and headed for the car, with Arkwright moaning all the way there. Jack eased him into the back while we took a breather outside where he couldn't hear us.

I held an invisible cigarette in my hand.

'According to this tape, Mary Witney had a troubled childhood with parents she didn't get along with, so she went to see a therapist; there should be a record of that somewhere. Then she left her home and came to London.'

Jack peered at the gap between my fingers. 'And was going to university here.'

'One of the best, apparently.' I considered the dichotomy of a brilliant student ending up in a shadowy world of violence in the capital; Mary wouldn't be the first teenager it had happened to. 'But at some point, she fell in with a group who enjoy inflicting pain on people, which might explain the marks on her body. Somehow that developed into torture and death: definitely her own and maybe for others.'

'Mr X and Missy?'

'I might have considered them to be figments of a troubled teen's overactive imagination, especially if she'd been unfortunate enough to read *Fifty Shades of Grey*, but her violent murder means there could be something in what she said.'

Jack rolled his eyes. 'A secret organisation of twenty-six people, each named after a letter of the alphabet, who torture and kill?'

'Stranger things have happened, partner. Experience tells us her claims are far from impossible. And remember what her last words were on that cassette.'

'We are the night killers.'

'Which sounds pretty ominous, don't you think?'

'Could there be more than one tape?'

I held the shoebox up. 'Perhaps the noises in the background can shed light on that.'

He handed me the car keys, and I gave him the box. He embraced it as if it were a baby.

'What did she mean about being the night killers?'

We climbed into the car and ignored Arkwright's complaints.

'I don't know, but I doubt it's anything good.'

BACK AT THE STATION, we left Arkwright with Constable Sutton to give his statement. I gave her and Grealish a quick rundown regarding the tape. Then Jack and I took the cassette and the player down to the Forensic Services Unit after having it checked for fingerprints.

The Forensic Services Unit of the Met Police, also known as SCD 4, is part of Met Operations, also known as Met Ops. It's divided into six units and we needed to speak to someone in Forensic Investigation - Specialist Crime. There are five storeys of open-plan office space in New Scotland Yard, and we headed to the middle one. We passed officers perched on stools, those who worked on laptops at a hot-desking bar, while others sat on high-backed sofas nearby, arranged to create a sense of little enclosed meeting rooms. There were conventional desks aplenty, banks of lockers for possessions, and even toilets tiled with colour schemes inspired by police car liveries.

Contrary to popular belief, there are no corners in the human eye, but as we strode down the corridor, heading for the suite dealing with audio equipment, from the edge of my vision, I glimpsed the impressive visage of the London Eye not so far away. That got me thinking about other tourist attractions in the city, and the image of Mary Witney's savaged body outside the London Dungeon fewer than twelve hours ago. Was the tape Dr Cooper discovered under Mary's fingernails connected to what was inside the box? Was her tale only a fantasy? I pushed open the door of the technology suite and hoped we'd get some answers. As we walked into the studio, the weight of discovering Mary Witney's killer transferred from my mind and into the shoebox, and it felt heavier than the sun.

'You must be Inspectors Monroe and Flowers.' A kid looking not much older than Abbey stuck out his hand and beamed at us. 'I'm Tom, one of the Digital Forensic Technicians.'

I gave him the box. 'There's a tape in there we need you to listen to.'

He grabbed it and couldn't contain his excitement.

'I know. Your boss informed mine about why you're here.' He opened the box and removed the tape and the player. 'Damn! This is some antique. You might get a few quid for it on eBay.'

I didn't know whether to be annoyed or encouraged by his enthusiasm.

'This is part of a murder investigation, Tom.'

He lost his smile. 'Yes, of course, I'm sorry, Inspector.' He placed the box and the player on the side and took the tape to an extravagant-looking desk full of buttons, sliders, and switches.

Jack beamed at them. 'I feel like I'm sixteen again.'

Tom stared at him. 'You were a technician?'

He shook his head. 'I was in a band, the singer and lead guitarist.' He turned glassy-eyed as he spoke about something unknown to me. 'The rest of the group were only in it for the touring, but I loved being in the studio.' Nostalgia overtook his face, and he looked the saddest I'd seen him since his separation. 'I believed we'd record the twenty-first century *Sgt Peppers*, but it never happened.' His shoulders slumped so much, I thought he'd slide onto the floor.

Tom regained his smile. 'But, Inspector, you could use your audio skills to fight crime.'

I stood next to the kid. 'That's why we've come to you.' I glanced over the array of equipment around us. 'Can you determine what the noises are in the background?'

He continued to grin. 'No, I can't.'

'What?' I was too tired to punch him.

The smirk grew wider. 'Don't worry, Inspector.' He took the cassette and placed it into a tape deck hidden amongst the modern-looking bells and whistles. 'I have to convert it into an audio file first.'

'MP3?' It was one of the new things Abbey had taught me.

'No, I'll turn it into a FLAC.' Confusion seeped out of me. 'MP3 is a lossy format, which means parts of the music are shaved off to reduce the file size to a more compact level. FLAC files are up to six times larger than an MP3, they are half the size of a CD, but have better audio quality. If anything is lurking in the background, that format should pick it up.'

I nodded without understanding what he said. 'How long will this take?'

'Give me twenty minutes and I'll have it transferred from the cassette, and then I'll separate the layers.'

So we watched him work his magic, playing the tape so we got to listen to it again, while he hunched over his mixing desk and the computer attached to it. Mary Witney's voice filled the room as it moved up and down on the digital screen in waves of blue lines on a black background. Tom separated Mary's words into one layer, discovered two others, and then dragged them into sections. They were too quiet to determine what they were.

I pointed at them.

'What are those?'

'I'll increase the volume and find out.' His hands were so quick I didn't see which controls he manipulated to change the sound. Then he played the first section. It was a low murmuring, an unmistakable noise.

'That's the wind coming off the Thames,' Jack said.

And it wasn't any help. 'Play the other one.'

It was a voice, repeating the same phrase, loud and clear.

Valentino's Pizza Van for the best pizzas next to your eye.

We listened to both clips more than once, and I guessed Jack's mind was doing the same as mine: trying to work out where Mary Witney had recorded her words if it wasn't the place we'd found the tape. The flat in Tower Hamlets wasn't that close to the river.

'Why would you have pizza next to your eye?' Jack said.

I shook my head. 'Perhaps it's a new hipster thing.'

Tom removed the tape and handed it to me with a small digital memory device.

'I've made copies of everything and these are yours.'

Jack gazed at the equipment as we thanked Tom and left. All I heard was the sound of the river and Mary Witney talking about being the night killers.

8 VIDEO GAMES

Constables Grealish and Sutton had been busy in the Murder Room, organising the existing evidence into an electronic case file, printing the most critical information, and pinning it on several boards. It was Jack's turn to type up the report from the visits to Mary Witney's flat and the Digital Forensic Technician. Because of that, I volunteered to get us lunch.

I strode back from the sandwich shop and loitered on Victoria Embankment, staring across the river to where we'd found her body. I removed my phone and called home; I hadn't spoken to Abbey all day. It rang for two minutes with no answer, so I sent a text.

What do you want to eat tonight? Shall we watch a movie?

Our relationship had been rocky for a few months, and I didn't know why. I continued to work stupid hours, still spending little time at home even though I'd promised Abbey I'd cut back on my shifts, so maybe that was something to do with it. Or perhaps it was a typical teenage rebellion which would blow over at some point. But at least we'd had the night at the gig together; and she'd hugged me in public, with other people watching.

A flock of seagulls fluttered above me as the river ebbed and flowed out of my reach. I remembered the sound of the Thames in the background of Mary's tape, listened to her voice in my head again as she spoke about her parents.

The brutality of childhood and the indifference of parents; does this happen to us all?

My mother and father were apathetic towards me until one of my father's church-going friends got me pregnant. Then it was all about avoiding family shame and ensuring I kept well away from anyone who might spread the news about my 'mistake' around town.

Had I been indifferent to my daughter's needs these past few years? It wasn't my fault she'd been groomed online by an adult from her school, but my lazy response to the bullying which preceded it continued to haunt me. Abbey had spent time with a clinical psychologist after that, and those sessions appeared to have helped her. Despite that, I worried about what was inside her mind.

The birds became more brazen, flapping closer to me and the sandwiches in my hand. How long had it been since Abbey and I had enjoyed a movie night? I remembered the last one was a Hitchcock classic: Tippi Hedren sitting on a bench outside a school as crows settled on a climbing frame behind her. She was smoking, distracted, and by the time she noticed a crow pass above her, it was too late. The frame and the roofs near the telegraph pole, plus the fence, were laden with birds and nothing could stop the attack on the children. It was an image which overwhelmed my brain as the gulls squawked around me and Mary Witney's non-face sprang up from the trolley in the morgue.

Dr Cooper's voice whispered in my head as I turned away from the river and returned to the station.

Two birds with one stone, Jennifer.

The excitement was palpable in the room as I entered; I doubted it was because I'd brought Jack a Philly steak sandwich. He took it from me as he relayed the good news.

'Sutton and Grealish have done some sterling work and tracked down CCTV footage from last night.'

'Is it a video of the murder?' I tried not to get my hopes up too much.

He unwrapped his food. 'I guess we're about to find out.'

We gathered around a gigantic computer screen. Constable Sutton held a digital memory stick.

'There are two separate files, one from Queen's Walk where they discovered Mary Witney, and another from cameras along Westminster Bridge. A bloke in the tech department stitched them together for me.'

She placed it into the side of the computer, found the combined footage and hit play. Like most CCTV film, it was grainy and black and white, with no sound, but we could see the teenage girl standing outside the London Dungeon; until she disappeared, pulled into the shadows by hands unknown.

'Sorry,' Sutton said. 'That's the wrong file. Here's the full one in reverse order.'

I wasn't sure why she was starting it that way, but the final few minutes of Mary Witney's life played out for us in black and white and in reverse. She jumped out of the gloom, rushed backwards down the Queen's Walk before staring at the South Bank Lion, then across Westminster Bridge where she gazed at the statue of the Boudiccan Rebellion. Then she took a left turn off the bridge, ran past

Big Ben, continued running, stopping before going inside the last place I imagined her visiting. Most of the frames were blurry, and it was difficult to make out clear faces, but there was no mistaking which building Mary Witney had begun her journey from that night.

Sutton froze the video clip on screen as I spoke. 'Is this actual footage?'

She nodded. 'Constable Grealish and I have watched it several times. We've checked each frame to identify those chasing her, but you can't see them.'

I reached over and hit play. Mary Witney left the building and started her journey at normal speed, strolling at first, but then picking up pace into a slight jogging motion, with no apparent urgency in her movements. She never turned her face to the cameras, but it was the same girl found murdered outside the London Dungeon. I watched it all again, that last trip before the shadows snatched her.

Jack slumped into a seat next to me. 'This puts a fresh perspective on the murder.'

'You're right, partner. It's not every case we get where the victim's final movements start at the Houses of Parliament.'

I rewound the clip and examined the first few seconds again. Mary Witney stepped out of the building, and then, for a brief second, turned back and spoke to someone out of sight inside. The image was blurred, so it was impossible to see her and who she was talking to.

'Is Parliament open late on Mondays?' Constable Sutton said.

'It shuts at ten-thirty on a Monday.' I'd visited the place enough times to have memorised the opening hours. 'And if you observe the CCTV footage, you see Big Ben is at ten o'clock when Mary goes past on her way to Westminster Bridge.'

'That's too late for Parliament tours,' Jack said. 'So why was she there?'

'Let's find out.' I stood and moved to Sutton and Grealish. 'That's excellent work, you two.' I even allowed them a little smile. 'One of you take the cassette tape we found at Witney's flat and compile a transcript. When you've done that, see if you can locate a site in London, somewhere near the Thames, for the Valentino pizza van.'

Jack walked with me as we left the station. 'Fancy us going back to Parliament on a case this year.'

He didn't sound happy at the prospect, and I understood why. It had only been a few months since we'd investigated Edwin Blair's death - the Home Secretary Oswald Blair's son. Our meetings with Blair had been uncomfortable, and I don't think either of us fancied returning to Westminster.

'Perhaps Mary worked there.'

'Do you think?' He didn't hide his scepticism.

'The Houses of Parliament run a student placement programme, and we know Mary was getting ready to attend university in London. Maybe this was part of her studies.'

'What if Mary's words on the tape are just a fantasy?'

He sounded bitter, and I wasn't sure why. Perhaps it was the thought of heading back into the centre of British politics.

'I doubt we'll be bumping into the Home Secretary while we're there.'

Parliament was fewer than ten minutes away on foot, so we set off on a walk. I studied Jack's face, detecting a slight twitch in his lips as he spoke.

'What if Witney was a streetwalker and there's some sex ring going on with staff in Parliament?'

'Involving torture and murder?'

'It's possible.'

Boadicea and Her Daughters observed us as we exited the Embankment and headed towards Big Ben. My stomach rumbled, and I realised I'd left my sandwich back at the station. And something was eating at my partner.

'Why don't you tell me what's on your mind, Jack?'

'What does that mean?'

'You don't believe Mary Witney is a prostitute and neither do I. You think this murder links to a paedophile ring.'

We stopped walking together.

'Don't you?'

'We have no evidence of that.'

'But it's possible?'

'Anything's possible.' My stomach wailed again. 'You know what happened the last time someone claimed there was a paedophile ring operating inside Westminster?'

In 2019, a police inquiry into allegations a VIP paedophile ring was operating in Westminster and had murdered three boys found parts of the accuser's account were unfounded, compromised and contradicted. The accuser fled to Sweden when his claims proved false. His accusations were against powerful figures in the military, the security services, and politicians. The embarrassment of that investigation had left a bitter taste with my colleagues in the Met. I couldn't understand why Jack would want to rekindle such allegations, since we had no evidence to base them on.

'Just because those were lies doesn't mean it can't happen, Jen.' He glanced from me and towards our destination. 'When you see what happens to kids like Mary, don't you worry about Abbey?'

The change of direction in the conversation from the professional to the personal threw me.

'I'm permanently worried about her, Jack. Why do you ask?'

He reached into his jacket, pulled out a piece of paper and handed it to me. His face had collapsed into a trembling shape of sadness.

'Jean is suing me for divorce and custody of the boys.'

I placed one hand on his arm while reading through the text announcing the end of his marriage.

'I'm sorry, Jack. I'm sure you'll be able to see Tom and Jack Jnr.'

'I'm worried about the kids. Jean's hours at the hospital have increased, and the boys spend more time on their own. Who knows what they'll get up to without me?'

I returned the paper to him. 'Do you want to return to the office and supervise Sutton and Grealish? I'll look inside the Houses of Parliament on my own.'

As quickly as he'd became morose, it disappeared. 'I can't do that, partner; we're a team.'

He set off ahead of me. I caught up with him and we entered the Central Lobby. Members of the public and staff wandered around as we approached the desk in the centre. I explained who we were and the reason for our visit. I glanced at the tiled floor, the collection of marble statues, and the ornate ceiling above. Then I returned my attention to the woman with the name badge.

'Are there any cameras in here, Nora?'

She shook her head. 'No fixed ones, only those the TV stations bring with them.'

'Were there any here at ten o'clock last night?'

'I'll check for you, Inspector.' She looked at a computer screen. As she did so, a tall man joined her. His curls were midnight black and his eyes a piercing blue, drawing me in like magnets and holding me there. When he opened his mouth, I might have guessed he was American from the whiteness and perfection of his teeth.

'Is there anything wrong, Nora?'

He didn't acknowledge us. She beamed at him as she replied.

'I'm checking something for the officers, Ted.'

He nodded, and then turned to me.

'Are the Met wanting to book a private tour of the building?'

I wasn't sure if he was joking or not. I introduced myself and Jack.

'We're here as part of a routine investigation, Mr...?'

'Ted Valance - Communications Manager at the House of Commons.' He glanced over my shoulder and dismissed us as soon as we knew his name. 'I'm sure Nora will look after you.' Then he departed to speak to a Member of Parliament across the lobby.

Nora finished on the computer. 'We had no TV cameras present then, Inspectors.'

Well, that was great. 'Do you have a staff rota for yesterday?'

Her smile disappeared. 'I'd have to get permission to pass that information on.'

Jack looked as disappointed as I felt. I handed her my card.

'Call me when you have it, Nora.'

We left the surroundings of British democracy no better off than when we'd entered the building. I checked my phone, finding no messages from Abbey. And my stomach was doing a terrible impersonation of a volcano about to erupt. At least Jack appeared to have cheered up a little.

'Let's return to the station, Jen, and track down the location of that tape recording.'

'I'll walk you there, partner, then I'm heading home.'

He peered at me through curious eyes, but didn't question my decision. I needed something to eat before my brain would work, but that wasn't the hunger which drove me.

I had to speak to Abbey and reassure myself I wasn't turning into the indifferent parent my mother and father had been.

I headed for last night's leftover pizza when I got home, only to find a space in the fridge where I'd abandoned it. The noise from upstairs told me Abbey was in, unless we had burglars. The lack of food in the house meant I needed to go shopping. How long had we existed on takeaways and their offspring? I grabbed what was left, two slices of ham just in date and a pack of unopened cheddar cheese. I found bread in the cupboard and used it to make a sandwich. It was dry and tasteless, but it subdued the revolution rumbling inside my guts.

The cat glared at me, perhaps jealous of my food. I assumed Abbey had fed it, or it had foraged for smaller animals in the garden. The cheese left a harsh taste on my tongue, with a bitter quality making me wonder if it would have been a better idea to fast for the day.

My feline friend scowled at me through peculiar eyes; had they always been that mixture of red and yellow combined like the paint used to decorate the walls of hell? It was Abbey's choice of a pet after she'd badgered me for ages about it and I'd given in for some peace. We'd had it for five years, and every time I saw it, the moggy still made me feel like a stranger in my home. Was that the real reason I'd let Abbey have her way with the cat? Or had I already been looking for a companion for her because I realised how work was taking over my life? I'd got a cat for my then nine-year-old daughter because I knew I wouldn't be in the house much? It was a terrible thing to imagine, but I wasn't dismissing it out of hand.

At least cats were superior to dogs. They made less mess, less noise, and could fend for themselves; they didn't need looking after. Rufus, this one staring at me, was a prime example of an animal hanging around to do me a favour. But even before I'd brought it home from the pet shop, I'd known it was a predator; there was a look in its eyes as it glared at me through its cage which I recognised from predatory humans. That same expression was on its face as I threw it a piece of ham and it contemplated the meat as if I'd done it a kindness.

What was it Mary Witney had attributed to her mother regarding the hierarchy of life? We all existed on one level, top: middle or bottom. Which level was I at and was it higher or lower than the cat peering at me? By the glare in Rufus's eyes, I guessed it believed I was beneath it.

Predator. I couldn't get that word from my head. Most criminals I chased were predators. I'd tracked down killers as obsessed with playing games with the police as they were with the mechanics of murder. Perhaps Jack was right and this connection, however flimsy, between Mary Witney and the Houses of Parliament, would lead to a criminal ring. It wouldn't be the first time an MP had been involved in illegal activity.

I finished the sandwich as something loud hit the floor upstairs. Rufus gave me one last lingering look and slipped out of the kitchen. The pale ham lay on the ground, unwanted and unloved. I removed my jacket and got my phone to send Jack a text.

I'm working from home for the rest of the day. Message me if anything urgent comes up. I'll see you in the morning.

The mobile fell from my hand and onto the table. I'd have a chat with my daughter and then take a long bath before ordering a Chinese takeaway. I crept upstairs and pushed open her bedroom door without knocking as she listened to an audiobook. It took me a minute to realise it was *The Outsider* by Albert Camus. It sounded as if Morrissey was reading it.

Her head tilted towards me in a gesture of acknowledgement when she saw me; she'd cut her long hair in half, so it didn't lie on her shoulders anymore, but rested on her ears instead, shiny velveteen purple and not midnight black. It wasn't the only thing Abbey had changed about her appearance: crucifixes replaced the angel earrings I'd bought for her fourteenth birthday. She wore a Ramones shirt over dark leggings, which made it look as if she'd lost weight since I'd seen her last night.

'Are you okay, Abs?'

Her eyes narrowed, highlighting the makeup caked around them. She looked a lot older than fourteen, and I wondered if I should be worried she was trying to grow up before she should. Wasn't I the same at her age, dressing inappropriately and listening to music my parents hated? At least I liked most of what she listened to.

'I'm going to be a singer in a band called Psychomania, so me being Abigail Flowers is no good. Neither is Abbey, nor Abs. I need something more appropriate.' She peered at me, waiting, I guessed, for that information to sink in before she continued. 'My name is Raven now. So don't call me anything else.'

I put both hands over my mouth to curtail the laughter, my gaze darting from her to the wall. Magazines lay scattered everywhere: fashion and celebrity publications where every image was of a thin young woman or one where a prominent bosom could carry a crate of ale across its lofty towers. The laptop was open on her bed, the screen running with random numbers like a scene from the *Matrix*.

'You're fourteen years old, Abbey.' I added emphasis on her name; there was no way I would call her Raven. 'You're not joining a rock band.' All the joy we'd shared the night before vanished in an instant.

'And I thought you loved me?' I wasn't about to get involved in a spot of emotional blackmail. Her eyes, encircled in ruby red glitter, bored into me. 'At fourteen, didn't you wish your mother supported you with your dreams and ambitions?'

The mention of my mother, the change in Abbey's attitude, my fears and worries, and the memory of Mary Witney's body meant my irritation got the better of me.

'My mother was an alcoholic who showed no interest in me unless I brought her booze.'

I was taking a step backwards, banging my elbow into the corner of the bookshelf, knocking a paperback copy of *Interview with the Vampire* onto the floor, when someone rolled out from under the bed. A bald teenage girl gazed up at me.

'Hi, Ms Flowers. Did you catch many criminals today?'

My arm throbbed with pain. 'Are you all right down there, Francine?'

Francine West had a smile brighter than the sun. Abbey had gone through several traumatic experiences in the last year, including being groomed online by the school welfare officer, before dicing with the probability of going to a juvenile detention centre after attacking a girl. So her close friendships had fluctuated like daffodils in the wind. Still, Francine, with her unusual condition, was the only one I guessed understood something about the difficulties Abbey had endured. She grinned at me while flicking at the small cross hanging from her ear: a perfect copy of the earrings my daughter wore.

'My new name is Ladybird, Ms Flowers. You know, like from the movie.'

'What were you doing under the bed?'

The grin never left her face. 'I dropped my phone and it rolled under there.' She turned to Abbey. 'Maybe we should give your mum a different name, Raven.'

'I can think of a few,' my daughter said.

I ignored Abbey's jab at me. 'Mobile phones don't roll, Francine.'

A haze of cannabis lingered around her as she got up. 'I'll remember that, Ms Flowers.' She looked like an anorexic beetle, small and skinny and dressed all in black. She grabbed a hat from the floor and used it to cover her hairless pate.

My head was a fog of conflicting emotions. I was there to be nice to Abbey, but what rushed through my veins wasn't a mixture of sweetness and light; it was painful and pointy and possibly inherited from my mother.

'Have you girls been smoking dope in here?'

Abbey gazed at me and burst out laughing. 'Don't be stupid, Mum; it's only Ladybird's body spray.' She switched her gaze from me to Francine. 'It's because she stinks so much.'

Francine stared at her friend in mock horror, rolling her

eyes, and then grabbing at her cheeks. When she'd finished, they fell onto the floor with the giggles, and I felt okay because these teenagers were behaving as I expected them to; as I wanted them to. The fire in my veins drained out of me. I sat on the bed, next to the over-excited laptop, as the girls settled down. I needed to turn the conversation back into something pleasant.

'Tell me about this band you want to join.'

Their faces lit up like the alien spaceship at the end of *Close Encounters*. They spoke together, their mouths in synchronisation as the words tumbled from their lips.

'We made loads of new friends at the show last night and we've been on the Hex Pistols Facebook page all day and there's heaps of other girls who want to be in bands or be singers or write songs and we've got a private video group set up and we'll probably put a benefit gig on and other stuff and we'll get an Instagram account for promotion and use Twitter to get some fans.'

I was exhausted just listening to them, but the joy in their faces, the pure happiness spilling from their eyes, was addictive. How could any parent refuse their kid something like this?

'Does this mean I have to buy you a musical instrument?'

They gazed at me.

'We hadn't thought that far ahead, Mum. But that would be great.'

There was so much energy bursting between them, I imagined they'd explode. Instead, they threw their arms around each other and bounced up and down on the carpet.

'Okay, girls. I'll leave you to make your plans and let me know later. I'm off for a bath.' I got up from the bed. 'Do you want to stay for food, Francine?'

I might consider them starting a band, but it would be a while before I addressed them by fake names.

Francine's smile was wide enough to jump off her face. 'Yes please, Ms...'

I held up my hand. 'Call me Jen.'

'Can we have Chinese, Mum?'

'You read my mind, Abbey. Check the menu while I have a soak.'

I left them giggling and laughing, joy rising through me because I'd turned a potential family argument into a personal triumph. I had no idea how far this rock group thing would go; they might have changed their minds by tomorrow, but I understood I had to keep it under careful control. If I'd refused what Abbey wanted, she'd only have done it anyway and kept me in the dark for most of it. At least now, I'd be there if anything terrible happened.

Not that I thought it would.

10 THERAPY

A lengthy message from Constable Sutton waited for me the next morning: our existing cases were now with other teams. I considered protesting, but realised it wasn't worth it, concentrating on the Witney investigation instead.

Sutton and Grealish had checked every London university's admissions offices and found no mention of Mary Witney. There was no trace of her anywhere on the internet: no social media presence, no accounts with Facebook, Twitter, Instagram, or all those video services most young people used. And no sign of an email address.

They'd also been unsuccessful in tracking down the place where she'd recorded the tape: the Valentino pizza van probably operated illegally, so feet on the ground would be the only way we'd find that. But it was the last sentence in the message which sparked my brain much more than the coffee I was drinking.

We have an address for Dolores Witney, Mary's mother.

The father, Phil Witney, had drunk himself to death two years before at thirty-six. Considering what Mary had said about him on the tape, I assumed he wouldn't be missed. There was no sign of Dolores Witney initially, and when I saw the address Sutton and Grealish had found for her, I knew why: the Wallace Psychiatric Hospital, Beckenham.

Abbey was warbling upstairs as I prepared to leave, a mangled version of *Pet Sematary* by the Ramones which made even Rufus flee. I didn't bother shouting to her; I'd send a text later, though I assumed she'd spend most of today trying to find the most expensive guitar she could online. Spending a bit of money on her was at least better than getting into another argument. I shouldn't have said that to her about my mother, about her drinking, and I wondered if it would play on her mind. Abbey had shown no interest in her grandparents, so I'd volunteered no information either.

A thought struck me as I went to get Jack and head to the psychiatric hospital: considering his unexpected revelation about his youthful days in a band, maybe I could convince him to teach Abbey how to play the guitar. It might cheer them both up, and I'd have an extra set of eyes watching her. And he could tell her a cheaper guitar would make her a better musician. So much for me spending money on her.

I collected Jack from the bed-and-breakfast place he'd been staying at in Woolwich since his wife kicked him out. I waited in the car since he didn't want me inside. He looked like he'd just woken up when he slid into the passenger seat.

'What a mad world, eh, Jen?'

'Is that a joke?'

He brushed burnt toast from the top of his shirt. For a man who'd prided himself on his appearance for all the time

I'd known him, he'd become rather slovenly while adjusting to his new life as a bachelor.

'Sorry, partner. I was listening to one of those eighties radio stations while I got ready, and they played some Tears for Fears.'

'Everybody wants to rule the world, Jack.'

He rubbed at his hands as if trying to get warm, even though it was a blistering summer's day this early in the morning. I noticed the length of his fingernails and wondered if he was turning into a vampire.

'Sutton and Grealish have done some sterling work for this investigation.'

There was a glint in his eyes as he spoke, and I hoped he wasn't getting any romantic notions about either of them.

'They have. You should talk to them about becoming Detective Constables.'

He nodded in agreement. 'Why not? I'm sure they'd be keen to get out of those uniforms.'

He said that with such relish, I imagined the Benny Hill tune ringing in my head. My father used to watch videos of the programme all the time when I was a kid, and I hated it.

'It's probably best if I mention it to them.'

Detective Constables and Police Constables have the same rank. They have different operational roles, with many similarities, but detectives don't need to wear a uniform. Sutton and Grealish had been doing the work of Detective Constables for a while with no change in their status. If they were interested, they'd have to pass the National Investigators Exam, Advanced Detective Training Course, and complete a two-year probationary period. Still, it would be a start on the ladder of progress within the Metropolitan Police.

'Do we know why Dolores Witney is in a psychiatric hospital?'

'No. I think Sutton tried to get details from Wallace's staff, but they wouldn't give any information over the phone. Do you believe it's relevant to her daughter's murder?'

Jack shrugged. 'Who knows with a case like this?' He checked his mobile. 'I assume you got the same message as me this morning.' He didn't wait for a reply. 'Mary Witney was invisible online, which is unheard of for a teenager in this day and age.'

It made me wonder how many accounts Abbey had across the internet, even after I'd warned her about the dangers in the aftermath of what happened last year. Her talk of using Instagram and Twitter for her new band concerned me.

'Let's hope her mother can provide some insight into the enigma of her daughter.'

If I was in her position and some stranger came along and wanted me to describe what my daughter was like, could I do it? Yes, I believe I could. I know Abbey likes cats and old movies and wants to be a singer or guitarist in a band, and I've met her friends. How many other parents could say that? If I spoke to Jack about his sons, asked him to talk about their interests, could he? I dismissed the notion as soon as I thought of it, the memory of his divorce papers fresh in my mind.

'What are we going to ask her, Jen?'

I pulled into the parking bay and slipped our police permit onto the dashboard.

'Let's see what we learn about her daughter.'

'And at what point do we tell her Mary is dead?'

I considered the question as we strode through the front

doors. A large tank of exotic fish greeted us as we entered; a school of different coloured inhabitants behind the glass nibbled away at invisible food. The walls shone white, contrasting with the thick blue fuzz of the carpet we marched across to the reception. The woman at the desk flashed me a tired grin, her lips struggling to move.

'Welcome to Wallace Psychiatric Hospital. How can I help you today?'

I made the introductions and we showed our ID cards. Then I gave her the unpleasant news.

'We're here to inform one of your patients about the death of a relative.'

The smile shrank into her mouth. 'Oh dear, how terrible.' She glanced between us. 'You didn't have to travel here. You could have provided the information over the phone.' My unmoving face must have confused her. 'It's better if the staff pass on dreadful news to our residents.' A slight grin crawled over her lips. 'We need to keep the possibility of disturbance down to a minimum, you see.' Then the smile grew into an unmistakable sign saying NOW GET OUT.

Jack leant on the desk, his voice rising high enough to make me move a little to my left. 'I'm afraid we have to insist on speaking to Dolores Witney.' He paused, I assumed for dramatic effect. 'This is a murder investigation.'

The receptionist raised her hand to her cheek, her mouth forming a silent sign of shock. It took her all of ten seconds to consider the implications of refusing two Metropolitan Police officers.

'If you'll give me a second, I need to get the duty manager.' She indicated we should grab a seat opposite the reception. So we did.

I patted Jack on the arm. 'That was forceful of you, partner.'

He crossed his legs and ignored my jab. I fiddled with my phone as we sat, but we didn't have to wait long for the duty manager to arrive and take us to see Dolores Witney. We walked down the corridor, past a games room, and another one where it appeared as if the residents took an art class.

We stepped through a door with a sign on it: *Be Nice, Be Polite, Be Friendly.* A group of smiling faces surrounded the words, and it felt like they all gazed at me. The duty manager provided a guided tour on the move, saying how each resident had a private room.

'I must be there when you speak to Dolores.' He pushed the door open, and we entered. I noticed he didn't knock before we did. I understood why when we stepped inside.

'Where is she?' I wondered if this would turn into a locked room mystery rather than a murder investigation.

'Dolores is on her way, Inspector. One of my colleagues is bringing her from therapy.'

Jack spoke to him while I scrutinised the place.

'Can you tell us why she's in here?'

He held up his hands as I stared at the rack of books stuffed along the shelves beside the bed. There was a TV in the corner, a room at the far end I assumed was a bathroom and a table with fresh flowers.

'Dolores is a voluntary resident at Wallace.'

As I considered who financed this, Jack drew my attention to the top of the bookcase. I was craning my neck to see what had caught his eye when a large man in a white uniform entered with a woman I guessed was Mrs Witney. More than time had battered her face; according to the records I'd read, she was in her late thirties, but the person before me wore the expression of someone who'd lived through more than one lifetime, and none had been easy.

The lines around her eyes told tales best kept away from children and people of nervous disposition; her hair was down to her shoulders and whiter than snow, with just a tint of premature grey in it. A plain top and ordinary trousers hid a frame which looked unfed for weeks. The duty manager must have recognised my concern.

'Sometimes, some of our residents lose their appetite, so we have to administer the right nourishment in more unorthodox ways.'

I didn't ask what they were as he introduced us to Witney. The other member of staff left the room as Dolores considered what she'd heard. As she did that, I glanced to the top of the bookshelf and what Jack had spotted: high above our heads and all those books, nestled near the ceiling on its own, was the duplicate of the cassette player we'd found at Mary Witney's place. Was it a coincidence or something else? From where I stood, it appeared identical to the one from Mary's flat.

Dolores sat down and stared at me as if I was the only person there.

'This is about my daughter, isn't it?'

I'd informed many people about the death of a loved one, but it never got easier.

'Yes, it is, Dolores.'

She clasped her hands together.

'Tell me how she died.'

11 DR FEELGOOD

Silence entombed us, the only noise in the room coming from the duty manager as he fiddled with the buttons on his uniform. Dolores Witney was a victim of Medusa, so cold, so unmoving, it was hard to tell if she was breathing. I'd delivered terrible news to the family, friends and loved ones of the deceased and seen the entire range of reactions. People deal with grief in different ways: some wail and weep, others express their emotions through anger and violence, and the rare few remain stony silent, frozen as if their life is on hold and they're waiting for it to restart.

But it never did.

I held onto my chest, finding the pain which was always there of the child I'd lost so many years ago. My skill was to shut off those parts of me which caused the most harm. I learnt this at an early age, long before my loss, the perfect student for the emotional cruelty delivered from my parents. But sometimes I'd close off my emotions without realising it.

Dolores Witney moved her arm, her hand reaching down into a set of drawers near her bed. She opened the top one and withdrew a photograph of a teenage girl, possibly the same age as Abbey, smiling through a face of freckles and brilliant brown eyes. The kid gripped onto a metallic statue which looked like a trophy in the shape of a book.

'She was always the cleverest in her classes.' There was no feeling in her voice, no trembling of her fingers or lips. 'She'd won dozens of competitions by the time she was a teenager.'

She held the frame out to me, and I took it, the only photograph we had of Mary. I passed it to Jack, who stood to the side and behind Dolores. He used his phone to take snaps of the photo without her realising. The duty manager looked more uncomfortable by the second.

Jack returned the photo to me, and I handed it to Dolores.

'When did you last see Mary, Mrs Witney?'

It was the first time I'd seen any reaction in her, a noticeable flinch in her cheeks and a splash of darkness behind her eyes.

'Call me Dolores, Inspector.' She placed the frame on top of the chest of drawers. I wondered why she'd hidden it away.

I asked again. 'Have you seen your daughter recently?'

She stared at the duty manager. 'It's hard to tell, Inspector. The staff have me on such a cocktail of drugs, it's difficult to say what day it is sometimes.' He laughed nervously at her words and didn't explain. I continued with the questions.

'Was it in the last few months?'

The darkness disappeared from her eyes, replaced with a glint of light.

'It's possible. I have so many memories of her, and occasionally they all roll into one.' She still hadn't mentioned

Mary by name. I wondered how useful this was. Then she reached across and ran her fingers over the framed photo. 'She was such a troubled girl.'

'Troubled, how?'

'It started early, just like with me.' She glanced to her side, staring at Jack for the first time. 'But then I guess we're all troubled.'

The duty manager found his voice. 'Are you sure you want to talk, Dolores?'

'Why not, Robert?' She dismissed him with a flick of her hand and returned her attention to me. 'Here's a funny thing, Inspector. Before I came here, I watched *One Flew Over the Cuckoo's Nest* three times as preparation. So, I expected a world of locked doors, of crazed nurses waving syringes at me, and dead-eyed prisoners shuffling everywhere before throwing their faeces at the walls.' Her eyes flickered at me. 'It's nothing like that.'

'Why did you voluntary admit yourself, Dolores?'

She ran a finger over her forehead. 'Too many things crawling through here; thoughts which worried even me. For once in my life, I sought the advice of experts.'

Jack moved next to me. 'And who pays for this?'

The darkness flashed across her face.

'Mary's father may have been a violent, alcoholic misogynist, but he was a functioning alcoholic and a successful lawyer. His timely demise left a fair chunk of money in our joint bank account.' She held up her arms and looked around. 'The wages of sin are death and permanent comfort.' Dolores pointed towards the rear of the room. 'The en suite bathroom is as good as you'd find in a four-star hotel, but there's no plug in the basin, and the taps and the shower turn themselves off after a minute.' She glanced at Robert. 'So I don't drown myself.'

Jack asked the hard question. 'Are you suicidal?'

Dolores laughed so loud, I thought she'd swapped places with someone else when I wasn't looking.

'Dear me, no. I'm a danger to other people, not myself, sweetie.'

Her eyes sparkled, a twinkle in her gaze as disturbing as anything I'd ever seen; and I'd dealt with serial killers, gangsters, rapists, and the worst kind of scum imaginable. As that thought ran through my head, a loud, piercing shriek erupted from the corridor. I couldn't imagine it originating from a human throat, but since I assumed there were no animals in this hospital, I guessed it must have. The howl came again and on repeat. Robert lost his cool amongst the continuous cacophony.

'Shit!' His hands jumped from his pockets and fumbled with the keys. 'I need to see what's happening outside.' He appeared to be telling us to leave, but my hand on his and a warm smile convinced him otherwise.

'We'll be fine.' I glanced at Dolores. 'Detective Inspector Monroe and I are more than capable of handling this situation.' I squeezed his arm for extra effect. 'You sort out whatever that is.'

He deliberated for a second before rushing out without a backward glance or word.

Dolores relaxed her shoulders. 'That'll be Karen thinking it's a full moon again.'

I pulled over the chair from the corner and sat down, trying to appear casual. Jack stuck to the sides. I leant in closer to her; she smelt of fresh strawberries, and I saw the resemblance between her and Mary in the photograph, with even a few freckles dotted around her cheeks.

'I bet you've seen some sights in here, Dolores.'

She clapped her hands and laughed again.

'You wouldn't believe it, Jennifer.' Her lips glistened. 'Can I call you, Jennifer?'

'Of course.'

She moved forward, her hand on my knee. She left it there for a mini-second before removing it.

'So, back to the things I've seen during my time here. Well, there'll be nothing to shock a police officer of your experience, I'm sure.' She spoke as if we were long-lost friends. 'Most of the residents are okay. It's the employees you have to worry about.' She glanced at the door, perhaps expecting Robert to reappear, before returning to me. 'The ward staff are agency nurses, and their lack of commitment and interest in their professional duties is painfully obvious.' She pondered on her words. In that instant, I saw a slight tremor from her top lip. 'How did Mary die?'

The sight of Mary Witney's destroyed face slid into the forefront of my mind.

'Someone murdered her.' I paused for her to process the information. There was no change of expression, no more movement from her lips. 'Do you know anyone who would want to harm her?' The next image in my head was the set of scars on Mary's back.

Dolores's eyes narrowed, her head tilted to the side as she smirked.

'You mean apart from herself?'

Her words shocked me. Not the idea Mary might have self-harmed, but that her mother would be so casual about it. And then I remembered where we were.

'You said Mary was troubled, Dolores, can you tell me more about that?'

She crossed her legs and peered right through me. 'Are you aware of Herbart's theory of the threshold of consciousness, Inspector?'

In all the years I'd interviewed witnesses, suspects, relatives, and persons of interest, it was the first question to stump me.

'No, I haven't, Dolores.'

She grinned like the Cheshire Cat.

'From an early age, I tried to stress to Mary that the only important thing in life is experience; everything we are comes from that. Her father was a perfect example; his addiction to alcohol and hatred of women came from his father and his father before that: a perpetual road of self-loathing and odium which could have been traced back into eternity.' Her body shivered as she spoke.

'We're not all the products of our parents, Dolores. We have free will.'

'We do, Jennifer.' She was the Cheshire Lion now, warming to her task. 'And that's because we layer one experience on another and another and so on until the positive outweighs the negative and, maybe, we don't find ourselves in a world full of Philip Witneys.' She shook her head. 'Experience creates and defines character. We must seek as many experiences as we can, the good and the bad, and believe the positive will outweigh the rest.'

'And you taught this to your daughter?'

'As soon as she crawled towards me, I taught her this.'

Jack stepped from the side. 'And who decides what's good and what's bad?'

She scrutinised him. 'For someone like you, Inspector, I assume the world only exists in shades of black and white, where differing from right and wrong is as simple as following the Rule of Law.' She focused on him. 'Perhaps there's something about you which might bend or break if the prevailing wind blew in the right direction.'

I couldn't let her get distracted by Jack. 'Is this connected to Mary's murder, Dolores?'

'For my daughter, Inspector, all she ever wanted was encouragement. So that's what I gave her: the inspiration to experience everything she could, no matter how painful it might be.' She turned her gaze from me, her eyes searching for something in the room only she saw. 'But I started her too early, too soon. As talented as she is, as she was, at that crucial stage in her life, she couldn't separate the negative from the positive and so the two became confused in her mind.'

'You're saying Mary wouldn't comprehend when to cease with negative actions, things harmful to her physically and emotionally, because she didn't understand how to?'

'Not just negative actions, Jennifer, but negative people.'

She put heavy emphasis on that.

'Did Mary apply to go to university in London, Dolores?'

She shook her head. 'There's nothing any university could teach Mary she didn't already know about life.' Then she rolled her legs onto the bed and stared at the ceiling. The sound of feet outside the room heralded Robert's reappearance. He appeared flustered as he entered.

'I'm afraid you must leave. There's a situation in the hospital requiring immediate lockdown.'

I stood, reluctant to argue with him, and we could always return to speak to Dolores again; it didn't appear as if she'd be going anywhere soon. But there was one last thing I wanted to ask her.

'Is that your cassette recorder on the top of the bookshelf, Dolores?'

She twisted her head to me. 'When Mary was younger,

I bought two of them, one for her and one for me, to record messages for each other on tapes and leave them around the house.'

Robert raised his voice. 'You must go now, Inspectors.'

I nodded in agreement. Dolores turned her face towards the wall, and I took that as an end to the conversation.

Jack and I left as hospital staff busied themselves and tried not to look too stressed. He didn't speak until we got outside.

'What did you make of all that?'

'Dolores Witney is a unique character. I can't imagine having her as a mother.'

'And a violent alcoholic father.'

'We need as much information about Mary's parents as we can find.' I made a mental note to text Sutton and Grealish to get right on that. 'But if what she told us is true, it appears as if Mary found it difficult, if not impossible, to realise when things were bad for her.'

'Meaning?'

'Meaning those marks on her back might not have come from torture, but she consented to them. And if that's the case, then perhaps her death wasn't a straightforward attack but part of a game she played.'

As we reached the car, Jack took out his phone. 'This sounds like something from one of those S&M films, you know, *Fifty Shades of Grey* crap.'

I touched the door as I spoke. 'You're right, partner, it does. Do you realise what this means?'

The blood drained from his face. 'Jesus, don't say it.'

'Don't you like undercover work?'

He groaned as I took the phone from him, staring at the screen, at the image of the freckled-faced teenage girl who was becoming more of an enigma than I first thought.

Constable Sutton pounced on us as we walked into the Murder Investigation Room.

'I've got some great news, ma'am.'

I grabbed a chair and slumped into it in front of the computer. I'd been hoping to ring Abbey before working, but it would have to wait.

'Illuminate me with your dedication, Sarah.'

The surprise of me using her first name threw her off guard for a second. I had to remember to mention her and Grealish applying for the Detective Constable programme.

'We tracked down the Valentino pizza van.' She glanced at Grealish to let me know this had been a joint effort. 'It's been trading around Lambeth for the last three months, particularly the patch which crosses Belvedere Road and Chicheley Street.' She placed two pieces of A4 paper onto the table near me. 'Most of the buildings are businesses or posh apartments.'

Jack picked one up. 'Posh?'

'Expensive, too affluent for a teenage girl, I'd say.'

I took the other paper, showing a grid of the area, where most of the places had a red cross next to them: all but one.

'And what does that leave us with?'

She pointed at the only location uncrossed. 'This building is in direct line with the London Eye and the Thames. My sources tell me this is where the Valentino pizza van spends most of its time.'

I stared at her with growing admiration. 'Your sources?'

She blushed a little. 'Sorry, ma'am. I mean the sources Constable Grealish and I have cultivated in the area.'

'I suppose you've been talking to the locals.' And by locals, I meant informants. Using informants was a contentious subject within the police, especially at the Met. At one point, the Metropolitan Police paid more than £4m to informants over five years, with some people inside and outside the Met arguing it hadn't proved value for money. The theory is if you arrest a drug dealer on the information of an informant, you remove a dealer, but all you're doing is creating an opportunity for another one. There's little reduction in crime, just a shuffle from one location to another. And how do you know you're not making things worse?

The other argument is that informants can be a successful method if used proportionately and legitimately to support the police in keeping people safe. It's a well-established, highly regulated and independently scrutinised tactic. Officially, they're known as Covert Human Intelligence Sources, but they're snouts, grasses or narks to the rest of us.

Most informants have some criminal past, and one drug squad detective I knew viewed anyone he arrested as a potential snout. In the bad old days, before I joined the force and well before Sutton and Grealish did, a police officer kept the source secret and recorded no details of their meetings or payments. It was an unregulated system open to abuse from both sides, and there were high-profile examples of this splashed all over the media.

Home Office guidelines set out strict procedures for paid informants, especially on the use of juveniles: they have to be registered and have a police handler. A Police Constable couldn't register an informant without speaking to a Senior Officer first. So, unless either of them had talked to Jack without telling me, which seemed unlikely, Sutton and Grealish's use of informants on this case might produce serious repercussions. All of that passed through my brain as I stared at Sutton. She never blinked once.

'Yes, ma'am. We scouted the crime scene, while you visited Mary Witney's mother, and discovered the location of the pizza van from people we spoke to.'

She was intelligent, they both were, but Jack and I needed to have a quiet word with them sooner rather than later.

'Well done, both of you. So what is this building?'

Constable Grealish appeared as relaxed as her colleague. 'It was a four-story office block, but now it's a squat. About two dozen people live there.'

I turned to Jack. 'It looks like we're heading back out.'

He held up his hand.

'Give me five minutes, Jen. I need to visit the little boy's room first.'

He left as I delivered their instructions.

'While DI Monroe and I check this place, I've got more jobs for you.' I gave them directions on tracking down what they could about Dolores and Philip Witney, and to speak to Mary's neighbours. I put the Detective Constable programme on the back-burner for now. While I waited for Jack's return, I made some notes on the computer from our psychiatric hospital trip.

Was Dolores Witney implying her daughter had a mental-health problem which she'd inherited from her?

Or was she claiming Mary's personality was affected by how her parents, but particularly her mother, raised her?

Was any of this connected to Mary's murder?

Did Mary's apparent inability to discern what was bad for her take her into a situation which led to her death?

I was pondering those questions when Jack returned. 'Are we walking to this squat?'

I glanced out the window.

'Why not? The sun's shining, and it's only a quick stroll across the river, perhaps fifteen minutes at the max.'

'I have to eat.'

I hadn't thought of food since leaving the house that morning, but I understood his need.

'There are plenty of places on the way, especially near the Eye.'

We grabbed our stuff and headed out, with him chuntering about how much the tourist grub spots charged for their goods.

'They're far too expensive.'

'Then you should have prepared yourself a packed lunch.'

I scrutinised him as we made our way down the stairs, concerned about how he'd let himself go since being kicked out of the family home. Creased clothes had replaced his once immaculate dress sense, with the occasional stain on them. Jack's grooming had been second to none when he was married, but now there was always two days of stubble on his chin, and his previously male-model hair looked like it hadn't had a decent wash in a while. He'd also put on an extra few pounds around the waist and, more worryingly, on his face. Perhaps it would be a good idea to get him and Abbey together so he could teach her how to play the guitar; it would give him something to focus on away from work and junk food, and I'd be able to monitor her without Abbey thinking I was spying on her even though I would be.

We left New Scotland Yard and, once again, followed the path Mary Witney took on her last journey in life. As we headed towards the London Dungeon and Jack scoffed the sandwich he'd bought from a steakhouse bar, I realised why we'd seen no one following her when she ran across the bridge and to her death. I grabbed him by the arm, using too much force so he dropped some of the chips which came with his steak. He glared at me.

'What's wrong, Jen?'

'We didn't see anyone chasing Mary on the CCTV footage because there wasn't anyone running after her.'

He wiped a blob of mustard from his lips. 'What do you mean?'

We started walking again.

'She wasn't being followed from the Houses of Parliament, Jack, because Mary's killer knew her destination.' We looked around together, staring at the tourists and Londoners going about their business. 'This squat is at the end of her route; the murderer was waiting for her there.'

We'd reached the Dungeon. I couldn't look at the spot on the wall where someone had crushed her face. Jack finished his food with a giant burp and threw the rubbish into the nearest bin.

'So they knew each other. This was no random attack.'

I considered this as we continued to the section where Belvedere Road and Chicheley Street met. The champagne bar on the left got my mouth watering, even though it wasn't lunchtime yet. Beyond that was the International Brigade Memorial and Jubilee Gardens. The sun beat down on me, and I struggled to resist the temptation of that champagne.

The sight of the squat rising into the sky brought me down to earth.

Whatever this building once was, whatever business it housed, it was now being put to a different use altogether; boarded front doors and windows greeted us. We strode to the back and a smashed entrance. Jack didn't move and I was wondering what he was waiting for.

'When I was a kid, after my mother fled the old man to live with the postman, some squatters moved into the empty house next door. All kinds of shit happened there. Noises at night and rubbish outside all the time until the police arrived and removed them. They didn't leave without a hell of a fight, though.'

You'd be fined and flung in jail now if you tried to squat in someone's home, but squatting in non-residential proper-ties wasn't a crime. That's why most squatters had moved into abandoned buildings like this one.

'Let's hope there's no fighting today.' I went in first, stepping through the doorway and into a ground floor of vacant offices, around a dozen of them. The glass in the windows was gone or broken. We walked down the corri-dor, peering into each office, and finding nothing but graffiti, cracked bottles, and rubbish strewn everywhere: the only signs human life had been there.

Jack headed towards the stairs. 'Four more flights to go through.'

I followed him up, fumbling in my pocket for my phone. Jack had sent me the photos he'd taken of Mary Witney earlier; those freckles appeared to sparkle on the digital screen as my feet plodded up the steps. We found the same on the next three floors: plenty of trash, but nothing living. The heat increased the longer, and further, we went on. He wiped the sweat from his face.

'Didn't Grealish say twenty to thirty people lived here?'

I should have brought a bottle of water with me.

'She said two dozen.' I removed my jacket. 'Maybe they've all gone to the park during this heatwave.' I wished I was with them, or even in the Thames.

'They all left because they're scared.'

The voice came from above. I peered up to see legs disappear into the fifth floor.

Jack pointed up. 'Someone's here.'

We headed upstairs at a quicker pace, opening the door to the same layout as the previous floors: six offices on each side. As we strode through them, the differences between them and what we'd discovered below were clear: people had individualised each of the rooms into living spaces. Temporary beds were in every room, while some had portable toilets and sinks. The only thing missing was people.

I scanned the space for her. 'Where is she?'

'Are you sure it was a girl?'

'Definitely.'

We continued down the corridor, finding our resident in the last spot. She stepped from the shadows, a young girl, only a teenager, but her voice sounding a lot older.

'This is where Mary lived.'

She stood with a hip jutted to one side, her arm draped across her thin body, clasping the elbow opposite. Her head held high made her short hair appear harsh and unkempt. She wore a faded shirt with David Bowie's face on it; it was too long for her and fell well below her waist. Her static eyes appeared to be different colours, and she never took her gaze from us; ready, I guessed, to flee if she thought we were a threat. A car back-fired outside and Jack flinched, but the girl never stirred.

I stepped a foot towards her. 'Are you Mary's friend?'

'We all were. That's why the others have left.'

'You're scared?'

She scowled at me. 'They are, but not me.'

Jack moved next to me. 'Perhaps you should be.'

He was trying to help, but I didn't think it worked. I gave him a look which said leave this to me. I peered beyond the girl and into the room where she said Mary had stayed: inside, brightly coloured fabrics with vivid hues of red, blue, purple, yellow, and green hung from lines of ropes stretched across the walls. Cushions were thrown over the floor, leading up to a makeshift bed and small plastic seats around the side of it.

I spoke to her.

'Mary lived here?'

'She sometimes did, when she brought her mates with her.'

'Friends?'

'There was another girl her age.' Her eyes narrowed. 'And there were older boys.'

'Do you know what happened in there?'

She clenched her hands into fists. 'We kept away from it. The noises hurt our ears.'

I turned to Jack. 'Search the place while I talk to her.'

He nodded and did that. When I switched back to the girl, she'd gone.

'Shit!'

'You better come here, Jen.'

The room appeared beautiful on the outside, with all those festive multi-coloured fabrics.

But it was a grimmer picture once we got past the facade.

13   SMASH IT UP

The taste lingered in the air of burnt metal placed on our tongues. What I'd thought was a lush red carpet next to the bed was a blue rug covered in blood. Jack handed me latex gloves. We had nothing for our feet.

'Watch where you walk, partner.'

I bent my knees to get a closer look at the spot. Congealed blood stuck to the top, with older, drier areas beyond it.

'This has been here a long time.'

Stacked behind it and leading up to the bed was a bunch of psychedelic blankets. A white piece of plastic sneaked out from the corner. I put one hand on the end of the sheets.

'Help me move these, Jack.'

We lifted them. The closer I got, the worse it stank. You never get used to the aroma of that amount of blood, fresh or not. I reached across and pulled the bag out. The top was tied, with the name of a popular supermarket printed on it. It appeared full. Jack took it from me and placed one hand under the bottom.

'Somebody left their shopping behind.' He lifted it to his nose, grimacing as he did so. 'And it stinks worse than the carpet.'

I nodded towards the bed. 'Put it down, and we'll untie it.'

'Maybe we should call for the forensic team first.'

I was too impatient. 'Do you want to wait for them?'

'Nope.' He undid the knot. The rancid aroma made us both cringe. Then he pulled the bag open to look inside. His eyes shrank as he handed it to me.

As I peered into it, I thought someone had left frozen sausages inside which had defrosted and gone off. Then I saw some of them wore rings, gold and silver shining in the light. I dropped the bag onto the bed and called the station.

The forensic team turned up half an hour later. Jack and I spent the time searching the other rooms next door, but found nothing useful.

Athena Temple arrived five minutes after her team, standing in the corridor wearing a khaki uniform as if she'd just stepped out of a war movie. I approached her as one of her staff handed Athena a blue protective jumpsuit. Jack grinned at her.

'Did you arrive in a tank, Tena?'

Her assistant helped her to step into the legs. 'I know how much you love a woman in uniform, Jackie boy.' He winced at the bastardisation of his name. Or maybe it was because she was teasing him again.

'Where were you when I called, Athena?'

Her arms were covered as a colleague zipped her up. 'I was about to start a paintball tournament. You did me a big favour by dragging me away.' She glanced beyond me towards the plastic bag on the bed.

'Don't you ever do a full day's work?'

'These are just some sacrifices I make for you, Jennifer.' I watched as one of the forensic officers discovered the bag's contents and dropped it onto the floor.

'What?'

'I was going to shoot a few of the top brass to help you.'

'Top brass?'

'Chief Inspector Constantine and some of her colleagues. Your name cropped up a few times.'

'Me?' I couldn't tell if she was being truthful or messing with me.

'Your star has risen in the police firmament these past twelve months, Inspector Flowers. There's talk of promotion in the air.'

She was definitely winding me up. 'What were you doing with them?'

She stepped into the room, suited and booted.

'Someone needs to be on-site if those idiots shoot each other in the eye.' She winked at me as we strode towards the bag. The Forensic Officer had stopped shaking and joined their colleagues at work. 'So what's in this, Jennifer?'

'Be my guest, Doc.'

Athena grabbed it and thrust her head inside like a nag about to feed. When she pulled up, she grinned at me.

'A finger of fudge is just enough, eh, Jennifer?'

'Have you seen anything like this before?'

'I haven't. Did you notice something strange about it?'

'What, something stranger than a shopping bag full of severed fingers?'

She rubbed her chin in mock surprise. 'What is the collective noun for a collection of human digits?'

'Tell me what's strange about it, Athena.'

'Well, apart from some of them wearing rings and, on first glance, a range of skin tones, I couldn't see any thumbs.'

'No thumbs?' How had I missed that?

She held her hands up with the fingers down. 'How many people are striding through London looking like this?'

'That's if any of them are still walking.'

'True, true.' She looked over at the dried blood. 'Something terrible must have happened here.'

Before I replied, I noticed Jack in a heated conversation with a Forensic Officer across the room. I wondered who he'd upset now. The two of them strode towards us in tandem. Jack wiped the sweat from his head, droplets of it sticking to his gloves.

'You need to see this, Jen.'

We headed to the back and a large print of Klimt's *The Kiss* surrounded by peeling paint. The Forensic Officer took the bottom corner and lifted it, revealing a hole in the wall.

Athena pointed at it. 'Take it down, Rodgers.'

'Who'll put their arm inside?' Jack said as Rodgers removed the poster. It should have been one of her team, but nobody rushed to volunteer, and Athena didn't nominate anyone.

I held out my hand. 'Get me a torch.'

When Rodgers returned with it, I shined the light deep into the darkness in the wall. It was a narrow gap, but reached down to the ground. My head was halfway in before the smell forced me back.

Jack stared at me. 'Are there any more blood and body parts?'

'I don't think so.' I ran my fingers across my face. 'It smells like a huge dollop of rat shit.'

'Did you see anything?'

'There's something at the bottom.'

Athena tapped me on the shoulder. 'Make way for the wrecking crew, Inspector.'

The only thing bigger than her grin was the large hammer in her hands. Jack and I stumbled backwards as she struck the first blow on the wall. I hadn't seen someone enjoy themselves so much since watching Abbey and her friends at the gig.

Temple whacked away, sending dirt and dust into the air, forcing us back towards the bed in a convulsion of coughs. Jack brushed bits of plaster from his face.

'This better be worth it.'

It was an impressive deconstruction job from the Head of Forensic Science, so professional you would have thought she'd spent most of her life smashing things apart. She was still grinning when she finished and turned to me.

'I'm going to smash it up until there's nothing left.'

I coughed again to get the lingering dust from my lungs. 'You've done a damned fine job on it.'

'Would you like to look, Inspectors?'

We waited for the dirt to settle before approaching, stepping through the damage Temple had taken so much pleasure in causing. Her team had gathered more lights, illuminating what I'd peered at a few minutes ago. Rat shit covered the floor, making most people hold their noses. An object stood in the middle. I bent and picked it up, shaking the dust from it and holding it so everyone saw it.

Jack moved closer. 'Is that what I think it is?'

Athena slapped him on the shoulder. 'If I'd known there'd be music, I'd have brought my dancing shoes.'

The cassette was dirtier than the one we'd found in Mary Witney's flat, but here, in the squat where she'd apparently recorded the other tape, was the next chapter of her story: TAPE 2 written on the front.

Temple held an evidence bag towards me. 'Pop it in here, Jennifer.'

'We have to listen to this. It's part of a murder investigation.'

'It has to be checked for fingerprints and DNA first, Jen. You know this.'

'Jack and I need to hear this as soon as possible.'

She glanced at the destruction she'd done to the wall, and then back to me.

'You can wait a few more hours, Jennifer.'

'That could lead to more bags of fingers, Athena; perhaps something worse.'

She considered my words, stuck out her lips and blew. 'Get over here, Jackson.'

Jackson did as instructed, covered head to toe in baggy protection gear, so it was hard to tell if they were male or female. I wasn't sure if this was the forensic team's new dress policy, but it seemed like overkill. Jackson didn't speak as Athena took the tape from me and dropped it into the evidence bag.

I was reluctant to give it to her. 'Don't you have a mobile lab here?'

She spat laughter at me, something unhygienic for the Head of Forensic Science.

'The building is five minutes away, Jennifer.'

'How quickly can you get it done?'

Athena spoke to Jackson. 'Inspector Flowers and Inspector Monroe will owe us a huge favour because you, Jackson, will work as fast as possible to process this cassette. Do you understand?' Jackson nodded. 'Off you go, then.'

'Thanks, Athena.'

'I meant what I said, Jennifer. You owe me big time for this.'

'Do we owe you or your department?'

She glanced at Jack, who stared at the bag of severed fingers.

'I'll let you know when I do.' Her grin returned. 'Now get out of my crime scene.'

We didn't need another invitation to leave. It was still blazing hot outside as we dropped our gloves into the nearest bin. I followed Jack as he headed towards the river and the breeze drifting off the water. I carried my jacket, my throat drier than the desert.

He stared across the Thames. 'What happened in that room?'

I loosened the top button of my shirt. 'A lot of chopped digits at least.'

'This isn't just about the murder of a teenage girl.'

'We have to speak to the other squatters from that building.'

He removed his jacket, the sweat sticking to a top he wouldn't have been seen dead in six months ago, and rolled up his sleeves.

'Good luck with that. I'd guess most of them fled once they knew of Mary's death. Especially if they saw what happened to her face.'

He was right again. Would we discover anything worthwhile from digging into Mary's parents' lives or from her neighbours in Tower Hamlets?

'What did she do at the Houses of Parliament before her murder?'

'Once we have the list of people on duty that night, we might have an answer.'

'But that's only those at work. She could have been meeting any member of the public.'

'Then it's a needle in a haystack time.'

'We'll only crack this when we learn more about Mary. We need to listen to that second cassette.'

We walked back to the Yard quicker than when we'd left. There was no sign of Jackson or the tape when we arrived. I went to my desk and got the cassette player. I was playing with the buttons when an energetic young woman burst into the Murder Room. Sutton and Grealish turned to stare at her.

'We've finished with your evidence, Inspector.' She had a disarming smile and hair so red, I thought it on fire. At university, I fell in love with the art of John William Waterhouse, and she looked like she'd fallen from one of his canvases. I assumed she was Jackson.

'Did you get anything useful from it?'

'Only a single set of fingerprints.' She handed it to me.

'Do you want to hear this?'

She nodded.

The five of us sat around the table as I put the tape in the machine and pressed play.

I must discover who X is. I have to reveal his crimes to the world.

Not that I'm innocent in this. My guilt eats at my heart every second of the day, but X is a horror beyond what I thought imaginable.

And there's the girl. What do I do about her?

Mr X and Missy, the two of them playing games in the back of my mind. If only I could leave them in the shadows, but when they creep to the front, all I see is my path to this junction. She says we are the night killers and I can't argue against that.

What do they call the fear of blood? I've had it since my sixth birthday when I stumbled over and buried my knee in the glass from a broken bottle of beer. I've avoided alcohol, but the sight of blood always sends shivers through me.

Haemophobia, that's it. It's my earliest memory, my primary experience. I don't recall how I fell, or where it happened, or if anyone was with me, or if my parents stood over me. All I recognise is the surge of electricity shooting through my knee, my leg, and into every part of me. I don't know if I visited the hospital, or saw a doctor, or who patched up my injury. I still have the physical scar, a crescent half-moon chipping into my bone. I guess I wiped all the rest from my mind.

My mother accepted early that this childhood calamity had infused a trauma in me, which wasn't going away. She didn't understand why I couldn't shake this off. Experience was everything for her, but she insisted we should pick which ones we absorbed and learnt from. I always tried, but could never quite be like her in that respect. After that, other significant things happened: my introduction to nursery school, meeting new kids my age, realising how much my father liked to drink, and seeing how he enjoyed using his fists on others.

Twelve months after the accident, Dolores - she insisted I address her this way - informed me it was time to do something about my little problem.

'You're going to the doctor,' she said.

I grabbed at the scar under my knee; just home from school and still wearing those shorts I hated, I sucked the breath from my lungs.

'Not the Cutting Doctor,' I said.

She lit a cigarette and smiled at me.

'No, not the Cutting Doctor. That's for when you're naughty.' She blew smoke into the air where it swirled to form the shape of a raven. 'This is a different physician; one to repair what's wrong with you.'

The Cutting Doctor was the bogeyman she'd invented to punish me when I didn't behave. It was years later before I understood she inflicted the cuts on me, but when I was so young, all I knew was the blindfold over my face, my body pushed into a confined space, and the nicks and slices along my flesh where no one else saw them. Small cupboards were my bête noire for a long time after that, but now I can't think of anywhere more relaxing.

A doctor made us better. That's what she told me. And there were different doctors for me. The dentist fixed my teeth, the optician for my eyes, and there was even a foot doctor. But the Cutting Doctor was to remove that which made me bad.

'This isn't the Cutting Doctor,' she repeated. 'You'll see Dr Gideon.'

I thought of God because of the Gideon Bible I'd found inside my father's desk.

'Is God going to make me better?' I asked her.

'There is no God,' she said as she introduced a seven-year-old to atheism.

Dr Gideon was a talking doctor. But she did little talking. It was I who spoke, and she listened. For ten years, I sat with her for an hour once a week for forty weeks of the year. It's the longest relationship I've had with anyone. Apart from Dolores, but that doesn't count.

In that decade of speaking and listening, I'm not sure at what point my interest in her changed from curiosity to irritation to infatuation, and then to fear. I've tried to block our meetings from my mind, but I can't erase the aroma of the apples.

What do apples smell of?

Sweet, floral and fruity. The thought of them makes me want to throw up. Mr X likes apples. He brings them to the sessions, uses his knife to peel them as he gets Missy and me to do his work for him. But there's no force involved. We enjoy doing it. That's how we met.

I wonder what Dr Gideon would think of me now.

When I was ten years old, she started offering me an

apple at the start of each meeting. She'd eat one and hand me another.

'It's part of your five a day,' she'd say. 'A healthy body begets a healthy mind.'

Do I have an unhealthy mind? I said when I reached thirteen. That's when I began fantasising about her and undressing her in my head as she sat opposite. I removed those thick glasses first, those copious frames which hid the shine of her beauty and the sparkle behind her eyes. No more was her long dark hair tied back, but flowing loose across her face.

Then there were her clothes and the changes I made to them in my head. Gone was the plain jacket and trousers she wore, replaced with a varied succession of garments which fuelled my increasing erotic imaginings: lingerie, stockings, leather and lace, frills and flowers, gloves, boots and many things to excite a teenager's mind. But never nude; it left nothing to the imagination. And my imagination became everything to me.

And to consider Dolores paid for all of it.

Perhaps she knew.

'You need more experience,' she said. 'Feel the pleasure and the pain.' The key was not to dwell on each experience, but to collect them and mould them into something new and different. Experience brings change, and without change, we become stale and mouldy. She'd tap the side of her head three times and repeat that same mantra.

But I was incapable of change if I couldn't move on from that first remembered experience. That's what she thought. I had to eliminate that haemophobia.

And yet here I am, speaking to you, my unknown audience, with my guts still resembling the contents of an epileptic washing machine every time I see blood.

I'd hit fifteen when Dr Gideon and I had the breakthrough. It was only later I understood she'd recognised my problems from the beginning. She'd been waiting for the right moment to tell me what was broken inside my head.

'There's nothing wrong with you,' she said. 'You only have to understand you're different from most people.'

'Most people?'

'It's not a fear of blood you have. Because of what happened when you cut your leg, it caused a switch in your brain to go one way instead of another. Your mind and your body have been fighting against it ever since.'

In my head, she wore nothing but a black lace bra and matching stockings. My concentration waned. I imagined taking her pen and writing my name on her eyeball.

'What switch?' I asked with incredible difficulty.

'Those parts of your brain which produce pleasure changed, so you find enjoyment in seeing the pain in others. It's not an uncommon thing and affects many people in varying degrees.'

As she spoke, I dreamt of sinking my teeth into her thigh. For most of my life, the thought of blood in my mouth would have made me sick, but now I became excited. I crossed my legs.

'So it's true what Dolores says. Am I not normal?'

'What's normal is a subjective thing,' she said. 'There's more than one way to skin a cat, and more than one way to live your life.'

'Dolores says I must heal before I can change.' I sometimes wondered if she saw me not as a daughter. but as a butterfly she had to control; a thing she needed to help along with its metamorphosis. Only later did I recognise it was her metamorphosis she sought to achieve, and I was only a cog in that process.

There's more than one way to skin a cat. Where did that expression come from? And why did it send that familiar surge of electricity through me when Dr Gideon mentioned it?

When I reached sixteen, I understood Gideon couldn't help me, and Dolores didn't have my best interests at heart.

And then there was my father.

The image of him fades by the year as if my memory is being washed clean like one of these tapes recorded over, so the original content is replaced by something of lower quality.

But memories of my father are for another time, for another recording, if I last that long.

He was the worst man I'd ever met until Mr X came along.

But X wasn't like that at the start, being no better or worse than any of the others at the sessions. Missy and the other teenagers drifted around like gadflies: floating between the adults in a constant search for something. I understood why I went to the meetings, but for others my age, it was more to do with money and favours.

I told myself I went to control the haemophobia, but that was only a facade. I desired the pain. Only it wasn't pain to me. And it wasn't pleasure. It was an experience, and I had to keep seeking experiences which pushed me to the edge.

And so I return to Dolores and her theory of experience. She had a name for it, some philosophical terminology she explained to me when I was eleven or twelve, but I've wiped it from my mind. I have other more tortured memories now.

X wasn't the first to approach me with a private invitation. There were plenty of them desperate to get me into their sphere of influence. But it didn't matter how sophisticated they thought they were, and it didn't matter how much charm they convinced themselves they had, because none of them could come close to the arch manipulations of Dolores Witney. And none of them could inflict the violence on me that Philip Witney did. I was impervious to their silver tongues and loving fists, and I continued to search for more.

Missy introduced me to Mr X. She recognised something in me which also possessed her. It controlled us both, but it dominated him.

How can I talk about him without talking about him?

What I mean by that is how should I describe his actions? No words can create such horrors, whether written or spoken; you must experience his works to understand them.

I considered getting video on my phone of his behaviour, but it's risky. He searches Missy and me every time we meet and confiscates our phones. That's why I'm making these tapes. He wouldn't imagine someone like me using such old technology.

Maybe you're listening to this and wondering why I haven't gone straight to the police. But it's not that easy. Dolores was, is, the strongest woman I've ever known, but even she didn't have the strength to leave my father, no matter how terrible his actions.

So it isn't easy.

He might walk away from the police and seek vengeance on me, and Missy.

Then there's the other reason.

I'm as guilty as he is.

15 FAMILY TIES

'Jesus.'

Jackson crossed herself as she spoke, exposing a silver crucifix around her neck. I'd always found it curious how some people could balance their science with their faith. My father's fundamentalism made that impossible for him. I looked at her.

'I don't think He's involved, Officer.'

Her eyes widened, her lips shivering a little.

'No, that's not what I meant, ma'am.' She gulped. 'What's on that tape, some things the girl said, reminded me of a case I worked last year.'

Jack sat bolt upright, Sutton and Grealish shifted in their seats, while I dug a nail into my palm.

'Go on, Jackson.'

'Forensics was called to a suspicious death at a flat in Lewisham. A guy hanging from the ceiling, plastic bag over his head with fruit in his mouth. He'd choked to death.'

I glanced at Jack. 'Why weren't we in on this?'

'You and DI Monroe had a high-profile case then.' She

meant the Hashtag Killer. 'Plus, the investigators determined early on it wasn't murder, but a tragic accident.'

'Was it an autoerotic sex act gone wrong?' Sutton said.

Jackson nodded. 'Yes. The victim's husband was away with work at the time of death. He had a perfect alibi, and he explained the two of them had an unusual private life, but they always did it together or with others; never on their own, apart from this one tragic occasion.'

I raised my eyebrows. 'With others?'

'That's what rang the bells for me when I heard this. The husband said they attended sessions; that was his word, sessions, with like-minded people in the city.'

'Did he say where?'

'I can't remember, but I can check the case file.'

'Send copies to Jack and me.'

'Yes, ma'am.'

She left as I removed the tape from the player. I looked at the others.

'Thoughts on what we've just heard.'

Jack took the cassette off me, turned it over, and replaced it in the machine.

'This is what we spoke about, Jen: sadomasochistic sex games taken to the extreme.'

I watched Sutton and Grealish stifle grins. 'Don't worry, ladies. Inspector Monroe isn't speaking about his personal life.'

He frowned and hit the play button. The first tape had a recording on one side and was blank on the other. I expected the same for this one, but we had to check. The sound of dead air played in the background.

'We need to investigate the S&M scene.' He didn't appear too keen on that.

Sutton piped up. 'I can help you with that.' We all

turned to her as she blushed. 'When I was younger, I dabbled in a few leather and lace clubs.'

It was Jack's turn to stifle a smile. 'What's a leather and lace club?'

I shook my head. 'Forgive Inspector Monroe's naivety. He's led a sheltered life.'

Constable Sutton regained some of her composure. 'Leather and lace clubs are at the milder end of the S&M community.' She placed her hands together on the table, and then scratched at her fingernails.

I had a sudden flash of severed fingers in a Tesco bag. 'How does this help us?'

'It may be a way into those sessions Mary Witney found herself in.'

'OK. We need to think about that. Any other thoughts from the tape?'

Jack reached over to his desk and pulled out a folder. He removed large copies of the photo he'd taken of Mary from her mother's room in the hospital.

'She must have had a tough upbringing. Some of what she said on the tape confirms what Jen and I got from our visit to Dolores Witney.'

Constable Grealish joined in. 'The accident she had at six years old was traumatic enough for her parents to send her to a doctor, presumably a psychiatrist.'

'Dr Gideon,' I said. 'One of you see if you can find her when we've finished this conversation.'

Sutton nodded. 'What do you think she meant by the Cutting Doctor?'

It was the phrase sticking the most in my mind. 'Mary's claiming her mother would cut her as punishment for her behaviour.' A terrible parent behaving terribly to their child, inflicting scars no one else could see; and not only on the body. 'For over two thousand years, people used bloodletting as a way of maintaining good health. Even today you can still find so-called alternative healers who recommend it for curing many problems.'

Jack puffed out his cheeks. 'Are we saying Mary Witney had an accident as a young kid, never got over it even though her mother sent her to a shrink, and then she fell in with someone who pushed her into sadomasochistic sex games involving torture and death?'

Enough sarcasm dripped from his lips to sink the *Titanic*.

'It's one avenue for us to pursue.' I faced Sutton. 'Did you have any luck with background information on Mary's parents and her neighbours at Tower Hamlets?'

'Yes, ma'am. There are reports on both your desks.' She glanced at Jack. 'Constable Grealish spoke to the neighbours while I researched Mary's mother and father. We also received the staff list from the Houses of Parliament for Monday night.'

My legs creaked as I stood. 'Great. There's plenty of work for this afternoon.' The tape clicked to an end. 'I need you two to find Dr Gideon and see what the forensic team gathered from the squat.'

Everyone had jobs to do so scattered to their desks. Jack spoke to me.

'Do you think some leather perverts smashed Mary's head in and chopped off a group of fingers?' Irritation filled his voice, and I didn't know why. I ignored his question and gave him one of my own.

'Can you do me a favour?'

The smile returned to his face. 'Anything, Jen.'

'Will you teach Abbey how to play the guitar?'

His eyes bulged in surprise. 'Eh, yeah, sure. Anything for you and Abbey. Does she have a guitar?'

I showed him the photographs she'd sent me.

'She wants me to buy her something expensive.'

He laughed. 'Maybe later, after you get that promotion.' That was unexpected, especially after what Athena Temple said to me earlier. 'I've got an old guitar she can use for now. When do you want to start?'

'I'll speak to her at home and let you know.' I pointed at the paperwork on my desk. 'Let's go through these reports and hope we find something useful.'

I started with the parents.

Dolores was about the same age as me; another kid of the eighties who probably had posters on her wall of David Beckham, the Spice Girls, and Blur. She was from a modest middle-class home in Kilburn; her parents were teachers, and she was an only child. Sutton had discovered an uneventful childhood for Dolores and an average set of teenage years; until she met Philip Witney.

This chance encounter came during a college performance of *West Side Story*. Sutton's notes didn't mention which parts they played, but I had a hard time imagining Dolores as Maria. We had no photos of the young Dolores. Was Philip Witney a violent, angry man at this stage, as he allegedly was as a husband and father? I resisted the temptation to look at his report and returned to Dolores as a teenager.

I grabbed the copy of a newspaper article about a college writing competition Dolores won with an essay titled *God Died Years Ago*. There was no photo of her, just the outrage from her contemporaries about her piece, which appeared based upon her reading of Nietzsche and Richard Dawkins.

There was no mention of what she achieved at college, only that she worked several odd jobs after leaving and before marrying Philip, including as an usher in a cinema, and on an assembly line in a soap factory. She married Witney when they were both teenagers and stayed at home while he started his studies and subsequent career as a lawyer. She fell pregnant early in their marriage and appeared to give up work to look after her daughter.

The next details related to her confrontations with the police, which her husband played a significant part in keeping her out of jail, including arrests for drunk driving at twenty when two-year-old Mary lay in the back seat; a period of shoplifting incidents with her daughter as an unknowing assistant as Dolores stuck items of clothing into her baby carriage; periods of drunkenness in many bars; swapping labels and prices around in supermarkets; accosting strangers on the street and telling them to become, in her words, change agents. Plus, her exploits in the world of conspiracy theories.

It all made for unedifying reading. How much of it had affected Mary's upbringing was open to conjecture, but the details on her father contradicted the hints we'd heard so far from Dolores and Mary on the tapes.

His report was more extensive, about his successful career as a lawyer and the firm he founded in his late twenties. He was a year older than Dolores, brought up in an upper-middle-class household, and went to the same college as his wife, before heading to university and getting his law degree. There were many photos of him in the files, most of them from the media concerning the cases he'd won: defence cases against the police and the criminal justice system.

I found the largest photo of him and studied it. Even in

the image, he had a face which would stop you in your tracks: tousled dark brown hair, thick and lustrous enough to appear as if it flowed from the photo. His eyes were a mesmerising deep ocean blue, flecked with tiny darts of light; or perhaps it was just a printing error. His cheeks were firm and defined, features moulded from granite, with a brilliant white smile. I'd stood in many a courtroom where confident advocates had the jury in the palms of their hands with judicious use of their charm and good looks. I didn't doubt Philip Witney would have been the master of such techniques.

He died two years ago from an undisclosed illness. There was nothing in the report about alcoholism or violent behaviour against his wife and daughter, or anyone else. I stared at his face peering at me from the photocopied image, wondering if someone so admired and squeaky clean could be as bad as what his family claimed.

I pushed those papers to the side and turned to the interviews with Mary's neighbours in the Tower Hamlets block of flats. Constable Grealish had done an excellent job persuading six of the residents to speak on the record. Still, they said nothing helpful: Mary was rarely there, was friendly when she saw anyone, and kept herself to herself. No one had seen her with anybody else; she appeared to have no friends or acquaintances. I'd reached another dead end.

As I filed that information away, the report from Athena's forensic team popped into my email inbox. I peered over the top of the computer screen at Jack.

'I found nothing useful in those reports. What about you?'

He shrugged. 'The same for me, though I got the impression Dolores Witney should have been inside a psychiatric hospital a long time ago, and that Philip Witney was the complete opposite.' He sounded impressed. 'Before his untimely death, he was an upstanding citizen and a pillar of the community.'

'He must be the first defence lawyer you've ever admired. Shame he's dead or you could have bought him a drink.'

He ignored the jab. 'Have you just got Athena's report?'

'I'm looking at it.'

The bloodstains on the carpet contained three different blood types. There were thirteen severed fingers in the plastic bag, ten of them identified through the missing persons' list. As an aside to the official report, Athena stated a collection of severed fingers should now be known as a baker's dozen or the last supper.

'Have you seen the names identified from the fingers?' Jack said from behind his computer screen.

'I have. They're all between the ages of fourteen and twenty-two. And all listed as missing with no fixed address.'

This meant they were living on the streets and were probably runaways. Did Mary run away from home?

My back ached, and the front of my head had acquired a troop of tap dancers practising on my cerebellum. The clock on the computer ticked beyond six, and it was time to leave. I stood and told the others to stop what they were doing.

'Let's put this to bed for tonight and return refreshed tomorrow.' None of them disagreed with me. I looked at Sutton and Grealish. 'You did excellent work with these reports.' I didn't mention we'd got nothing useful from them. 'In the morning, I want you to track down this Dr Gideon Mary mentioned on the tape.'

They both nodded and packed their things away. Jack came to me.

'And what will we do next?'

'We'll address that tomorrow, partner. Now I have to go home and convince Abbey to let you be her guitar tutor.'

I didn't go straight home. My head was too full of noise to engage with Abbey.

So I walked over to the Houses of Parliament. The weather was cooler, and I was hungry for the first time since the morning. I ignored all the food temptations on the route. I planned for us to cook together like we used to before Abbey grew into a stroppy teenager and before I became obsessed with work.

It was early evening. Even so, the tourists flocked on the bridge, their attention focused on the sights and sounds of the capital. I stared across at the home of British democracy. Who did Mary meet there? Did she go to see one of the MPs?

Then she left, heading for the bridge, before pausing where I stood. What was it about the statue of Boudicca and Her Daughters that made her stop? If she thought someone was chasing her, why would she wait there? Was it a case of catching her breath?

I waited with a group taking photos and videos of the bronze sculpture: Boudicca, queen of the Celtic Iceni tribe who'd led an uprising in Roman Britain, was mounted on a scythed chariot drawn by two rearing horses. People bought souvenirs, including small versions of the statue, tea-towels with the image on it, and the usual British tat some liked to collect.

Did this sculpture mean something to Mary? She claimed to be going to university, even though her mother denied this; perhaps she was interested in history. It should be easy enough to find out which school she attended and her exam results. Would that help in discovering her killer?

As she did, I continued along the route, but slower, pausing again at the next statue: the South Bank Lion. This stone animal had rested in many places around the city: first on the Lambeth bank of the River Thames, then it was shifted close to Waterloo station, before arriving at its current location. Did Mary identify with the lion's strength or its nomadic life? Why did she pause at these two tourist attractions if someone chased her?

The questions lingered in my mind as I walked to where she died. The Dungeon had closed at five, but visitors continued to head towards it. Several of them moved to the wall where the killer bludgeoned Mary. The tourists strode to the place of the terrible discovery, posing and taking selfies as they appeared to be having an enjoyable time. The concrete was clean now, but they gawked at the spot. There'd been nothing in the media to connect Mary's death to the squat and the severed fingers – yet – but I wondered if these people would make their way there next. Perhaps these two spots would become part of one of those murder tours the capital did so well. And maybe more would be added to them before this was all over.

There were still thirty minutes left for the London Eye to operate, time for the last rotation, and some morbid gawkers pointed at it, checked their phones, and then ran in that direction.

Why did Mary spend periods between the squat and her flat in Tower Hamlets? I thought of only one reason: to keep the mysterious Mr X from where she lived. And if he killed her, did he also sever those fingers? And what part had Missy played in it?

People came towards me in fancy dress, another set of revellers determined to enjoy their time in the capital. They looked as if they'd just stepped off the *Titanic*. Some swigged drink from flagons, while young men carried small pieces of wood under their arms. There were at least four Kate Winslet lookalikes with damp hair, while a man dressed as the captain of the unfortunate vessel held onto a portable device playing that song by Celine Dion. I put my hands over my ears and marched away from them, heading back to my car at the Yard.

A thousand thoughts swam inside my head regarding Mary Witney's death, and right at the heart of them was a constant continuous belief this was only the tip of the iceberg.

I'D BEEN DRIVING for five minutes when I realised I couldn't be bothered to cook. Every part of me ached, and I needed food soon. I texted Abbey and asked her what she wanted, getting a one-word answer in reply.

McDonald's!

All my good intentions of bonding over the cooker went up in flames, but I didn't complain. The idea of healthy eating in the Flowers household was out of the window again.

Abbey was sitting on the sofa when I got back, head-phones in her ears and staring at her laptop. It continued to be a warm evening, but she wore a thick black jacket and a dark scarf around her neck. I placed the food onto the table and stepped into the kitchen for napkins. I expected to find a mess, but it was immaculate. I grabbed what we needed, including a bottle of ketchup, and returned to the living room.

'Did you tidy up?'

She seemed oblivious to my presence, her eyes fixed on the screen as I stood there. I dropped the sauce onto the table with a thump. The noise brought Rufus running into the room and shook Abbey from her reverie. She pulled the headphones off and grabbed the food.

'I'm starving.'

The burger was in her mouth quicker than I could reply. I threw my jacket over the sofa and sat to eat. I thought about scouring the TV for news of what we found at the squat, but spoke to her instead.

'Have you had an interesting day?'

Bits of salad stuck to her lips. 'It's been great. Did you look at the photos I sent you?'

'Of the guitars? I've been too busy for that, love.' I'd let her finish her food before mentioning Jack and his old guitar.

'You mean with the finger bag crimes?'

'Finger bag what?'

'That's what everyone is calling it on the internet. They say people got chopped up in a squat near the river and the police found fingers in a plastic bag. Are you involved with it?'

'Let's not talk about that while we're eating.'

I stared at the fries covered in tomato sauce and

pictured the Tesco bag of fingers again. Abbey slurped her coke while I sipped at mine and imagined it mixed with bourbon. It took her fewer than five minutes to finish her food and drink. She twisted her computer around to show me the screen.

'I've been watching guitar tutorials on the internet.' The sparkle in her eyes sent a warm glow through me. 'I want to get one as soon as possible.'

If she didn't, would her enthusiasm for it wane? A few months ago, she wanted to be a writer or draw comic books, but that was only a passing phase. I put my drink onto the table as the ice slipped between my teeth.

'You know I'm not happy with this idea of you forming a band, don't you?'

The sparkle disappeared, and her eyes narrowed. 'Yes.'

'So, we need a compromise.'

Abbey picked up my drink and finished it.

'All my life has been a compromise.'

She appeared fourteen going on forty-five.

I dug my nails into my knee, switching my gaze from her to my hand; the last supper of fingers.

'One more shouldn't be difficult then.'

'I don't see why you care.' Her stare cut right through me, and I understood what was coming. 'You're never here, anyway.'

How soon our good intentions wither and die when faced with harsh reality. How many times had I come home with work clinging to me, a day's worth of vileness wrapped around me like a cheap vest, and then walked into here and exposed my daughter to the darkness no one should ever have to experience, never mind a teenage girl? Abbey wanted a mother who focused on her; she needed a parent to spend time with. She didn't want someone obsessed with casework and murder investigations, a mother who speculated about suspects and victims, office politics and promotions. Abbey needed a parent who didn't spend all her time focusing on the dead.

But if I didn't think about this dead girl, who would? Jack would say there were plenty of people doing jobs like ours, that we were expendable. He'd be right, but once I started a case, once I'd got under the skin of a victim, had peered into their lives, I couldn't leave it alone; and if it meant putting the dead before my daughter, then that's what I'd always done.

That's what I'd always done. What a terrible thing to admit. So, what was wrong with me?

Abbey continued to stare at me, her words ringing in my ears and my heart.

You're never here.

She meant not only my physical non-appearance, but something worse, my mind visiting somewhere else even at home.

'I'm here now.'

'What do you want me to do, Mother?'

'I don't understand the question.'

'I think you do.'

Fourteen going on sixty-five.

'Think again.'

She kicked her legs out as she stood, knocking the table and sending the empty plastic cups rolling onto the floor.

'You should live at work and leave me here with Rufus.'

The cat glared at me from the side of the room, and I knew I was seconds from losing my daughter, possibly for good.

'I've got a guitar for you, Abbey.'

She froze to the spot, her face turning towards me like the girl from *The Exorcist*.

'What?'

I picked the cups up and put them onto the table, bits of ice rattling around inside and matching the cells revolving in my brain.

'This is the compromise I mentioned.' Her eyes never left me as the cat rubbed against her leg. 'I can't afford to buy you one of those new guitars you looked at, but I've done better.'

She picked Rufus up, and he purred against her chest. Why did she wear that oversized scarf when it was like a furnace inside the living room?

'How?'

'Did you know Jack used to be in a rock band?' Abbey shook her head. 'Apparently, he's a top-notch guitarist, and has offered you not only the use of his guitar, but to give you lessons.'

I waited for her to wail against the suggestion and throw the cat at me. Instead, she showed more maturity than I expected.

'When can I start?'

My back found the perfect nook in the sofa and I felt as relaxed as I'd done in weeks.

'I'll speak to him tomorrow, and we'll sort times out. How does that sound?'

Abbey stroked Rufus's head and smiled at me. 'Great.'

Then she scampered from the room without another word, and I contemplated how close we'd been to an irreparable rift. I wouldn't get carried away; there was still time for me to muck this up.

I cleared the rubbish from the table and emptied it into the bin in the kitchen. Abbey was singing upstairs, and even with Mary Witney's death possessing my thoughts, I felt good. Only when I returned to the living room did I notice the light flashing on the answering machine; Abbey must have missed it when watching her guitar lessons online.

I touched the cold button and played the message. A shaft of ice cut through my heart when I heard the voice.

'Hello, Jennifer. I got this number from one of your colleagues at the police station.' A long pause while the whole of my body trembled. 'I need to see you. It's about your mother.'

The call finished with a click, and my legs gave way; I tumbled onto the sofa behind me. It had been twenty years since I'd heard that voice, but even after all that time, I couldn't mistake it.

My father had returned.

17 FIFTY SHADES

If you stare into the sky at night, all you see is death. Those stars shining bright above you are nothing more than the last gasps of celestial bodies; those twinkles you might have wished upon when you were a child are only the remnants of cosmic life now long gone. Even the biggest object hanging above our heads is only another lifeless hunk of rock.

I didn't play the recording on the answering machine again; it was unnecessary since my brain wouldn't let the memory go. It was just like the echo of dead stars hovering above my head, only it reverberated around the insides of my skull all night and into the next day.

When I sat across the breakfast table from Abbey as she spoke about playing the guitar with Jack, I saw her lips moving, I heard her words, but layered over the top of them was his voice on that tape; the recording I'd deleted so my daughter wouldn't hear it.

She knew very little of her grandparents. What I'd told her had been brief. I'd said they never liked me and left for America when I went to university, and I intended to let her keep on thinking that. I wasn't interested in whatever it was he wanted to say. Dementia had committed my mother to a care home, making it easy for her to forget everything they'd done to me. I had no interest in my past, concentrating on the present.

The drive to work comprised of me turning the radio up full blast to drown out that echo: Bowie sang about heroes before the Stranglers segued into no more of them; Bolan wanted to get it on while Iggy was just a passenger. Kate ran up a hill before Polly Jean rubbed it till it bled.

It felt as if all my internal organs were bleeding when I walked into the Murder Room. The other three had beaten me there, their cheery smiles not doing enough to kill that voice.

'Morning, partner.' Jack handed me a sheet of paper. 'These are the names we've got of the people whose fingers we found in that bag at the squat.'

I glanced at them, wondering what to do and getting nowhere since his voice was still inside my head.

'What are the girls doing?'

'Sutton is going through lists of registered psychiatrists, psychologists, and therapists for Dr Gideon. Grealish is trying to find addresses or family for those people missing their fingers.'

I pushed the paper next to my computer. 'What should we do then?'

Jack rubbed at the stubble as it turned into a new beard. 'Are you okay, Jen? You look like you didn't get much sleep.'

It's about your mother.

I told him a half-truth. 'I argued with Abbey last night.'

He grabbed my arm, guided me into a seat and took the one opposite.

'Was this about her rock star dreams?'

My hands were in my pockets, searching for the cigarettes I'd given up years ago.

'Yeah. I only calmed her down by mentioning your offer of the guitar and lessons.'

I think his laugh was supposed to make me feel better.

'And how did she take that?'

'She was over the moon.' I imagined Abbey flying over that dead grey rock. 'She wants to begin as soon as possible.'

He laughed again. 'Well, I've only got this murder investigation to keep me busy, but apart from that, I'm free any time. Why don't we start this weekend, say Saturday morning at your place? And you can cook me lunch.'

It was my turn to laugh. 'You trust my cooking?'

'No, but it must be better than mine.'

I wondered why my face felt strange until I realised I was smiling. I got my phone and texted Abbey the news. As I finished, Constable Sutton approached and handed both of us a sheet of paper.

'Here's a list of those Leather and Lace clubs I mentioned, and some of the capital's raunchier parties.'

I placed it with the other lists. 'Do we get dressed up, or down, for these gatherings?'

'You can wear whatever you want, ma'am, plus they have events during the day. There's one this lunchtime. It's for charity.'

I nearly fell off the chair.

'For charity? Today?'

'Yes, ma'am. The popularity of the *Fifty Shades of Grey* books and movies has brought BDSM into the mainstream.'

Jack pulled at his emerging beard as if he'd tear it out hair by hair.

'BDSM?'

'It's a condensed abbreviation for bondage and discipline, dominance and submission, and sadism and masochism, sir.'

He looked like a kettle ready to boil over.

'I caught Jean reading that Fifty Shades of Crap once.'

Jean was the wife who'd kicked him out when she discovered he'd been writing love letters to an imprisoned serial killer. The relationship between Jack and me only just survived that revelation, but his marriage had sunk between the waves.

I picked up Sutton's list and read through the names: Fetish Knights; Latex Lovelies; Rubber Runs; Torture Garden; the Velvet Underground; Heaven and Lace; Leath-ernecks; Club Antichrist; Killing Kittens; SubDomRom-Com. I stopped before reading the rest.

'None of these seem likely for a charity event.'

Sutton pointed to the paragraph at the bottom of the page and read it out; she must have memorised it earlier.

'*Fifty Shades of Giving.* Come along for an afternoon of dressing up and laying down your cash to help support the NHS and social care facilities across the country. Dishy doctors and naughty nurses will be on hand to administer the right medicine to those who don't behave.'

Jack resembled a balloon ready to burst.

'I know the health service is in trouble, but I didn't realise they were this desperate.'

I did my best to wind him up. 'Are you desperate to go with me?'

He crossed his arms, and then his legs as if his body was trying to get away from him.

'One of us has to stay here and read through the case files, Jen. Plus, DCI Merson will want an update.'

He'd rather face Merson than visit a fetish charity event.

'I'll let you off, but only because you're helping Abbey with the guitar lessons.' The relief seeped from his eyes. 'So, who will join me there?'

Constable Grealish's silence was conspicuous; her head turned away and faced the computer screen. But she needn't have worried; Sutton wasn't slow in volunteering her services.

'I'd be happy to come along with you, ma'am.'

Just how happy would she be?

'You'll have to change out of that uniform, Constable.'

'Yes, ma'am.'

I scanned the details.

'The charity event runs from 1 to 4 pm at the ExCel Centre.' Sutton nodded. 'Is it like a fashion show?'

She shrugged. 'I'm not sure, ma'am.'

I wasn't a hundred per cent convinced by that.

'Okay. We've got the morning to continue with the rest of the investigation and then grab a bite to eat before we head to the Docklands.' I turned to Jack. 'Do you want to compile all the relevant information into a report for Merson?'

'I might as well. Better to be prepared for when she calls me into her office. What are you going to do?'

My fingers danced across the keyboard as I replied.

'I'm doing my research into bondage and discipline, dominance and submission, and sadism and masochism.'

Jack did his best impersonation of a hyena.

'Don't get yourself too excited.'

That seemed unlikely. While it appeared as if our murder investigation involved extreme acts of torture, I needed a refresher on what was and wasn't legal concerning BDSM. It didn't take long to track down the relevant details.

British law does not recognise the possibility of consenting to actual bodily harm. Such acts are illegal, even between consenting adults, and people face prosecution if they get caught breaking the law. Some individuals and organisations had complained that people can consent to activities such as boxing and body piercing, which also result in pain, but apparently cannot consent to BDSM. This led to the situation that, while Great Britain and especially London are world centres of the closely related fetish scene, there are only very private events for the BDSM scene.

In 1987, a group of men were convicted of assault occasioning actual bodily harm for their involvement in consensual sadomasochism over a ten-year period: this was the infamous Operation Spanner carried out by police in Manchester. The Spanner case ruled consent was not a valid legal defence for wounding and actual bodily harm in the UK, except as a foreseeable incident of a lawful activity in which the person injured participated, such as surgery.

Since the original case, there had been several police raids, arrests and prosecutions for both gay men and heterosexuals based on the possibility they had engaged in illegal SM activities. The gutter press, now extended to cover most of the internet, feasted on stories like this and spread them far and wide for the titillation, or outrage, of the public. The *Fifty Shades* phenomenon and its popularity had left some people confused by the whole thing. A quick online search brought up many questions relating to what was legal and what was illegal.

I want to spank my wife, rough sex, you name it. We have a safe word ("cabbage") if things don't go according to plan, and we stop. I've just read that even with consent, the bobby can still nick my wife or me for ABH. What happened to the doctrine that whatever two consenting adults do in the bed is none of the government's business? My wife is planning to dress up as a constable and detain me with cuffs and abuse me. I consent to all the bruises she gives me. If the actual police come and raid my house and arrest my wife and me for ABH, can we claim a breach of Article 8 of the Human Rights Act?

Sutton had brought me a cup of tea before I started reading, and I nearly spat the drink all over the screen halfway through. Maybe she should stay in uniform when we attended this charity event. But not everybody was happy with *Fifty Shades* bringing BDSM into the mainstream, with some saying its popularity was laying the groundwork for the "Sex game gone wrong" as a hastily pieced together excuse for murder. And perhaps it wasn't just as an excuse for after the fact; what if there was premeditation? The more I dug, the more dirt I discovered, including the statistic that over twenty women had died in the last ten years in a so-called sex game gone wrong.

I found a post online where a woman said she asked her boyfriend to choke her because she'd "seen it in porn and read that it strengthens your orgasm." They copied what they'd witnessed in the *Fifty Shades* film, and she ended up bursting a blood vessel in her cheek and hurting her windpipe.

There were genuine risks involved in this community of pleasure and pain, so rules, regulations and safe words were the norms. That's if you didn't want to get hurt too much, or killed.

'Should I get lunch?'

I hardly recognised Constable Sutton at first. She'd changed from her uniform and into a pair of jeans, comfortable shoes, and a patterned red and white top which wouldn't have looked out of place in Paris. The clock on the computer showed it was two minutes to twelve.

'Where does the time go when you're having so much fun?' I reached into my jacket and pulled out a twenty-pound note. 'Buy some sandwiches for all of us from the canteen. Make sure there's meat in mine.' It sounded like a line I might hear at one of those BDSM parties.

Sutton took the money from me.

'Did you find anything useful online, ma'am?'

I switched the screen off. 'I'll need a long shower when I get home.' And this was before attending the so-called charity event.

She pulled a face at me before leaving. Jack sidled over.

'Have you been converted yet?'

'That might come this afternoon. No pun intended.'

He grinned. 'Do you think it'll be useful?'

It was a good question.

'Perhaps. It could provide some insight into Mary's mind, or the killer's. I don't see what else we can do unless we get something from the staff at the Houses of Parliament or there's a link from those fingers in that bag.'

As if on cue, Constable Grealish approached.

'I've got addresses for all the people linked to the severed fingers.' She lifted her notebook. 'Nine of them are from outside London, with the farthest away coming from Aberdeen. I've spoken to the police stations closest to the missing persons' last known abodes and asked if they can send officers to interview family and friends. I thought Sutton and I could investigate the three London addresses.'

Sutton returned with the sandwiches and cold drinks and handed them around. I picked some dry lettuce from my sandwich and dropped it into the bin.

'Constable Sutton will be engaged this afternoon, introducing me into the world of leather and lace. Once DI Monroe has kept DCI Merson on everyone's good side, the two of you can check out those addresses.' Jack was too busy eating to disagree, plus I believe he was happy to do anything other than accompany me to the ExCel centre. 'Did you have any luck finding Dr Gideon, Sarah?'

She beamed, seemingly pleased I'd used her first name.

'I've narrowed it down to twelve, ma'am. I have to make more enquires.'

We finished our lunch, and then Sutton and I made the twenty-five-minute drive to the docklands. Outside were a group of police officers, both men and women, dressed in tight-fitting uniforms with lots of flesh on show; this wasn't how I'd expected my day to go when I'd fallen out of bed this morning.

But at least that voice had vanished from my head.

For now.

18 RUBY THURSDAY

Outside the building, there weren't only people keen to partake in the charity event. A small crowd, around twenty of them, protested against the occasion. These guardians of traditional morality flapped their placards proclaiming 'No one has dominion of one person over another apart from God.' The badges they wore identified them as the Christian Action Group (CAG).

'God is your Master, you are His Servant,' one of them shouted at me as we walked up the steps.

I waved at them. 'That's my favourite Depeche Mode song.'

I thought it inappropriate to use our police ID cards to get into the event for free, especially since it was for charity, so I put the ticket price on my debit card. I questioned how that would show up on my bank statement and made a mental note to make sure Abbey didn't see it. As we wandered inside with the other customers, I wondered what we were doing there; what we'd learn from this about Mary Witney's death and her killer. Was I clutching at straws coming here, leather and lace ones, which might not be good for my environment? Sutton must have read my mind.

'At this event, you might get an idea of those involved in the BDSM community, ma'am, without having to go to one of the more hard-core clubs.'

I guessed she was trying to protect what she thought were my delicate sensibilities, forgetting that I'd seen the worst of humanity and that a few people dressing up while engaging in sex was hardly comparable to the terrible things I'd witnessed.

I grabbed a glass of fizzy orange from a tray carried by a staff member dressed like Wonder Woman; perhaps I'd strolled into a comic book convention by mistake. Unfortunately, the drink didn't have any champagne in it.

'Don't address me as ma'am while we're in here, Sarah.' The bubbles fizzed between my teeth. 'Call me Jen.'

'Yes, Jen.'

I searched the arena, seeing stands and tables with individuals and groups offering goods and services for charitable donations. We strode together down the aisles, dodging people, most of whom appeared to be as surprised as me. As far as clothing was concerned, it wasn't much different to what you'd find at any LGBT parade, with lots of leather, lace, tassels, flashes of flesh, but nothing which would offend most of the population. The occasional whip dangled between fingers, but it didn't concern the security.

We spent an entertaining, but fruitless hour traversing the centre, talking to many people but getting no further forward in identifying Mary's killer. I was about to suggest to Sutton we left when a familiar voice spoke behind me.

'Of all the perv joints in the world to walk into, fancy seeing you here.'

I turned to face someone from my recent past.

'Are you still peddling half-truths on the internet, Ruby?'

The last time I'd spoken to Ruby Vasquez, she was recovering in a hospital bed after being shot by her father. Now she stood taller than me, helped by the six-inch heeled knee-length black boots she wore. The skin-tight leather dress she'd squeezed into left nothing to the imagination, especially how her breasts appeared to be on the point of tumbling onto the floor. Ruby's hair was as red as ever, blazing like the sun, and long enough to dangle below her shoulders. She leant towards me, nearly taking my eye out with that prominent cleavage, so I saw she had genuine journalistic credentials.

'I'm working for a proper newspaper now, Inspector Flowers.'

'Which one?'

'*The Daily Mail.*'

'Jesus!' I think I cracked a rib with laughter. 'You should have stuck to your online blog, Ruby.'

She pursed her purple lips at me. 'I still run that.' She sneaked a lingering look at Sutton. 'A girl has to keep busy.'

'So why are you here? I thought the *Daily Fail*'s readers would hate this.'

Her laugh was coquettish enough to draw admiring eyes from the men and women around us.

'On the surface, most of them do, but underneath every stiff British upper lip is their inner pervert desperate to get out.'

I shook my head, ready to leave and return to proper work.

'Good luck with that.'

Ruby grabbed my arm before I could move, pulling me closer to her. Her perfume was jasmine, freesia, and rose water: intoxicating enough to send most weak at the knees. Next to me, Constable Sutton looked like she'd faint.

'That's just a front, Jen. I'm here for her.'

She released me, my body snapping back.

'What are you talking about?'

She nodded behind me. 'Watch and listen, Inspector.'

There was a large stage a hundred yards ahead of us. A man wearing an expensive suit held up his arms to get everyone's attention. I was close to Sutton.

'What's happening, Sarah?'

'This is the start of the main event, Jen: the big charity auction.'

'What are they auctioning, a bag full of leather clothes?'

'It's for a date with the chief sponsor.'

A round of applause spread through the room, accompanied by wolf whistles as a woman walked onto the stage. It was my second surprise of the afternoon. I stepped closer.

'It can't be.'

Ruby followed me on one side.

'I thought you might like this, Jen.'

'That's Carrie Spector.' Her appearance shocked me. 'What's she doing here?'

'You've met her before, then?'

I gave a silent nod. The last time I'd seen Carrie Spector, she was sitting in a restaurant with the unelected King of East End crime, Tommy Cromwell. Not only that, but she was the mother of his teenage daughter.

'Once or twice,' I said. 'What do you know about her, Ruby?'

She squashed up to me.

'You know who her husband is, right?'

The surprises kept on coming.

'Did she marry Tommy Cromwell?'

'The wedding was a month ago, very low key.' Which explained why I hadn't heard about it. 'Apparently, Tommy is ill, with rumours of terminal cancer, and Carrie is taking over his criminal empire.'

I twisted my head to her. 'That can't have gone down well with his brother, Pete.'

'There's talk on the street of war coming.' She narrowed her eyes at me. 'I'm surprised the police aren't aware of this.'

'We probably are, but I don't deal with the likes of Tommy Cromwell. That's for the Organised Crime Unit to handle.' I glanced over my shoulder to see Sutton taking photos of the stage. 'Why are you interested in Spector and Cromwell, Ruby?'

She grinned at me. 'Why should I give you all my best stories before they're published, Jen?'

'Because you owe me.' After her father had died trying to kill Ruby and her mother, I discovered she'd once had a twin sister who'd died at birth. And I'd revealed this to her while keeping the details from the media.

Ruby considered what I said as the announcer on the stage started the bidding for an evening with Carrie Spector, only now she was Carrie Cromwell. Perhaps her brother-in-law Pete would put in a proxy bid so he could have a private word with her about who was really in charge of the Cromwell Empire.

Crime in the East End had been rife for centuries. Take an intense concentration of people, add high levels of poverty together with cheap alcohol, and you have a recipe for social disaster. Jack the Ripper and the Kray Twins used the East End as their private hunting ground, but I didn't care what the Cromwells got up to; my colleagues in Organised Crime would deal with them. All I focused on was finding Mary Witney's killer and whoever it was with the taste for runaway teenagers' severed fingers.

The auction raised hundreds of pounds in bids for the pleasure of Carrie Cromwell's company, and then the hundreds turned into thousands. Ruby leant close to me.

'It's interesting, wouldn't you say?'

Sutton kept on taking snaps, including of the people bidding.

'What am I missing here?'

Ruby was back on my shoulder, wafting her exotic perfume up my nose.

'What would you guess the bids are for?'

'You told me it's for a date with Spector, or Cromwell, or whatever she's calling herself now.'

'Well, they're trying to win time with her, but for most of them, it's not for a date.'

I lost patience with her, or maybe I was just sick of the way she smelt.

'Spill the beans, Vasquez, before I arrest you for wasting police time.'

Her laugh sounded like the slow tinkle of piano keys.

'Now, now, Jen, don't be grumpy. Let's see how the auction ends, shall we?'

I'd had enough, grabbing hold of Sarah's arm to leave.

'Enjoy your new job, Ruby.'

She stood in front of me and blocked our way.

'They're bidding for one of her franchises, Inspector.'

I turned to scan the crowd, inspecting the bidders, picturing them raising their amounts so they could control lucrative Cromwell criminal activities. Then I faced Ruby again.

'Let's say I believe you. What franchise are they bidding for?'

She shrugged, the leather rippling against her flesh.

'I'm unsure, Jen. That's what I'm trying to find out. You don't think I squeezed into this outfit and these heels for fun, do you?' She winked at Sutton, who tried to hide her blush, but failed miserably.

'Where did you get this information?'

Ruby tapped the side of her nose. 'A good reporter never reveals her sources, Inspector.'

I couldn't help but laugh; thankfully, the bidding had ended just at that point, and the applause of the crowd drowned out my high-pitched shriek.

'You must send me some links to all these stories you've written.'

She looked hurt, her eyes shrinking as her lips grew bigger.

'There's no need for that, Jennifer. We helped each other before and we can again.'

I was ready to leave. Whatever the new Queen of the East End was up to, my colleagues would deal with it. I barged past Vasquez, with Sutton following in my wake. A few people complained about my brusqueness, but I didn't care. It had been another wasted afternoon, and even though it had been a temporary distraction, my father's voice played that message in my head again.

'There are plenty of photos on my phone, Jen.'

The sun returned with a vengeance, and so did my anger.

'You can call me ma'am now, Constable Sutton.'

She shrank into that multi-coloured top she wore. 'Yes, ma'am.'

'I'm not lying, Inspector Flowers.'

Ruby stood behind us and was a better target for my frustration than Sutton. I turned on her.

'Do you know how to speak without duplicity, Vasquez? How many innocents were hurt because of your internet posts last year? How many continue to suffer because of your words?'

Vasquez was a magnet for other people's desperations; beyond the fancy perfume, I could smell it on her, that clingy, throat-churning aroma of someone crawling over others to get what they wanted in life. Her face was unmoving as she spoke.

'I only reported on the Hashtag Killer and the vigilantes, Jennifer. I didn't control their actions.'

'Bullshit,' I said as I headed down the steps, the wind brushing clarity through my head.

'If you don't want my help, that's up to you. But I might know who's been chopping fingers off runaways if you're interested in that.'

My legs stopped at the same time as my heart. When it moved again, so did I, turning to see Ruby Vasquez heading back into the ExCel centre.

'What now, ma'am?' Sutton said.

What now, indeed?

19 VELVETEEN

I drove the three of us from the Docklands to North West London. Ruby Vasquez sat in the back, promising to tell me what she knew about the events at the squat near the London Eye. Before we left, I texted Jack to keep him updated. His response was brief.

Ruby Vasquez!!

The journalist told Sutton and me what she'd been up to since leaving the hospital last year.

'My mother is doing a lot better now. She's off the booze, cleaned up the house and herself, and you'll never believe this.' She leant over the seat, her red hair popping over the leather, which seemed appropriate considering what she wore. 'My father had an ancient life insurance policy which paid out handsomely. So, that's another favour I owe you for shooting him, Jennifer.'

'You're welcome.'

'It meant I had enough money for a down payment on the flat. And I didn't have to worry about getting a job straight away.'

Constable Sutton turned to see her, with barely an inch

between their heads. Vasquez had a massive grin on her face, the sunlight bursting through the window and lighting up her luminescent red hair.

'How come you ended up working for the *Daily Mail*, Ms Vasquez?'

Her smirk grew wider. 'Please, call me Ruby.' She thrust her wrist into the small space between her and my back. 'And what's your name?'

Sarah shook her hand, and I noticed she left it there longer than usual.

'I'm Constable Sarah Sutton.'

'Cool. I'll call you Sarah, then.' Ruby returned to me. 'What happened to that big bag of testosterone you were partnered with last year, Jennifer? What was his name again, Mutton or Mackerel or something?'

'Detective Inspector Monroe is working at the station. When I told him I'd bumped into you, and what you're wearing, he said he couldn't wait to see you again.'

Ruby sat back in the car and stuck out her impressive chest. Since last year, she'd had a boob job, or she wore the latest Wonderbra underneath that impossible dress.

'Would you like to take some pictures to send him? I can pout into the lens.'

'I'm sure he'll survive without.'

'It's a shame what happened to him and his wife.'

I twisted my neck in surprise. 'How do you know about that?'

'I told you, I'm a journalist. We know these things.'

'Working for a downmarket tabloid doesn't count as real journalism.'

She shrugged. 'They offered me a decent job once I'd recovered from the attack and, even though we got that insurance bonus, I wasn't going to turn down the money.'

'So they sent you on an assignment at that BDSM charity event.'

I watched her in the mirror; when she laughed, all that red hair vibrated like a snake on the loose.

'I'd hardly call it BDSM.' She leant forward again. 'Would you, Sarah?'

Sutton pulled at her seatbelt and gulped.

'I explained to Inspector Flowers it was more of a Leather and Lace gathering.'

'Yeah, that *Fifty Shades of Grey* stuff has mixed up the scene with the public.' Ruby pushed bits of red hair from her face. 'Still, at least they were doing things for charity.'

'I thought you said the event was only a front for one of Carrie Cromwell's criminal activities?' I would have to get used to calling her that.

'Part of it, but most was for charity.'

'Are you ready to tell me what you have on Carrie's crime gang?'

'In about ten minutes.' She pointed through the window. 'Turn left, then right, and you'll be at my building.'

We parked outside the front. Ruby took us inside and up the stairs to a studio flat on the second floor.

Sarah scrutinised the place. 'It's nice.'

Ruby dropped her bag onto the sofa. 'It'll do for now. There's a living room, bedroom, bathroom, and balcony if I want to stare across the road outside.'

It was a decent place for a single person. 'It's better than what I had at your age.'

She smiled at the two of us. 'Make yourself comfortable while I slip into something less bone-crushing.' She stepped into the bedroom before popping her head out. 'Unless either of you wants to come in here and help me out of this dress.' I scowled at her while Sutton blushed again. 'No?

Well, it was worth a try.' She laughed as she closed the door.

I got on the phone to Jack while Vasquez changed her clothes.

'How did it go with Merson?'

'Same as always; Merson's never happy unless she's getting the credit for something. How's it going with Vasquez? Christ, I can't believe you bumped into her again; and at a sadomasochistic charity event of all places.'

'She says she has details about the severed fingers at the squat.' And I told him about Carrie Cromwell.

'Well, it'll be a stroke of luck if she does. Do you want me to speak to someone at Organised Crime about the Cromwell family?'

'Yeah, you should. They could confirm Vasquez isn't lying.'

As I spoke, she came out of the bedroom wearing a t-shirt and jeans. She had bare feet, spotlighting her bright purple toenails. I caught Sutton glancing at them.

'Is that Jack the Lad you're talking to, Jennifer?'

I hung up the phone.

'Tell us what you meant when you mentioned someone chopping fingers off runaways.'

Ruby walked over to a set of drawers next to her giant flat-screen TV. She opened the top one and pulled out a pile of papers.

'You know I've always been interested in crime stories, Jennifer.' She indicated for us to sit down, so we did on a sofa opposite her. There was a coffee table between us where she placed her collection of documents. 'Once I moved here, I spoke to some of my contacts on the street, looking for the right story to get back into the game while taking any assignment my regular employer gave me.'

'Seeking their version of what's immoral in society?'

'I don't make moral judgements on anyone, Jennifer. I took the work when I needed it so I could follow up on my projects.'

'Which are what?'

'I had a few at first, but none of them sparked my interest enough: drug dealers with political connections; alcoholic celebrities; Royal perverts; and even a few bent coppers.' She waited for me to bite, but I didn't. 'Then I heard of an enclave in the BDSM community taking things to the extreme.'

I put one hand on the table, the glass cold under my skin.

'What do you mean by extreme?'

She glanced at Sutton. 'I'm guessing you were at today's charity event for a professional reason and the two of you weren't on a date.' She waited for another response I didn't give her. 'Not that there's anything wrong with that.' Her gaze lingered even longer on Sutton this time. 'In fact, I would encourage it.' She must have seen the blood rushing to my knuckles. 'You've done your homework about the BDSM scene in London?'

Sutton found her voice. 'We have.'

Ruby grinned. 'Good, good. So you understand about setting rules and safe words before engaging in any BDSM activities.'

'We do,' I said.

'Well, there are always those willing to break the rules and take things to the limit.' She held out her hands. 'Do you know what I'm talking about? Of course you do; you're coppers. Anyway, a little bird told me this big secret three months ago. Certain members of the BDSM community got together and created their own niche cell with no rules and no safe words.'

Now I was interested. 'Which means what?'

'It means this group, and I don't know how many there are or who they are – yet, engage in their sessions and don't stop until, well, they physically can't go on.'

Sarah rubbed at her fingers. 'So, if someone screamed for the others to stop, they wouldn't?'

'Exactly. They played hard to see who would be pushed the furthest. But then accidents happened.'

Daggers grasped at my heart. 'What type of accidents?'

'It was injuries at first. Ears sliced off, people losing toenails, even loss of blood leading to them being rushed to hospitals. And then there were the severed fingers.'

'Are these the ones at the squat?'

'Yes, and at other places.'

'Deaths?'

'That's the rumour.'

Sarah seemed confused. 'The more extreme they got, wouldn't they have driven people out of their niche group?'

'That's what I thought until I heard they'd involved outsiders in their activities.'

'Outsiders?'

'Individuals outside their group, people who weren't part of the BDSM community.'

'What individuals?'

Her eyes narrowed and I recognised the sorrow in her face.

'Runaways, the rumour goes, and missing homeless kids.'

Sarah gasped. 'They snatched them off the streets?'

'At first, they might have, but they soon realised how

dangerous that was. So they sought safer measures and looked for someone to facilitate the procedure.'

She stopped talking and the three of us sat in silence, struggling to process this information. And then I understood why she was at the charity event.

'This group, whoever they are, paid for what they wanted, to get the runaway kids they desired while ensuring this facilitator wouldn't go to the media or the police.'

'That's what I've uncovered so far.'

'And you know who this facilitator is?'

'I believe so.'

I let the silence linger for a minute. 'Carrie Cromwell.'

Constable Sutton gasped, and Ruby Vasquez nodded again.

'Look at me. What a terrible host I am. I haven't offered you two a drink.'

Which was the last thing I wanted. 'Tell me who your source is.'

She pulled at her lips as if a child scolded by her mother.

'I can't do that, Jennifer. Confidentiality has to be respected.'

'Then we'll have to take you to the station for questioning, Ms Vasquez.'

She mimed shock horror. 'Have we returned to boring formality? And here was I thinking we were friends. Do you want me to provide the handcuffs?'

Sarah leant forward, her hand on Ruby's.

'A young girl is dead, Ruby. Other kids have had their fingers sliced off. Who knows what else might have happened to them? We need your help with this.'

She left her hand there, and Vasquez didn't remove it.

Then she tapped Sarah on the arm, got up and walked into the bedroom. When she returned, she held something.

'There's a party in a club tonight. My contact will be there.'

I stood to face her. 'Where is this club?'

She handed me the card. 'This is it.'

It was plastic, like a credit card, but thinner and lighter. It was black on both sides, with three words printed in white on one side.

'The Velvet Underground.' She nodded at me. 'Does it cost a banana to enter?' It was depressing to see neither of them get the joke.

'Entry is free with that card. But you must wear different clothes.' She looked me up and down dismissively. 'You won't be allowed in dressed like that.'

'This is a proper BDSM club?'

'It is.'

Would I go to a BDSM party? To catch a killer, I would.

'There's no address on this.'

'It changes every time, to keep the riff-raff out. You need to scan it through an app on your phone to find out tonight's location.'

'Can't you do it for me?'

'You can only use the card through a mobile app. Once you scan it, it's registered into your account.'

'I'm guessing you have to pay for this app?'

'£100 gets you one free entry.'

'That's hardly free.'

'It keeps out the riff-raff.'

I removed the phone from my pocket. 'What's the name of this app?'

'It's called Velveteen.'

It wasn't difficult to find, with a purple icon of a pair of stilettos shaped like lips. I paid and downloaded it.

Sarah followed my example.

'Can we claim this back as police expenses?'

'What makes you think you're coming with me, Constable Sutton?'

She smiled as if I wasn't her superior officer.

'Otherwise, I'll have to go with Ruby.'

The Vasquez grin was warmer than the sun. The app had downloaded, and I opened it. It was straightforward to use with a scanner which used my phone as I passed it over the back of the card. I guessed it had a chip inside, though it didn't feel like it. I handed it to the others, and they did the same.

'Where did you get the card, Ruby?'

'I bought it online. From one of those sites you keep the kids and sensitive souls away from.'

The app pinged, and an address came up on our phones. And I'd lost a hundred quid from my account. The party started at ten o'clock.

'We'll meet you inside. I need to go home now.'

Ruby laughed and clapped her hands.

'Excellent. It's time for a girls' night out.'

That was just what I needed.

20 FASHION

We said our goodbyes and headed back to my car. I texted Jack an update but failed to mention tonight's rendezvous; Constable Sutton must have guessed it.

'You didn't let Inspector Monroe know about the club?'

'No point giving him a heart attack. We only need to find Ruby's contact.'

'You don't want to risk losing them.'

'I'll put the fear of God into them, don't you worry, Sarah.'

She appeared unconvinced and checked her phone.

'We've got time for clothes shopping.'

I shook my head. 'No. I must go home and check on my daughter. I'll wear my own gear.'

'You know what Ruby said. Even with the app, you might not get in if you're wearing the wrong outfit.'

'I don't see how I've much choice.'

'You can borrow something of mine, ma'am.'

I turned to Sutton. She was ten years younger than me, but we had similar physiques. What was there to lose?

'Make sure it's nothing outrageous.'

'I promise it'll be fine.'

I had my doubts. 'You'll come with me while I check on my daughter. Then we'll go to yours before heading to the club.'

I wasn't sure what filled me with more trepidation: wearing some of Sutton's BDSM clothes or having a conversation with Abbey. Or the prospect of finding a message on my answering machine from my father.

It was seven o'clock when we got to the house. I left Sutton in the living room and headed upstairs for Abbey. She wasn't home, and a phone call only reached her answerphone. I sent a text and waited. I grabbed two bottles of Desperado from the fridge and handed Sarah one; then I slumped into the sofa and offered a toast to her.

'I hope you like tequila.'

'Who doesn't?' She lifted the alcohol towards her face.

I took a large drink. 'How old are you, Sarah?'

'I'm twenty-five.'

She looked younger and made me feel older.

'Do you remember being a teenager?'

'I was a quiet kid. Kept my head down at school, got good grades, passed all my exams, and then went to university. My parents were happy I stayed out of trouble. What about you?'

How much personal information did you tell a junior officer, even if you were drinking alcohol in your house and would soon visit a bondage club? Not a lot.

'About the same as you. It's my daughter Abbey I'm concerned about.'

'She's fourteen?'

'Yes. She's had some tough situations this past year.

Abbey appeared over them, but I think I'm seeing a delayed reaction now.'

Sarah placed the bottle on the table.

'Perhaps, or maybe it's a teenage thing.'

I finished my drink, wanted another one, but I knew it wasn't a good idea. There was a long night ahead of us. And as if by magic, I received a text from Abbey.

I'm staying at Francine's tonight.

At least she didn't call her Ladybird. I got off the sofa and resisted the urge to call Francine's mother. Not trusting Abbey now would only make things worse.

'I hope you're right. Finish your drink, and we'll get a taxi to your place. Where do you live?'

'In Barking.'

I held the phone, the taxi app on the screen. How did we exist without mobile phones and apps doing everything for us?

'I guess you've heard all the jokes?'

'You mean about me being barking mad?' I nodded. 'They started before primary school, and I still get the odd wag at work thinking they're the funniest bloke in the world and the first person to say that.'

She didn't seem upset about it. Ever since I was a kid, I'd suffered through all the flower jokes, wishing I had a pound for every time some moron called me petal. Just focusing on my surname brought the memory of him crashing back. I gritted my teeth. Even though I'd been reluctant to do it, I checked the answering machine: it was empty.

What would I have done if he'd left another message? He wasn't someone who went away because you ignored him. I pushed the thought of him from my mind, craving more of the taste of the tequila clinging to my lips.

The taxi appeared not long after I'd booked it. It was a ten-minute drive, with me spending each of them thinking about what to wear. When we got to her place, it wasn't what I'd expected: three bedroomed detached, with front and back gardens, on a quiet-looking road. She must have seen the surprise on my face.

'I grew up here. It's the family home, and I'm an only child.' Sadness filled her voice. She took me inside. 'It's too big for me really, but I hate to leave it.' She showed me into the living room.

'Are your parents around?'

'My father died five years ago. My mother is in a care home.' Pain creased her face. 'She has dementia.'

'I'm sorry.' It put all my problems with Abbey into perspective. I didn't tell her about my mother. Perhaps I would at some point, but not now when we were preparing for an unofficial undercover operation. Or maybe it was just two people going to a nightclub. That's what I'd say if Merson or Cane asked me in the morning.

'At least she's being looked after properly.'

'Do you see her much?'

'I visit her once a week.' She stared at me. 'It depends on how hard the boss works me.' Then she broke into a grin. 'We better get you sorted with an outfit. The club opens in an hour.'

'Don't remind me. I'm not looking forward to this.'

'The club or the clothes?'

'Both.' I took a seat. 'What have you got?'

She scrutinised me from top to toe. 'Are you six foot tall, with a size nine shoe?'

'About that.'

'Great. There are drinks in the fridge. I'll be right back.'

She headed upstairs. I looked around the living room.

She was correct; the house was too big for one person. There was a giant TV at the far end of the room, much larger than the fifty-inch screen we had. She owned a full bookcase, a stack of CDs next to a music centre, a three-piece sofa, coffee table, potted plants near the window, and a thick, luxurious carpet which made me want to take my shoes off and run my toes through it.

A lot of banging came from above me before it stopped, and Sarah called down.

'Come here, Jen.'

I removed my jacket and did as commanded. I got to the landing, looked at the art nouveau prints on the walls, and counted at least three bedrooms and a bathroom.

'Where are you, Sarah?'

'In here.' She was in the far bedroom.

I pushed the door open. The room was as big as Abbey and my bedrooms put together, with a huge double bed in the middle and walk-in wardrobes either side of it. Sarah was at the one nearer to me, holding an outfit in front of her.

'Is that for me?'

'What do you think?'

I strode forward, catching my reflection in the mirror. The lines on my face increased daily, and the bags under my eyes were large enough to fall into. I took the items from her.

'Leather trousers, leather shirt, and a leather jacket. Are you trying to tell me something, Constable Sutton?'

She laughed at the amusement in my voice.

'Yes, Inspector Flowers: you'll look great in leather.'

'Cheers.'

And she was right. Once she left the room to sort her outfit out, and I squeezed into the trousers, I had to admit that, as I stared at myself in the full-length mirror, I didn't appear too bad. I could have passed for a Joan Jett lookalike on the nostalgia circuit. As my skin stuck to the leather, I wondered what Abbey would say if she saw me like this. Jack would have a heart attack.

Sarah knocked on the door. 'Are you decent?'

'That's debatable,' I said as she entered. And what an entrance it was. She wore a black lace top, exposing the corset underneath it. Her skirt was six inches above her knees, her legs inside patterned stockings. Jack wouldn't survive seeing her like this.

'How did you get involved in this?'

She grabbed a small jacket from the bed and put it on.

'It's a short story. I'll tell you about it when we sort out some shoes downstairs.'

The footwear didn't take long. I picked the shortest pair of heels she had, about two inches. She settled for four.

'I'm amazed you can walk on them.'

'I've had years of practice. Plus, I enjoy towering over the men. They find it very intimidating.'

'No doubt.' I watched her step into them. 'Have you always been into alternative lifestyles?'

Sarah's laugh was like a ray of light settling on me.

'Don't worry, Jen. I'm not a secret Dominatrix. I like the look and feel of these shoes and clothes. I guess it started when I first listened to Goth music at fourteen.'

'Now I'm getting worried about Abbey.'

We laughed together. 'I'm sure she'll be fine with you around, Jen.'

And there was the rub; I was never there for Abbey. I peered at Sutton and considered how little I knew about her.

'How long have you been a copper, Sarah?'

'I joined at twenty-two, so three years now.'

'And before that?'

'School, college, university, then twelve months travelling the world.'

'A gap year before joining the force, I suppose. Did you go with your friends?'

'No. I travelled on my own.'

Impressive. 'What did you study at university?'

'Criminology.'

'Wow. I bet you got a First.'

She raised an imaginary glass to me. 'I enjoyed my three years there.'

'Have you considered promotion at the Met?'

She shrugged, the corset flexing against her chest. 'I try never to look too far ahead.'

'Jack and I discussed you and Grealish joining the Detective Constable training programme. You've been doing the practical work for it anyway, so you might as well get the rank recognition. It takes two years.'

'Is there a pay rise?'

'Nope.'

Perhaps it was something she wasn't ready to talk about, but she changed the subject.

'Do you trust Ruby?'

For someone she'd only met a few hours ago, Sarah had quickly settled into using Vasquez's first name.

'Are you aware of how she spread the Hashtag Killer's crimes around the internet and on social media?'

'I heard about it and saw her online posts. Some still perceive her as a hero.'

'But others view her as the person who fuelled the rise of vigilantism in this country. She's capable of manipulating people and events to further her own needs.'

'Couldn't she have changed for the better?'

'We'll wait and see. We need to monitor her tonight.'

It was nearly ten o'clock. 'I'll order the taxi, Jen.'

As we waited, I wondered if I'd done the right thing. Should I have told Jack about this? Should I have tried harder to speak to Abbey? Should I have deleted that message from my father?

I found the photo of Mary Witney on my phone and focused on her. I'd catch her killer, no matter what it took.

21 CLUB CULTURE

The queue was massive when the taxi dropped us at the warehouse. The leather itched as soon as I got out of the car. As we strode towards the line, one of them split away and approached me: a bronzed man with a Groucho Marx moustache, wearing red-and-white skin-tight circus pants and a sleeveless shirt showing off his manicured muscles. He sucked on a cigarette which wasn't a cigarette and blew smoke at us, grinning at me as if about to perform a somersault. He sounded like Mickey Mouse on acid.

'Do you new girls want a tour?' He waved his fingers in the air like fat maggots crawling from a fresh corpse. 'I've got all the right tools for showing you a good time tonight.' He opened his mouth wide enough to fit a twelve-inch pizza inside in one go and wriggled his tongue at me. I was thinking of a diplomatic response so as not to offend the regulars when Sarah stepped in.

'It's amazing you had so many poorly chosen words in two sentences.'

He opened his mouth even wider and lifted his tongue

to show more studs on it than flesh. He glared at Sutton, but she was unmoved.

'Are you blind, love?'

'No, my vision is fine. It's just unfortunate I've used it to see you.'

I was readying myself for physical aggravation when Ruby appeared from the shadows and dragged Sarah and me from the man with the steam coming from his head.

'On your own for two seconds and look what happens.'

She'd changed into another exotic outfit, dressed like a harlequin crossed with a nurse who'd bought her uniform from a 1970s Soho sex shop. Hanging on her arm was a handbag in the shape of a skull, looking as if made from human flesh; I assumed it was a fake.

'It'll take ages to get inside, Ruby.'

'This is where you witness the power of the press, Jennifer.'

She left us standing on the side and strode to the front of the queue and the security prowling around: two burly blokes well over six feet tall with muscles waiting to burst from their suits. I recognised the bald one as someone I'd put behind bars five years ago for aggravated assault. I hoped he wouldn't remember me, expecting this outfit to confuse him enough not to recollect the time I'd pushed him against a wall. Ruby whispered into his ear, and then waved us over. To the annoyance of the rest of the crowd, we got inside before anyone else. A girl at the counter, dressed like a ballerina whose leotard and tights left nothing for the imagination, smiled our way.

'She's not a natural blonde,' Sarah said to me as the three of us handed Miss Nude Swan Lake our phones, and she brushed a scanner over the Velveteen app. She grinned at me.

'Welcome to the Velvet Underground.'

I was about to make a quip about Andy Warhol when Ruby pulled me inside the club.

'You two get a drink and have a mooch while I find my contact. If you encounter any trouble, ask one of the Dungeon Monitors to help you out.'

She was off before I protested. I asked Sarah what a Monitor was. She pointed towards a tall man behind us dressed in a gimp suit.

'Most clubs have Dungeon Monitors walking around with "DM" on an armband or lanyard. They're employed by the club for safety reasons and sometimes to play with if you're feeling lonely. DMs are hired because they're friendly. You can tell them if you're overwhelmed, confused, or don't know how to approach a situation.'

While I considered this, people filed in behind us, with a few dirty looks aimed my way. I couldn't say if it were because we'd pushed to the front of the queue, because of what I wore, or maybe some of them recognised me as a copper.

A bloke decked in a velvet outfit and feathers henpecked a woman next to him. She had a pile of fruit on her head and barely wore a dress made of see-through lace. A towering Dominatrix strode past with a semi-naked man on a leash; he had an apple in his mouth and slippers on his feet. A voluptuous lady in a glittering gold top, tight leather shorts, and hold-up stockings wobbled up to me on six-inch heels. She held a rope between her fingers.

'You look like you want to be tied up.'

'What?'

Glitter covered her face and it shimmered as she spoke.

'I'm an expert in shibari, the art of Japanese rope bondage.' She offered a hand to me. 'Don't worry, my dear.

Shibari is more than a fetish; it's a skill you can use for mental stimulation and relaxation, and you seem super stressed to me. If you let me be the rigger to your bunny, you'll find all the tension in your body fade away once the rope kisses your sweet flesh.'

After over fifteen years in the police, having dealt with the hive of villainy this nation threw at me, this was the first time I'd frozen on the spot. I wasn't shocked by what she said; more the realisation I was tempted by the offer. Alcohol drifted in the air and tried to worm its way into my veins. As I fought off differing temptations, Sarah linked her arm in mine and faced the glitter woman.

'Easter's long gone, darling, and I don't think that rope would pass a health and safety check.' She eased me away and towards the bar.

'We shouldn't drink.' I reached into my pocket for some money. 'But I need one.'

I bought us both a gin and tonic as we surveyed our surroundings. Heavy dance music thumped against the walls as if the wrath of God thundered above.

Ruby was right; there was a strict dress code: leather, latex, rubber, metal, nylon, lace, drag, chains, studs and naked skin. There was a mixed age range there, as many who seemed older than me as appeared younger. I'd expected it to be mainly blokes, but I noticed plenty of women. The shackles and spikes grew in number as the night progressed and, if I gazed in all the wrong places, the sights and sounds of sexual activity were difficult to avoid.

We were on our second drinks and had rebuffed at least six intimate invitations from men and women when I decided we'd done enough blending into the scene, and we had to find Ruby.

'When did you see her last, Sarah?'

The DJ changed the music from hard techno to a cacophonous droning sound, pierced with human shrieking which I wasn't sure came from the speakers or people in the room, so I missed her reply.

'What did you say?'

She moved closer to me, her lips next to my cheeks.

'About twenty minutes ago, she headed for the loo with a giant spotted dog.'

'What?'

'I assume it was someone dressed in a Dalmatian suit.'

The music, if you could call it that, hurt my ears. I shouted at Sarah.

'That's the perfect disguise if you're about to spill secrets. Where are the toilets?'

She lifted her hand and pointed towards an alcove on our right. We finished our drinks and headed there, striding past a muscular youth covered in tattoos and piercings, two women joined at the hips and the lips, and a bearded bloke wearing nothing but a nappy. I pictured Ruby and wondered what her readers at the *Daily Mail* would think of this.

We got hemmed behind a group of people playing naked Twister and had to find a different route. The leather stuck to every inch of me as I spoke to Sarah.

'Do you visit many clubs like this?'

Her head was next to mine; her voice high to speak above the sound of the music.

'When I was younger, sometimes two or three times a week. It helped me to relax, so I didn't get stressed out at university.' She looked around the club, and I followed her gaze. 'The outside world is so vanilla, but in places like this, everything is multi-coloured.'

The DJ changed the tune and *Master and Servant* by Depeche Mode burst from the speakers.

'What do you mean by vanilla?'

'Boring and bland.' We stood squashed between two drag queens, Sarah's legs pushed up against mine. 'But it's more than that. As a woman, if you go to a club, especially on your own, there's always a sense of danger surrounding you. Do you know what I mean?' I nodded. 'Here, I feel much safer than in any other club. People are aware of the boundaries. You understand your yes and no here, and it's empowering.'

'This is a whole new world for me.'

'The fetish community isn't hidden from the rest of society, Jen. We just have to ensure we keep the idiots and instigators away or they'll ruin it for everyone.'

I scanned the room, seeing people smiling and enjoying themselves. She was right about that sense of fear, which was missing. Even at the gig the other night, where it was mainly women and girls, there was still that feeling the evening might spill into violence at any second; I didn't get that here.

'It must be difficult to find decent-sized venues.'

'From what I've seen, councils across the country are prioritising luxury developments over cultural institutions, gentrifying areas and forcing out those who are different and diverse. It's making nights like these harder to support.'

'You're fighting against politics and economics.'

'These kinds of events have always been political, particularly in London or an urban space where the economy has gone in such a way that living becomes more expensive and more difficult. To inhabit these spaces as a gay person, as a person of colour, as a person who doesn't fit some strange idea of "beautiful", it is a political act of bravery. That's a crucial thing to focus on, even more so than the fact that some people like getting spanked.'

'Some will view events like this with horror.'

Space had opened up around us.

'You can't control other people's sense of morality, Jen. Fetish parties are legal in the UK, and plenty exist above the radar. We don't harm anyone.'

I noticed how quickly she'd settled back into claiming this as her community.

'The only people who get harmed are those who want it.'

'You could see it like that, but those in the BDSM community don't perceive it as harmful.'

'But there's still at least one killer within that community.'

'Killers exist everywhere, Jen. All communities harbour those who want to hurt others; you know this better than most. It's the nature of humanity.'

As she spoke, I spotted Ruby across the other side of the club.

'Let's see if our journalist friend can help us find a murderer.'

I didn't notice anyone wearing a dog outfit as we moved through the crowd towards Ruby. The noise and the shrieking increased as we walked.

And then the music died, the murmuring of the mass pierced by a single scream.

Sarah and I pushed our way through the people stumbling from the body on the floor. The man dressed as a dog had lost his canine head, his dead eyes staring at me as blood poured from his throat. Ruby stood near him, up against the wall, peering at the skull handbag at her feet. Sarah rushed to the dogman as I went to Ruby. She pointed at her bag.

'In there.'

I looked inside. Between the lipstick, perfume, and tissues was something no one would want to see anywhere. I tilted the bag to remove the contents onto the floor. Sarah called our colleagues as two severed hands fell at my feet.

22 DOG EAT DOG

The Scene of Crime Officers arrived at the club within twenty minutes. They secured the area and took witness statements. Jack turned up not long after. I'm not sure what shocked him the most: what I wore, or the sight of two fingerless hands at Ruby Vasquez's feet. His mouth formed a large O as he spoke.

'Did Halloween come early?'

Before I replied, an added distraction approached us.

'You throw the best parties, Jennifer.'

Athena Temple resembled a 1920s flapper, crushed into a pencil-thin dress, with a dark bob which must have been a wig, and enough pearls around her neck to open a jeweller's shop. I scratched at my waist where the leather made me itch.

'What did we drag you from this time, Athena?'

She crouched down to inspect the discarded hands.

'I was at a late showing of *Pandora's Box*. It was playing with a live score.' She didn't hide her disappointment as she stood. 'Murder always gets in the way, doesn't it, Jennifer?'

'I guess so.'

'Where's the body?'

'Over here.'

We trooped across to the space near the toilets and the deceased in a dog suit.

'Woof woof,' Athena said.

Jack already had his hands and shoes protected.

'Did you see what happened?' He directed the irritation in his voice firmly at me.

'No. Ruby was going to talk to him when we heard a scream. When we got there, he was dead.'

The blood curled up around his face in a small pool. Athena crouched again, getting a hand on the side of his face.

'This was expertly done. The blade cut deep into the vein, severing the artery in one swoop.'

'It's someone with experience with a knife?' Sutton said.

Athena checked the head and the wound before rising.

'It wasn't a wild, random hack.' She turned to me. 'Do we have the weapon?'

'No. But there's a blood trail leading out the back. Your team is processing those spots.'

She looked over at Ruby sitting on a bench, but spoke to me.

'And what do we know about those hands?'

'A warning, I think.'

'A warning?' Jack said. 'For who and why?'

I explained why we were in the club. I ignored Jack's grimace and focused on Athena's grin. She was enjoying herself.

'You've become an undercover officer, Jennifer?' She looked me up and down. 'And I thought you were finally revealing your true nature.'

Jack butted in. 'Does Merson know about this?'

There was an argument brewing, but I didn't want it here. I grabbed his arm and dragged him away.

'This isn't the time and place for this, partner.'

A thousand suns blazed inside his eyes.

'I am still your partner, then?'

'Look, Jack, I should have told you about this, I accept that, but you wouldn't have come here, to this club, wearing these clothes, would you?'

I waited for a further explosion, but it didn't arrive. His face relaxed, and his lips parted.

'Well, I wouldn't have worn those clothes, that's for sure. Where did you get them?'

I let go of his arm, weariness sweeping through me.

'I borrowed them from Sarah.'

He glanced at her. 'She's a dark horse.'

'She'd eat you alive, Jack.'

We returned to the others. The tension between us dissipated, but I recognised something brewing inside him, which would need a release soon. I was surprised to see Grealish talking to Sutton.

'Are you working overtime, Constable?'

She swatted the jab aside with precision.

'We have the victim's jacket from the cloakroom, ma'am.' She handed me a wallet, presumably his. I checked the details.

'Our victim is Daniel Hathaway, thirty years old, with an address in Balham.'

'Would you like me to inform his next of kin, ma'am?'

It was five to eleven, and with Abbey away, I had nothing to go home to; unless I wanted to speak to Rufus and see if my father had left another message.

'That's OK, Constable Grealish. Inspector Monroe and

I will do it. Are there any cameras in here or outside the club?'

Sarah shook her head. 'The organisers always choose venues where outsiders can't spy on the participants.'

It was more bad news. Jack and I went to Athena as she organised her team. Someone had placed the severed hands inside individual evidence bags. Jack picked them up and peered at them.

'These seem older than the ones we discovered in the squat.'

Athena slapped him on the back.

'Well done, Inspector. We'll make a detective of you yet.'

'Is he right, Athena? These hands aren't linked to the bag of severed fingers we found?'

'From a cursory glance at both of them, I'd say none of the severed fingers belongs to these hands, but I'll run DNA and blood tests to be sure. Are you assuming the same person committed both crimes?'

'I assume nothing.' I turned to leave. 'I look forward to your findings.'

Jack and I left her to the job and returned to Sutton and Grealish. Grealish seemed amused at what her colleague wore. I pulled at the leather around my chest.

'We have to return to your house, Sarah. I can't see Hathaway's next of kin dressed like this.'

'You got that right,' Jack said.

'There's something I need to do first.'

I left them and moved to the far side of the club where Ruby Vasquez sat, deep in her thoughts. She looked up at me.

'Have you come to give me a hand, Jennifer?'

'Do you have any idea who might have done this, Ruby?'

'You mean amongst my many enemies?'

'You have enemies?'

'Well, let's see. Last year I championed the deeds of a vigilante killer.' She clutched the skull handbag close to her. 'And I work for the *Daily Mail*.'

I couldn't help but laugh. 'You have a point.'

Jack stared at the two of us.

'I don't think your partner likes me.'

'Someone definitely doesn't. You realise those hands placed in your bag are a warning, and that Hathaway's dead because he's been speaking to you.'

'Who?'

'Daniel Hathaway. The man murdered here tonight.'

'I didn't know his proper name. I knew him as Zed.'

'Zed?'

'He liked to keep our communications simple.'

'Zed or just the letter Z?'

She arched her eyebrows. 'I never really thought about it, but you could be right.'

'How did you meet him?'

'He approached me at one of the club nights, said he recognised me from my internet blogs. He claimed he had information to sell. When I asked what he had, he only gave me a taster at first.'

'And what was that?'

'Zed dropped heavy hints about a crime gang involved in the fetish scene. He told me about Carrie Cromwell's alleged involvement with events at the squat. He promised to provide more details tonight and would name his price.' She glanced over at his body. 'And then this happened.'

'He sold you information?'

Her voice trembled as she spoke. 'He was about to. Until he got his throat slit.'

'Do you want police protection, Ruby?'

She put a hand on her heart.

'Why, Detective Inspector Flowers, I'm touched by your concern.' She jumped off the seat. 'But I'll be fine.'

Jack stood with Athena as he waved me over.

'You know where I am if you need me, Ruby.'

'Thanks, Jennifer. But there's one last thing.'

'Yes?'

'Don't forget about Carrie Cromwell.'

That name echoed in my head as I joined the others.

'Time to go, Jack.' I glanced towards Hathaway. 'His name was Zed.'

Athena laughed. 'Zed's dead, Jen.'

Jack drove us back to Sarah's place, where I changed into my clothes. I thanked her for all her help.

'Consider what I said about the Detective Constable training programme.'

I explained what Ruby had said to Jack as he took us to Daniel Hathaway's house.

'Do you think Hathaway is the letter Z from Mary Witney's alphabet group of sadomasochistic killers?'

'Let's hope we find something at his home, to shed some light on that.'

He parked outside the property. Grealish had discovered Daniel Hathaway lived with his mother; now we had to tell her that her son was dead. I knocked on the door and waited. I was about to rattle the wood again when the sound of shuffling feet heralded someone coming.

She opened up, standing there with a dressing gown half-open, flashing both of us with a body which, from what I saw before turning away, was a lot older than the mid-fifties Grealish said she was. Mrs Hathaway had left her youth behind like an abandoned shopping bag at a bus stop.

Jack introduced us.

'Can we come in, Mrs Hathaway? It's about your son, Daniel.'

'Danny? What's he done now?'

I gave her my most sympathetic smile. 'It's best if we speak inside, Mrs Hathaway.'

She hesitated for a second, looking over my shoulder at the house next door. Then she showed us in, taking us into the living room and offering tea. Jack declined for both of us, and then informed her of her son's death. The lines froze under her eyes, her hand rising to her cheeks. I helped her into a seat as she asked all the inevitable questions.

Are you sure? How did he die? Who did it? Why? What happens now?

I got her permission to search through his things while Jack did his best to answer all her questions. She told us he worked from home as an independent stock trader. He had an office out the back, so I checked that first.

The room was painted grey, with walls covered in Van Gogh and Matisse prints. There was a laptop on a desk, an open notebook, and a stack of papers sitting under a Pepper Pig-shaped paperweight; magazines and books dedicated to the world of trading stocks and shares crammed the shelves. I sat at the computer and touched the keyboard. The machine sprang to life and wanted a password. I was about to leave it for Cybercrime when I hit a random key. The screen flickered awake, and an image of water lilies stared at me.

I browsed through his files. Most of them were spreadsheets for his trading, columns and rows of data of what he'd bought and sold. Most of what I found was in the red. If these were true, he had some serious debt. It might explain why he'd risk things with his fetish group and sell information to Ruby.

The rest of the documents didn't give me any details on his life as Z or anyone in the BDSM community. I also couldn't find anything connected to Mary Witney or Carrie Cromwell. A quick flick through his web viewing found plenty of sites dealing with stocks and shares, but nothing out of the ordinary. If he'd visited fetish or BDSM websites, they were well hidden.

I closed the laptop and returned to the living room, standing behind Mrs Hathaway. Her shoulders moved up and down as she sobbed. Jack gave me a nod which said 'I've got this.' I crept past them and went upstairs. Finding Daniel's bedroom was easy; it was crammed with books about financial management and how to make a million before thirty. I searched under the bed, in the cupboards and drawers, and through his wardrobe. There was nothing useful, though it was strange I found no fetish clothes anywhere. Did he keep them somewhere else and out of sight of his mother?

As I came down the stairs and into the living room, Jack was speaking, giving her details about the support groups available for crime victims' relatives. He handed her his card and stood. She wiped a tear from her face.

'Thank you for coming, Officers.' We both gave her a silent nod and turned to leave. I needed to sleep. 'You should have the tape Danny left me.'

We stopped dead. I got the words out first.

'What did you say, Mrs Hathaway?'

Her legs creaked as she stood.

'Danny came to me yesterday. I knew he was worried, but he wouldn't answer any of my questions. But he gave me something for safekeeping. He said it was very important, and he could only trust me with it.'

'What did he give you?' Jack asked.

Mrs Hathaway reached under her seat. 'I always sit here. No one would ever peek underneath.' She pulled out an envelope. 'I didn't open it, but I could tell there's a tape inside. I used to make loads of tapes of music off the radio when I was a teenager.' She leant towards us. 'You won't arrest me, will you?'

'Why would we do that, Mrs Hathaway?' I said.

She dropped her voice to a whisper. 'Taping music off the radio was illegal then.'

I smiled at her. 'No, Mrs Hathaway, we won't arrest you.' She breathed a sigh of relief. 'Can we have the envelope?'

She handed it over. I opened it, removed the contents and stared at the writing on it.

TAPE 3

23 ALPHABET SOUP

Soon, there'll be an opening for a new letter in the alphabet. That's what Mr X told me. And he said I could take that place.

If I passed the initiation tests.

'What tests?' I asked.

I'd always been good at tests, had passed every exam I'd taken with flying colours, but I didn't think what he meant would be the same.

'Tests of your mind and body,' he said. Missy sat in the corner, observing us, examining me. Perhaps the tests had already started. 'Tell me about your father.'

But I couldn't speak about him without mentioning her. There is nothing without her; I'm nothing without her. I have no early memories of him, only her. After putting me into therapy, I remember her taking me everywhere. He worked away, leaving only the two of us.

She took me shoplifting, and we broke into houses; she made me change bottles of hair dye in the stores, slipping the contents of one box into another; we visited train stations and gave strangers the wrong directions for their journeys. We stood outside schools, and she whispered to the mothers about the fathers waiting to pick up their children, telling them terrible lies about these men.

I asked her why she did these things.

'To prove that nurture is greater than nature,' she'd tell me. Life was important as long as we became agents of change. Our bloodlines were secondary to environment and experience. Every day, she'd ramp up her teachings, impressing upon me that what I did was more important than where I came from; that what I did was more important than what people wanted me to do. Control was everything.

I had more to say on this, but Mr X interrupted me.

'You're delaying. There's no place in the alphabet for those who hesitate. Tell me about your father.'

'He was the unhappiest man I'd ever met,' I told X.

My father was the opposite of my mother regarding the significance of existence. He hated life, but didn't know what to do about it apart from making everyone else as miserable as him. 'Misery loves company' was his motto. The only change he desired was to inflict pain upon those who were happy. He'd never had time to live a proper life and loved to tell me why.

'You come into a world you never asked for, a bawling child who knows, somehow, the terrible things awaiting them. You grow up with other mewling kids; go to a school you hate, with teachers who don't understand you and adults who want to push you around. They force food into you which animals wouldn't eat, put you in clothes passed on from the dead, encase you in sounds and smells which scratch at your senses, all hoping to craft you into another cog in the machine which batters the majority to make wealth for the minority.

'People endure this because they're sold on the lie there's a chance they'll crawl out of their assigned place in society and snuggle at the feet of the gods. Get a house, get a car, get a TV, then a computer and a phone; then throw them away and get newer versions. Install and then upgrade, climb up the ladder, be better than those around you. That's the only worth you have in life. And if you're desperate enough to scramble over the lives of others for a modicum of temporary happiness, you can prepare for your death. Then, maybe, if you follow the delusional messages attributed to imaginary beings and cults, you can pretend you'll end up in a world better than this one.'

He told me these things not as a rant, but in calculated and precise moments, his voice never wavering, and his body never losing control. I guess he wanted to write these things down, more as catharsis than delivering a manifesto, but when he tried, his mind wouldn't work; the sentences he said out loud wouldn't form onto the paper or screen the way he envisaged them. It only made his anger worse. In his studies, in his work as a lawyer, communication came easily to him; but he told me that this life of his was all a lie and so easy to project to the world; when he tried to express his true feelings, that's when he struggled to get his message across.

Perhaps this unhappiness forced him to propel his hate into the rest of the world, and he arrowed this hatred at one special section of humanity: women and girls.

My father hated half the population, fifty per cent of the world. He never hid that fact, at least not from my mother and me.

'They fawn all over you,' he'd say to me, sometimes forgetting I was one of this venomous species. 'Showering you with terms of affection until you sink below platitudes of gratitude and love, but none of it is real. They despise you. You need a shower after meeting any of them.'

Often, he'd say these things while Mother laid food in front of him, or as she cleaned up his mess. Later, I'd listen to his grunts and groans from the bedroom. But her silence roared the louder.

My father was as useful as a prick on a priest. That's what my mother said, and I agreed with her. 'If there were a school for ugliness,' she'd shout at him, 'you must have passed with flying colours.'

She didn't mean he was ugly on the outside, for he was the exact opposite, a handsome man with chiselled cheeks, impressive jawline, and magnetic eyes which lit up the whole of his face. His physique was striking, with finely tuned muscles in all the right places and not a sliver of fat on him. I inherited his looks but not the body, and I was weasel-shaped compared to his Herculean form.

No, my mother spoke about the ugliness inside him, that dark, festering personality which cheated and lied and manipulated and beat the goodness from others. I always wondered what she first saw in him, and no doubt it preyed on her mind on many a night.

It was the darkness of his soul which I believed had transferred to me when Dr Gideon explained about the flipped switch inside my head, that indicator pointing me away from the norms of society and towards something much more unusual. My mother had framed it differently.

'It's all about their desires,' she said. 'Males have this gaze which they can't control or understand; most of them, anyway. They lust after us while hating us, and the contradiction makes them even worse.'

'Your father sounds like a failure,' X said to me. 'But your mother is much more interesting. Tell me about her.'

But I didn't want to. I looked at X and knew I needed to escape his reach. What had once been excitement mixed with trepidation had changed into something which would end my life or transform it into something where I wouldn't recognise myself anymore.

Perhaps this was the ultimate action my mother wanted me to experience. I always heard her voice inside my skull, even when X glared at me and Missy played with her toys, telling me I had to endure everything this man would bestow upon me.

That was until I stared at him and his blood-red eyes like a wolf peering from a forest on fire. No box Pandora ever opened could contain so much evil as was in his head. I had to get away from him, but I wouldn't abandon Missy to his designs. Even though she'd sunk to his depths and it was hard to see her coming back. But I couldn't leave her with him. She gazed at me, possibly reading my mind, counting out to thirteen on fingers which weren't her own.

'Tell me about your mother,' he said.

There was no choice. The marks on my back told the world, told our world, I was his to do as he saw fit. It was the life I'd chosen. But then we'd thrown the rules away and, unless I acted soon, I'd be just another throwaway girl. Vampires desired fresh blood to feed on, and so did he.

'Tell me about your mother.'

He knew bits about her, snippets I'd weaved into a conversation as we'd cut and burnt and sliced our way through willing flesh; knew how she'd treated me since childhood. I think he wanted to hear more and needed that kindred spirit he'd searched for all his life. Perhaps that's why I'd been drawn to him over the others: because he reminded me of her.

'Tell me about your mother.'

So I spoke about the good things I remembered.

Mother had told me imagination is more powerful than reality. What we see around us, what we touch, and hear, and smell, they all wither away, but thoughts live on, passed down through generations. Even though people die, ideas exist on paper, walls, and tablets, even though wood rots, stone crumbles, and technology falls apart. But ideas and dreams and concepts live on beyond their originators.

We need to inspire the way people think and change their perceptions of the world and themselves, creating positive influences that last beyond us. The stories we write, the memories we make are the only things worth having. Each of us should aim bigger and try harder to be more than an individual grasping at selfish pursuits. We should deliver excitement and adventure to those around us to provide them with something worth remembering and disseminating down the generations.

He gazed at me in silence as if what I'd said had been in a foreign language, or from a forked tongue of a blasphemer.

'I've changed my mind. Your father sounds like the better parent.'

Then he laughed at me, a vast swath of hot air bursting from his lips. It was at that moment I decided not to run away, but to expose him.

But I know nothing about him, about his real self. I don't even recognise where they take me to in London. They blindfold me every time. Then we get in the car, and I assume he drives. They pick me up from a different place, mainly at night, but also the day. The first was from Kensington Gardens; last time it was Victoria Park. So far, no one has ever commented on me wearing a mask during the day. Perhaps the sight of another young girl, joking and laughing, puts them at their ease.

Missy is always smiling, even when she's doing terrible things. I look at her and know she's my way of getting to him. If I discover more about her, who she is, where she's from and get her real name, I might uncover the true him. They'd been together a while before I joined them. I think she suggested he take me under his wing.

But then I believe it was my reaction to the blood which convinced him.

I was nestled into the fetish community when I noticed him inspecting me one night. I'd conquered my fear of blood, but in this dungeon on this specific occasion, it paid me a repeat visit, the agony in my knee returning in one fell swoop and making me swoon as the bald bloke chained to the wall howled in pleasure or pain. The man I came to know as X caught me in his arms and pulled me close.

The leather mask stuck to his face and was the only thing he wore. Pressed against me, he transferred his excitement into my flesh, but we did nothing about it; sometimes, the denial was more pleasurable than the consummation.

If only I'd known then what I know about him now: he can only achieve arousal when observing someone in emotional distress. Inflicting physical pain is important to him, but it's the result of that agony which he desires.

'It's dacryphilia he told me. And I think you're the same as me.'

And I believed him for a while. But now, I know different.

I watched him with our latest volunteer, drawing a knife across the boy's chest. The kid moaned in pleasure, but X only had eyes for me.

'You'll be the last letter in the alphabet,' he said.

24 BORED TEENAGERS

It was two in the morning, and we'd listened to the tape for the third time. Only Jack and I were in the Murder Room. He touched my shoulder.

'We need to rest before we process this.'

But my mind couldn't relax.

'Mary said she'd be the last letter of the alphabet.'

He slumped into the chair opposite, the bags under his eyes leaking into the stubble.

'You think this man, this X, lied to her and led her on? That he used this claim of a group of extreme fetishists to intimidate and control her, and probably others?'

'I don't believe he controlled Mary.'

'What about this Missy girl?'

Indeed; another teenager occupying my mind. I rubbed at my flesh, remembering where the leather had touched it only a few hours earlier.

'I'm not sure if she's innocent or guilty in these events. Remember what Mary said about her on this latest tape.'

'I recall it exactly: counting out to thirteen on fingers

which weren't hers. That must mean those severed digits we found in the squat.'

'It's too much of a coincidence otherwise.'

He reached onto the table for the Coke from the vending machine. He wouldn't get any sleep after drinking that.

'How did Daniel Hathaway acquire this tape? Why did he give it to his mother for safekeeping?'

'Perhaps Mary gave it to him? She's hiding these tapes so Mr X won't find them. I'm guessing he handed it to his mother because he knew someone was closing in on him.'

Jack slurped at the Coke.

'Those things about her parents.' He shook his head. 'No wonder the kid was troubled.'

'Having met Dolores Witney, I can believe what Mary said about her mother. But the father is an enigma. She paints him as a terrible person, but the reports say nothing but good things about him.'

He wiped the sugary liquid from his lips.

'How many times have we encountered people who seemed the nicest in the world, but when we dug a little deeper, we discovered how vile they were?'

'It might be worthwhile interviewing those he knew, those he worked with.'

He slipped the tape into an evidence bag and removed his protective gloves.

'There could be more of these tapes. If we can find them, Mary might provide some physical details of Missy and Mr X.'

I peered at the cassette inside the plastic.

'She left these on purpose. We have to locate the others. She hasn't finished her story.'

Mary Witney's story wouldn't be over until we found her killer.

'You need to go home, Jen.' He checked the clock on the wall. 'We've got a meeting in twelve hours.'

I willed my eyes to stay open. He was right about me needing some rest.

'Who are we meeting?'

'I spoke to Detective Inspector Croft today, - yesterday - from the National Crime Agency. He'll give us information on the Cromwell organisation.'

Carrie Cromwell. Was she involved in this, as Ruby claimed? She'd spent time in prison for embezzling funds from her family firm, a charge she'd always denied, and had a daughter with Tommy Cromwell fourteen years ago. There was still the suspicion she'd stolen the money from her family for Cromwell. But they only married this year, presumably because of his terminal illness. How had she taken control of the Cromwell Empire when his brother was already there and had waited years for it? And why would she be involved in Mary Witney's murder and whatever this Mr X wanted?

'I can leave you to log the tape into evidence?'

He nodded. 'Go home and get some sleep.'

So I did. Go home at least. I expected little rest.

I checked Abbey's room when I got in. Her clothes were dumped on the floor, surrounded by comic books, novels, and music magazines. She was at Francine's, yet I'd spent another day away from her; another day barely thinking about her.

Was Dolores Witney a better mother than me? I wondered about this.

I sloped downstairs and stared at the answering machine. When I checked, there were no messages. Had I imagined that first one? Was that possible? Stress and lack of rest might play tricks on the mind, but could I do that to myself?

Those thoughts swirled in my head as I fell into bed. Sleep came eventually, longer and deeper than I'd had in an age.

IT WAS close to ten o'clock when I woke. I felt great, refreshed, yawning a little as I headed downstairs. There was no sign of Abbey as I put the kettle on. I texted Jack and said I'd see him at the station in an hour. He replied immediately.

No need. I'll pick you up at one-thirty, and we'll head over to the NCA's headquarters in Vauxhall.

That was good enough for me; I had three hours to eat, get ready, speak to Abbey and ruminate on last night's events. I left the water boiling and looked for her, my legs throbbing as I headed upstairs. I knocked on Abbey's bedroom door. When she didn't murmur after two minutes, I pushed it open to find the room empty; if I'd been paranoid, I might have thought she was avoiding me.

My phone was in the kitchen, so I got it as the kettle hummed. I took the tea out as I rang her number. After a minute, it went to voicemail.

'If you don't ring me in the next five minutes, I'll send a squad car out to look for you.'

I dropped two slices of bread in the toaster as I waited, feeling better than I had in a long time; even the pain in my legs had disappeared. My mobile vibrated on the table before I had the chance to get the butter from the fridge.

'I had my phone turned off.'

That was it, her only excuse; one as believable as Carrie Cromwell using her new ill-gotten gains for the benefit of the community.

'Where are you, Abbey?'

'I'm at Francine's.'

Should I call Francine's parents? Not yet. 'Will you be home later?'

'Will you?'

The kettle boiled as I did. I held the phone away from my face, picturing the image of a man in a dog costume with his throat cut. Rufus strode into the kitchen as I spoke.

'I'll be here at six, and we'll cook together. How does that sound?'

'Unlikely.'

Then she hung up on me. My fourteen-year-old daughter hung up on me. I slammed the phone onto the table, so hard even the cat jumped in the air. My head simmered as the toast burnt and I attempted to slow my beating chest. Then I spread enough butter across the hot bread to give me a heart attack, sipped at the tea, and stared at the kitchen wall.

I did that for ten minutes before heading upstairs, going into Abbey's room and rifling through everything I found. Did it make me a terrible parent? I was too annoyed even to consider it; and the irritation grew with what I discovered: a bunch of rolled cigarettes, some of which were cannabis, and a flick-knife.

The real knife thrust an imaginary dagger through my heart.

My teenage daughter had a switchblade, illegal in the UK, hidden inside a drawer in her bedroom. I crawled onto her bed and lay down, staring at the ceiling, wondering where it had gone wrong with her. I stayed there for more than an hour, my brain searching through dozens of ways in which I would deal with this and finding every one of them unsatisfactory.

The responsible parental policewoman thing to do would be to confiscate the knife, then find Abbey and drag her home.

But I didn't do either of those.

Next to Abbey's bed, the digital clock said I had thirty minutes before Jack's arrival, and I still wasn't dressed. I rolled off the bed, the knife in my hand as I reached over to drop it where I'd found it. No matter what happened with the rest of my day, I'd be here tonight and talk to her face to face.

I stretched to put the weapon back, distracted by a flashy-looking homemade flyer. What did Abbey say her alternative name was? Raven?

I grabbed the paper while slipping the switchblade into the drawer: an amateurish drawing of a girl swinging a guitar like an axe. Around it were details of a band, venue, and date and time.

Raven and Psychomania

At The Brood.

Friday @9

So few words, but I had to read it half a dozen times before the facts sank in. My daughter and her group would be on stage at the same place where we'd sweated and danced only a few nights ago. Had anyone's life changed so much in such a short space of time? Was I thinking of Abbey or Mary?

I placed the flyer back into the drawer and closed it. I reached deep inside me and flicked the switch from mother to detective; it wasn't hard to do. The music on the radio in the bedroom was something familiar and long-forgotten: one of those tracks by The Beatles that nobody sang, but could have been their greatest song. I turned off my mind, relaxed, and sat in the living room as I waited for Jack.

He arrived twenty minutes later. When I let him in, it took me a second to realise what was different about him.

'You've shaved off your beard.'

And he smelt of cinnamon and apple. He wiped at the dimple in his chin.

'It irritated me. I loved it for a while, but then it got on my nerves.'

'Welcome to my world.'

I locked the door and we stepped into his car.

He updated me on what I'd missed at work this morning as he drove to the headquarters of the National Crime Agency.

'Officers went to Hathaway's house and removed his laptop and paperwork related to his job. The computer and his phone are with Cybercrime.'

'Was there anything from the people at the Velvet Underground last night?'

'Is that the name of the club you visited? I thought they were an American rock band.'

'They were. So, was there anything?'

He shrugged and drove.

'Most of the names and addresses we got were false and the organisers, who'd promised to provide information, are now doing the exact opposite.'

'It's a community which values its privacy, Jack.'

'I value my privacy, but I'd help if I'd seen someone murdered; even if they resembled a large spotted dog.'

'Are you mad because Sutton and I visited the club without telling you?'

He puffed out his cheeks and blew out hot air.

'No. Maybe. Just a little.' He glanced at me. 'But I've kept secrets from you before, so I guess we're even.'

I didn't argue with him on that.

'Did you have a lengthy conversation with DI Croft?'

'Not really.' He gave me a long look. 'I wanted you with me for that.'

'Did you mention it was about the Cromwell crime family?'

'I did. I had to give him plenty of time to find anything useful for us.'

This meant he'd also had enough time to decide on the things he wanted to tell us and those he didn't.

But that wasn't on my mind when Jack found a parking spot.

All I could see was that flick-knife hidden in my house.

Detective Inspector Croft possessed a warm smile and a hard grip. When I released my hand from his, I expected a few missing fingers. We sat in an interview room, Croft placing a folder of papers onto the table. I assumed its contents were the bits of information which he deemed acceptable for us to see. When he spoke, I pictured Darth Vader without the mask.

'I hear you had an interesting time last night.'

It sounded as if he smoked sixty cigarettes a day. My body ached for the taste of nicotine, and my smile was as nothing to the radiance coming from his teeth.

'We were following up a link to the Mary Witney murder investigation and Carrie Cromwell.'

That information took him by surprise. He left the folder unopened on the table and sat back into his chair.

'There's so much organised crime in the UK, most of it goes unchecked. At the last count, we had a list of over five thousand criminal gangs and syndicates in Britain, employing over thirty thousand professional gangsters.' He glanced around the room and through the windows to his colleagues working outside. 'There are more gangs in Britain than staff members of the NCA; thirty thousand plus career criminals translate to more gangsters in Britain than belong to all three big Italian mafias. In the last twelve months alone, we've dealt with a Russian attempt to kill one of their former nationals on the streets of London; a North Korean cyber-attack; Eastern European slave traffickers; Scottish cocaine smugglers. And that doesn't include trying to track down the hundreds of billions of pounds laundered through London every year, plus the dramatic rise in the murder rate in the capital.'

I wondered where he was going with this impromptu crime lesson to two of London's more experienced police officers.

'You've got your work cut out for you.'

'That's why we're happy to see the Cromwell Crime Empire disappear with the death of Tommy Cromwell.'

It was my turn to look surprised. 'Tommy Cromwell died?'

'Last night, about the time you dealt with the murder of the dog-faced man.'

'That's a lucky coincidence,' Jack said.

Croft leant forward and opened the file.

'Here's a brief history of Tommy Cromwell and his empire.' He removed the first few pages. 'His father, Billy, started the syndicate with his brother John, in the early 2000s. Once they saw off their rivals, they got into drug trafficking, money laundering, extortion and the hijacking of gold bullion shipments, and security fraud. They have links to over two dozen gangland murders of informants and rival criminals.'

He wasn't telling us anything we didn't already know and was leaving out the rumours of connections to Metropolitan Police officials, plus supposed links with several sitting Members of Parliament. I glanced over at the contents of the file, staring at the Cromwell family's black and white photos.

'Billy and John died in 2010, murdered in one of those gangland fights the media love to portray as romantic and heroic, but they somehow never mention the two kids and their mother who perished in the crossfire, or the others injured inside that pub,' I said.

'This is true,' Croft continued. 'And then Tommy took over the organisation's reins while his younger brother Pete handled the security.' He pushed the photos of the brothers onto the table. 'Tommy was the brains, the one who kept all the parts ticking over. With his illness, the business fragmented and other gangs have taken over the separate bits.'

'What's happened to Pete Cromwell?'

Croft shrugged. 'He's disappeared off the face of the earth. Some say he's left London, others that he's on the run in Europe from various enemies.'

'Do you mind?' I picked up the folder and flicked through the other documents before passing them on to Jack. 'There's not much here about Carrie Cromwell or her daughter Holly.'

'She's never been involved with the business. She was in prison for a while, I'm sure you're aware, for embezzlement and fraud, but the only contact she had with Tommy was when they got together for their daughter.'

'That's not what we've heard; now she's the one controlling the business, and she's involved in some fetish-themed people trafficking.'

He burst out laughing. It was not a good look, twisting his cheekbones so he resembled the Elephant Man.

'Where did you get such nonsense?'

I wasn't about to mention Ruby Vasquez.

'We have our sources, Inspector.'

He grabbed the papers and slipped them into the folder.

'Well, I'm sorry to inform you, but your sources must have been snorting too much of their product. The Cromwell Empire is gone. Carrie may have siphoned some money from it before splitting it up, but from what I understand, she's using it for charity work in the city. So at least some good came from it.'

Croft stood as if the meeting was over, and I suppose it was. We shook his hand again, gave our thanks, and left the building. I stared across the street, and my stomach rumbled as if a freight train was going through it.

'Have you eaten today, Jen?'

'Not enough.' There was a café opposite offering an all-day breakfast; only it finished at midday. 'Do you think if we show them our police IDs they'd rustle me up some bacon and eggs?'

'I'll make sure of it, partner.'

We stepped inside. I ordered breakfast and a hot drink for me, while he got a burger and Coke. Then we talked about what just happened. When it came, I covered the sausage and bacon in brown sauce. Jack grimaced at me.

'How much of what he said do you believe, Jen?'

I bit into the meat. 'He could have mentioned all that over the phone or in an email. He wanted us there to find out what we have.'

'Which is very little.'

My second round of toast for the day stuck to my teeth.

'You know how busy they are. Either what he said is

true about Tommy Cromwell's business now being splintered and spread around other criminal gangs, or he doesn't believe it's worth bothering about if Carrie Cromwell is in control.'

'You think he's discounting her ability to run an organised crime gang because she's a woman?'

'Perhaps, but if he is, then it's a serious underestimation. She has an IQ of 160 and is sharper than a crate of new pencils.'

I finished the eggs and started on the black pudding, realising I promised Abbey I'd be cooking food with her in a few hours. And then there was that gig she was playing with her band tonight. Just the thought of saying "her band" in my head made me smile and worry at the same time.

'Are you grinning because you know something Croft doesn't?'

I told him about Abbey's group and her secret flick-knife. He wiped a stray onion from his top lip.

'Wow. That is a lot to process. What will you do about Abbey?'

The waitress came with our bill. I stared at Jack.

'Do you want to go to a gig tonight?'

He laughed. 'Why not? And you'll cook beforehand?'

'You want to eat again in a few hours?'

'This is only a snack.' He licked grease from his fingers. 'And there'll be booze at this concert, right?' I nodded. 'Best I put a lining on my guts first, then.'

I paid the bill, pushing away Jack's protests. We left the café and stood in the sun.

'We need a way in with Carrie Cromwell, Jack.'

He pondered the notion. 'Maybe through that charity event you attended.'

I thought about it as we headed back to the station.

WE RETURNED to the office so Jack could type up the notes and I'd write the report from the events at the Velvet Underground. Before we did so, the rest of our team had their updates to deliver. Grealish spoke first.

'Cybercrime has completed its check of Daniel Hathaway's computer and phone.' She handed a sheet of paper to each of us. 'His trading of stocks and shares online fell off the cliff in the last month, acquiring a debt of over ten thousand pounds with his bank.'

Jack whistled. 'And they allowed him to do that? My bank won't give me an overdraft of a hundred quid.'

'I spoke to someone at the bank. Hathaway had an excellent record with them, depositing sizeable amounts in the last two years, so they were prepared to allow him some leeway. And they also slapped a top rate of interest on his debt.'

Jack sipped at his Coke. He appeared to have developed an addiction to sugar over the last week.

'I bet they weren't happy when you told them he was dead.'

Grealish continued. 'The curious thing about his bank statements, though, if you look at the third and fourth paragraphs on the sheet I gave you, is the regular payments he made to a company called Prometheus Investments; one each for the last six months.'

So we looked at them. 'One pound each time. What were they for?'

'There are no more details on that, and the bank didn't know what they were for either. I searched for Prometheus Investments online, and there was little there, apart from a registered business number and a PO Box address. There's no website, no phone number, no email address, and no physical address. I compiled a list of businesses connected to them.'

She handed me the list; it was bookmakers, gambling sites, a charity, two online fashion shops and a block of luxury apartments.

Jack dug into his experience of quiz nights about myths and legends.

'Wasn't Prometheus a god?'

I impressed him with my knowledge.

'Prometheus was a Titan of Greek mythology, a Trickster figure who stole fire from Zeus and the Gods and gave it to mortals.'

Grealish interrupted the history lesson.

'Because I couldn't find anything through the usual internet channels, I dug around underneath and dropped some questions in the less than salubrious sites.'

My interest grew. 'I'm guessing you found something.'

'Just rumours about them, mainly from those who use illegal gambling websites and apps. Prometheus Investments provide individuals with funds for these sites, and they take a small amount from your bank account as a direct debit, but that is only a percentage of what the borrower owes.'

'How much?'

'The reports vary, but that single pound could be up to £10,000.'

Jack whistled again. 'Jesus, that's a lot of money.'

'No wonder he was desperate to sell a story to Ruby Vasquez,' I said.

As we processed that, Sutton provided an update on the forensic report on Hathaway's murder. A slice across his neck with surgical precision, in Athena Temple's exact words, was the fatal wound.

'The severed hands appear to have come from the same person. There's no way to identify the owner with no fingers for fingerprints, but they are male, aged between thirty and fifty.'

I took the printed forensic report from her and dropped it on my desk.

'I need you to do something else for me, Sarah.'

Jack gave me a mock evil eye, disapproving of my drop into informality with her. He was probably still thinking about our trip to the Velvet Underground.

'Yes, ma'am.'

'Get a list of the guests or patrons from that charity event. See if you can find out who won the main auction of a date with Carrie Cromwell.'

'Will do, ma'am.'

She returned to her computer as Jack dragged his chair towards me.

'You two must have bonded last night if you're calling Sutton by her first name in here.'

'Is that a joke?'

He arched his eyebrows. 'What do you mean?'

'You're asking if we bonded at a bondage party.'

He put his hand on his chest and grinned. 'I promise I didn't, Jen. I'm not that clever.'

'You got that right, partner.' We laughed together, and then he changed the subject.

'Are you borrowing more clothes from Sarah for the gig tonight?' There was a heavy emphasis on her name.

'I'll ask her if she has some for you, if you want?'

He continued laughing as he returned to his desk. I stared

at my screen, at the accumulation of data we had for two murders, a bag of severed fingers, and two hands minus their fingers and everything else. There was nothing to show for it on the monitor, but in my head, I knew it all led to one name.

Carrie Cromwell.

26 PSYCHOMANIA

It took little to talk Jack into coming back to mine so I could make him a meal.

'As long as Abbey's doing most of the cooking,' he said.

I laughed about it as we left work, but his comment had become prophetic by the time we walked into the house. Abbey flicked burgers like a professional and everywhere smelt of fried onions and sizzling beef as we strode into the kitchen.

She glanced at Jack before turning back to the frying pan.

'It's a good job I got enough for tonight and tomorrow.'

'You didn't trust me then?'

I dropped my bag onto the floor and threw my jacket over a chair. Jack didn't wait for a drink, heading for the fridge and beers for both of us. The bottle chilled my fingers as he handed it to me. Abbey frowned at him.

'Where's mine, Jack?'

He glanced at me while I shrugged.

'You need to keep your head straight if you're performing tonight.'

She left the meat in the pan as smoke drifted around the kitchen.

'How do you know that?'

How did I know that? I'd stupidly given it away that I'd gone through her room. Jack intervened to save my bacon as Abbey stopped the beef from burning.

'I saw it online, Raven.'

She grinned at him, and then at me.

'Mum told you about my new name?'

'She did, kiddo. And she said you're getting a guitar and lessons from me.'

Abbey turned the grill off.

'Yeah, starting tomorrow, right?'

Jack gulped his drink like a professional.

'That's correct. Not too early, though. I might have a hangover.' He winked at me. 'If you're singing tonight, I'll need a lot of booze to protect my ears.'

'You wish.' She punched him in the shoulder before shovelling burger and onions into buns for the three of us. 'There are fries in the oven.'

I grabbed some mitts. 'I'll sort those out. You get the plates ready, and Jack can get settled.'

We sat around the table, with me steering the conversation to Abbey's new career.

'How did you discover this band - what are they called? Psychokillers or something?'

Abbey snatched the Coke from Jack. I'd convinced him to slow down after he'd drunk two beers in twenty minutes.

'We're Psychomania. It's a new group, first gig tonight, and I picked the name.'

Jack gurgled his drink like he was a teenager.

'Isn't that a film?'

Abbey's eyes lit up. 'Absolutely. It's a biker horror movie

from the 1970s. Francine's brother has all these videotapes and a player at their house. We've been binge-watching them the last week to get ideas for lyrics. *Psychomania* is my favourite and a cool name for a band. Don't you think, Mum?'

It sounded terrible to me, but I didn't say so.

'It's great, Abbey.' I was just glad we were behaving like a typical family again. 'Who else is in this group of yours?'

She grabbed a handful of fries and dipped them in barbecue sauce, eating and talking simultaneously.

'Francine is on backing vocals, her brother, Rick, is lead guitar. His mate Dev is on drums and Dev's girlfriend Shelley is on bass guitar.' She turned sheepish as we stared at her. 'We're not the main band tonight, only the first support. We're playing for twenty minutes, which is good because we only have four songs so far.'

Jack squeezed his burger into near oblivion.

'Are they five minutes long, these tunes of yours?'

Abbey continued to devour the rest of the fries. It must have been nervous energy because I hadn't seen her eat so much in an age and I'd worried she might be anorexic.

'No, but we're doing some covers as well.'

'Will we know them?' I said.

Her smile lit up my heart.

'Wait and see.' She glanced at the clock on the wall and bounced from the table. 'I have to get changed before the guys come for me.'

She scampered out the kitchen and upstairs like a mini-whirlwind. Jack let out a loud burp when she'd gone.

'At least she seems happy.'

I threw my hand in front of my face and attempted to wave away his stink.

'Yes, it's wonderful, but what shall I do about the knife in her room?'

His chair creaked as he leant into it and patted his gut.

'Give her some space and speak to her about it tomorrow.'

'Maybe.' It was best to put off a difficult conversation.

'Are we working tomorrow?'

'At some point.' I looked at my mobile. 'Sarah texted earlier to say she'd tracked down the therapist, Dr Gideon. I have a phone number for her.'

Jack stood. 'You should ring her now and arrange a visit.'

'And what are you going to do?'

'Little boys' room.'

He went off while I rang Gideon. All I got was an answering machine, so I left a message. When I finished, Abbey came bounding down the stairs. When I looked at her, I thought I'd fallen back into the Velvet Underground: she wore a leather jacket, her Hex Pistols shirt, a short skirt and torn tights. She glared at me, waiting, I assumed, for me to tell her to get changed.

'Are teenagers allowed into this pub?'

She zipped up the coat and put on a pair of lace gloves.

'Yes, if you're with a parent or responsible adult.'

Jack came back into the room. 'Well, that rules one of us out.'

He stared at me as if reading my mind. I gazed at my daughter, who appeared way older than fourteen, and considered what to do. Then I chose a compromise.

'You can go tonight and sing, but I'm taking you there.'

Abbey glared at me. 'You can't drive, you've been drinking.'

She was correct. 'I'll rephrase that. You can go tonight

with this band, but you're coming with Jack and me in a taxi.'

I didn't know what to expect from her, but when she jumped forward and threw her arms around my neck, it was not that.

'Thanks, Mum. You won't regret it, I promise.'

She pulled from me, and I wanted her back in my arms again; instead, I smiled. Getting into her good books now might give me some leverage tomorrow when I broached the subject of the knife and the drugs.

Someone tooted a car horn outside, and Abbey ran to the window.

'That's the band.' Her eyes bulged wide, her body full of nervous energy and bouncing up and down. I clutched her hand, and static electricity flew through me.

'Tell them we'll meet at the pub.'

She sprinted from the house before she exploded. Jack stood there and grinned at me.

'And you told me you were a terrible mother.'

We grabbed our jackets to leave. 'You make sure you stay sober tonight, partner.'

He frowned as I called for a taxi. As I got outside, I glimpsed the rest of the band, all dressed in black so they'd be invisible in the darkness. As they drove off and Abbey ran back towards us, and I cringed again at what she wore, I thought that might be a good thing.

She continued to be a bundle of energy as we waited for our lift, chatting away with Jack about when he was a musician. I observed her, perhaps the lengthiest time I'd focused on her for a long while, and tried to remember what I was like at that age. I was the same, rebelling against the adults around me, wearing clothes my parents disapproved of, getting boyfriends they hated, doing and saying anything just to upset them. Wasn't this a rite of passage for all teenagers? At least I'd be with her tonight and, if everything passed smoothly, she might trust me again; trust me enough to talk about the things she'd hidden from me.

———

THERE WAS no queue scrambling outside The Brood when we arrived. Inside, the gig space was closed for the sound checks, and Abbey sprinted off to be with the rest of her group. Jack and I retreated to the bar. He bought the drinks while I monitored what was happening in the other room.

A familiar tone dragged my attention back to the bar.

'What would you two like to drink?'

Sutton and Grealish stood together as I turned around.

I tried not to show how pleased I was to see them.

'What are you doing here?'

'Inspector Monroe invited us, ma'am.'

Thankfully, Sutton's voice was so low, I didn't think anyone else heard her words.

'No formalities tonight, ladies,' Jack said. 'I'll get the first round in.'

Sutton took me to one side while he did that.

'I asked everyone I could at the station about who might have spoken to your father and given him your home phone number, but came up with nothing.'

'Thanks anyway, Sarah.'

I wouldn't dwell on it now. This was to be Abbey's night. The last image I needed in my head was her grandfather.

Fifteen minutes later, we all had drinks in our hands as we watched Psychomania take to the stage. Including us, there were a dozen people there. The lack of bodies didn't seem to bother Abbey as she grabbed the microphone and peered into the tiny audience. She found me and strode to the edge of the stage.

'We're Psychomania and this one's called *Death Dance*.'

The guitars and drums burst into life together, a squealing, shrieking cacophony that was one of the worst things I'd ever heard. It was as if the three of them had never played their instruments before tonight, and they probably hadn't. Abbey cradled the microphone and sang.

THE RUNNING *girl*
>   *She flees your world*
>   *The running girl*
>   *She flees your world*
>   *She's like an insect*
>   *In your grasp*
>   *Like an insect*
>   *In your grasp*
>   *A flea put to task.*
>   *All she has is the death dance*
>   *All she has is the death dance*
>   *All she has is the death dance*

IT LASTED ABOUT TWO MINUTES, gathering polite applause at the finish from the audience which had grown to about twenty. Jack grinned at me as I clapped, wondering how my daughter had written those lyrics.

My worry decreased slightly with the next track, a semi-humorous tune about a vegetarian end of the world named *Apocalypse Cow*. Then there was a number which I think was about the movie *Titanic* before two covers, *Wuthering Heights* and *Blitzkrieg Bop*. They finished with a song called *Knife*.

Abbey lowered her voice, only accompanied by a low hum from the guitar this time. She bowed her head as the instrument droned over the crowd before lifting her face to gaze around a captive audience. And then she sang like Nico.

A touch
    So cold
    A shimmer
    A sliver
    Just enough
    To keep me
    Thinner
    A kiss
    To lips
    Never
    To heal
    That tender
    Caress
    Never
    To feel
    You put
    Me away
    Saving up
    You said
    For a rainy
    Day
    A burnt
    Memory

A distant
   Distress
   Now just
   History
   For your
   Cold
   Mistress

THERE WAS silence when she finished, the guitar ending on the last syllable. The crowd appeared stunned. I was shell-shocked. Then whistles and applause spread through the venue and inside my brain.

Jack was the first to congratulate the band as they climbed off the stage.

'Well done, guys. That was excellent.'

Sutton and Grealish joined in with the praise. Abbey was the last one down; resembling a rabbit in the headlights, she stared straight at me, her eyes burrowing deep into mine. I stumbled forward, drunk on pride and confusion, and threw my arms around her. I fought back the tears when we pulled away.

'Will you still talk to me when you're famous?'

Her lips trembled as she spoke. All the confidence from the stage had vanished as soon as she faced me.

'Did you like it, Mum?'

'I didn't like it, Abs.' I shook my head. 'I loved it.'

'Time for more drinks,' Jack said as he slapped everyone on the back.

We stayed until the band had collected their gear before I made our excuses and took Abbey home. Jack hung around with Sutton and Grealish, and I reminded him about tomorrow's guitar lesson before he had too much to drink.

Abbey beamed all the way home in the taxi, holding my hand like she hadn't done since she was a little girl. I think she wanted to talk, but I saw the emotional exhaustion creeping through her.

'You were great, love,' I said one more time as she floated off to bed.

I watched her and wondered whether to be happy or worried about the lyrics she wrote.

Saturday morning started lazily. By the time I'd slipped out of bed, showered and got dressed, Abbey was cooking brunch. There was no burger and fries, but roasted vegetables and grilled chicken. I stood in the kitchen with my mouth resembling an open bin.

'You'll catch flies like that, Mum.'

'So who kidnapped my daughter and replaced her with a pod person?'

Abbey switched off the oven and pointed to the table where a glass of orange juice waited for me. I sat and drank it as she shared her thoughts about the gig.

'I had the greatest time.' She must have repeated that ten times as we ate.

The fruit juice cleansed my mouth as I watched her talk. I may have been joking about the pod person, but now, in this moment and last night, it was the difference between light and dark compared to the previous three months. I didn't want it to end.

'Jack will be here at two for your guitar lesson so I'll do the washing up.'

After that, I was hoping we'd visit Dr Gideon. I'd had no response to the message I left her yesterday, so would call again.

She grinned at me. 'That's if he gets here.'

I scooped vegetables into my mouth. 'What do you mean?'

'Didn't you see him with your two lady cops last night? I don't know which one he flirted with the most.'

I nearly choked on a piece of chicken. 'You're joking?'

'Nope. I'm surprised you didn't notice. Is it allowed for officers to be in a relationship?'

'Well,' I rubbed at my throat to loosen a stray pepper, 'junior officers shouldn't be involved with a senior officer. It leaves the situation open to exploitation.'

'If Jack's smiling when he gets here, we'll know he had sex last night.'

I grabbed at my drink, hoping it would cool down the heat racing through me. Abbey was fourteen, but I hadn't had that conversation with her yet. I'd tried two years ago, but she'd hushed me into silence.

'We get those lessons at school,' she'd told me.

I watched her drop the dirty plates into the sink, humming a Nine Inch Nails tune as she did. I barged straight in.

'Do you have a boyfriend, Abbey?'

It was her turn to form an O with her mouth. Then she smiled.

'Or a girlfriend?'

I was ashamed to say I'd never even considered that.

'Francine?'

'God, no, Mum. Franny's my best mate.'

I deliberated telling her an intimate relationship with

your best friend might be a good thing. But what did I know? I wasn't an expert in the field.

'I thought maybe, with you being in a band now, that you'd, perhaps...'

'Get involved in sex and drugs and rock-and-roll?'

I pulled at my throat, trying to dislodge the frog stuck there.

'Something like that.'

She came over and kissed me on the cheek. I couldn't remember the last time that had happened.

'You've nothing to worry about, Mum.'

'That's good to hear.' Though I wasn't sure I believed it.

She changed the subject. 'Did you listen to your message on the answering machine?'

My hands shook as I gripped onto the empty glass. 'What?'

'It must have been left when we were at the gig.'

My legs and back pushed up against the fridge, fingers pressed into my chest.

'Is it the same as from the other day?'

She looked confused. 'I didn't see one then. This is the only message I've noticed all week. It's some doctor or other.'

'Doctor?'

'Yeah. She wants to meet you or something. She must have tried your mobile last night, but you won't have heard it at the gig. Did you give her the home number?'

'It must be Dr Gideon.'

I'd left both numbers in my original message. I went into the living room and played it.

Hello, Inspector Flowers. This is Dr Gideon returning your call. I'll be in my office tomorrow, Saturday, from four o'clock.

I deleted the message. Four would be perfect, once Jack and Abbey had finished their lesson. And it would give Jack and me a chance to talk about what we'd ask Gideon. I texted him about my plan.

He arrived at two, carrying a guitar and an amp. I hadn't considered the noise they'd make and wondered if I should warn the neighbours. He'd dressed as if about to interview a suspect: Armani suit, velvet shirt and tie, new brogues, and clean-shaven. My surprised look must have amused him.

'I thought it best to stay professional since we're going to see Gideon.'

I didn't argue with him, leaving the two of them in the living room while I sat outside in the sun. Rufus joined me, peering at me from a safe distance. A distorted fuzz burst from the house every few minutes, and the cat jumped into the air. People walked by and looked at me. I thought about Dr Gideon's message on the answering machine and wondered about my father's one.

Did he leave that message? If so, why hadn't he called again? Sutton told me she'd checked around the station to see who had passed my number on to him and didn't find anyone who'd admit to it. Personal numbers were off-limits without permission, so maybe that's why nobody owned up.

Or did I imagine the entire thing? Abbey said she couldn't remember seeing any other messages this week. But why would I do that about a man I'd hadn't seen for nearly twenty years?

Was it stress? And if so, why now? These and a thousand other questions swarmed inside my head as I waited for the lesson to end. Abbey was the first out of the house, with guitar clutched to her chest and a Cheshire Cat grin.

'Jack said I'm a natural, Mum. He said I'd be playing it in the band in a few weeks.'

I scooped up Rufus before he could escape.

'What about the guitarist you already have?'

She swung the instrument in her hand like a gunslinger.

'Oh, he's crap. We'll be much better when I'm singing and strumming.'

Jack stepped outside. 'It's difficult playing and singing together, Abbey.'

She considered his words. 'It never stopped Lennon and McCartney.'

I was impressed with her musical knowledge. 'Give Jack his guitar back, Abbey. We have to go soon.' For once, I didn't feel guilty for leaving her alone.

'I'll leave it and the amp with her, Jen. She should practise as much as possible.'

'Great.' Abbey was off before she saw the horror in my face. 'What have I got myself into?'

He laughed at me. 'You're about to have the best time of your life, partner.'

He was still saying it thirty minutes later as we stepped from the car outside Dr Gideon's office. There was a bank next door and a pub opposite, one of those places where drinks were cheap and the punters low rent. The doctor's workplace was on the second floor of a modern block of other offices, surrounded by accountants, solicitors, and a media company. Jack tried the door, but it didn't open. I pressed the buzzer and peered into the small camera above our heads. A red light blinked, and then the entrance opened.

'It's easier to get inside a prison,' Jack said as we entered.

A morose looking woman with a beehive greeted us.

'You must be the police detectives Dr Gideon is expecting.'

I showed her my identity card. 'Is Dr Gideon here?'

'She's with a client at the moment, if you wouldn't mind waiting?' She pointed towards some comfy chairs and a coffee table.

Jack picked up a glossy magazine, a copy of *Town and Country*, and opened the pages to an article which appeared to be about how difficult it was to be a member of the Royal Family. He lifted it so it was between the receptionist and us and spoke to me.

'What do we know about Dr Gideon?'

'Only what our dedicated researchers discovered.' I got my phone and found the file Constable Grealish had sent me. 'Dr Helen Gideon is a Psychoanalyst. With a medicine and psychiatry background, she first trained in Psychoanalytic Psychotherapy at the Thomas Clinic, London, and then in Psychoanalysis at the Institute of Psychoanalysis, London. She's a member of the British Psychoanalytical Society and the International Psychoanalytical Association. She's registered with the General Medical Council and the British Psychoanalytic Council.'

'That's impressive.'

I didn't know if he was speaking about her achievements or the new article he'd flicked to in the magazine, something about male vanity and how the rich and famous used innovative medical procedures to take twenty years off their appearance. The receptionist coughed.

'Dr Gideon will see you now.'

We got up, and she led us into the doctor's main office; a profusion of healthy green plants gave it the feel of a friendly jungle, while comfortable, supportive-looking chairs begged to be sat in, and nature-based artwork adorned the walls. About ten diplomas hung on the far wall, all of them advertising Gideon's expertise; her clean, clutter-free desk added to the feeling of openness and space.

A tall woman with an athlete's physique stood behind the desk and held out her hand towards me.

'You must be Inspector Flowers.'

It was a firm grip from soft flesh. Her long dark hair flowed down onto her shoulders, and even before she turned to Jack, I sensed his knees wobbling.

'Detective Inspector Jack Monroe,' he said as she took his hand.

'Please, have a seat,' Gideon said once she got her hand back.

So we did, and I focused on her wall of qualifications.

'That's an impressive collection of credentials you have, Doctor.'

'The more certificates on show, the better.' She settled into her chair. 'There was a study taken a few years ago which asked two hundred undergraduates to look for one minute at a photo of a clinician's office, furnished in a modern, minimalist style, and to give their impression of the therapist who worked there. All the images came from the perspective of the client's chair, but some students viewed a version with bare walls and no family photos on the desk. In contrast, other students scrutinised a version with a certificate-adorned wall and family photos on the desk. There was no therapist present.

'The key finding was that students who saw an office with certificates on the wall rated the therapist not only as more skilful, experienced, better-trained, and more authoritative, but also as more friendly, kinder, welcoming, pleasant and interested in clients. This was before they even met them; the more certificates, the better. Students who saw an office with four or nine certificates and diplomas rated the therapist as even more friendly and proficient than students who saw an office with just two or no certificates. And for the perceived energy and dynamism of the therapist, nine certificates were better than four.'

I counted the ones on the wall. 'You have ten.'

'Always aim high, Inspector.'

I wondered if she was already analysing us.

'Is therapist your official title, Dr Gideon?' Jack said.

'I'm a Psychoanalytic Psychotherapist, Inspector.'

'And what exactly does that entail?' I said.

'Psychoanalytic Psychotherapy draws on theories and practices of Analytical Psychology and Psychoanalysis. It is a therapeutic process which helps patients understand and resolve their problems by increasing awareness of their inner world and its influence over relationships, both past and present.'

'You did this with Mary Witney for a decade?'

She didn't answer my question. 'It's terrible what happened to Mary. Have you caught her killer yet?'

'That's why we're here, Doctor.'

Her eyes narrowed. 'Am I a suspect, Inspector?'

'We want to build a profile of Mary, Dr Gideon, for our investigation. You spent a decade with her, so anything you tell us would be an enormous help.'

I gave her my broadest smile. And then Jack blundered in with his size ten boots.

'Did she have a psychological condition which made her seek pleasure in other people's pain?'

Her gaze cut through him like a knife. 'Mary wasn't a sadist, Inspector, if that's what you're implying.' She switched her focus to me. 'She may be dead, but doctor and patient confidentiality still covers Mary's time with me.'

Her hesitation was not unexpected; we'd need to use more guile to get anything useful from her.

'She first came to you when she was seven. Isn't that a

little young to start therapy?'

She clasped her hands together as if performing for the media.

'Mary's mother was keen to bring her to me, and since Dolores was an acquaintance of mine, I couldn't say no. Mary was suffering trauma from an accident to her knee, which had produced a mild case of haemophobia, a fear of blood. I knew with time she'd overcome her dread.'

'But that anxiety transformed into something else, didn't it, where Mary mixed up her feelings regarding pleasure and pain, so it was difficult for her to separate one from the other?'

Gideon grinned at me. 'Are you a trained Psychoanalytic Psychotherapist, Inspector?'

I smiled back. 'Just a layperson expressing her thoughts, Doctor; we came here for your expertise.'

Jack went straight for the jugular. 'Did you know Mary was sexually attracted to you?'

She didn't flinch. 'It's not uncommon for patients to fixate on their therapist. Mary's early teenage years were difficult for her to process.'

'Difficult, how?' I said.

'Her mother can be - how can I put this delicately? - she can be assertive to the point of aggression. She's an emotionally belligerent woman, and I came to believe that...' Gideon placed one hand in the air as if the rest of her thought had trailed off into the ether.

'What did you believe about Dolores Witney, Doctor?'

She didn't speak for a minute. 'I don't suppose it matters now, considering what's happened to them both, but I eventually understood Mary's issues were more to do with her mother than her accident when she was six.'

Jack gave it another try. 'Didn't you tell Mary those

parts of her brain which produce pleasure were changed, so she found enjoyment in seeing the pain in others?'

Gideon glared at him as if he was a shadow made real.

'I have no recollection of ever saying that, Inspector.'

'You said Dolores was an acquaintance of yours, Doctor. What did you mean by that?' I said.

'We were at school together.'

'Friends?'

'Acquaintances.'

The woman was a block of granite. I explained to her how Mary died; her expression never moved an inch.

'Is there anything you can tell us which might provide insight into who killed her?'

'Inspector, I wish there was something about my time with Mary which could explain what happened to her, but I'm afraid there isn't.'

Jack's face turned purple next to me, and I decided it would be prudent to leave. I got out of the chair even though the whole of my body screamed to stay there.

'Thank you for your help, Dr Gideon.'

She stood. 'You might find the insight you want in here, Inspector.' She opened a drawer and pulled out an envelope. 'I received this last week.' She emptied the contents onto the table: a card and a cassette tape. Jack put on his protective gloves as I spoke.

'Have you listened to it, Doctor?'

'I don't have the technology for that.'

Jack picked up the card and read it out loud.

Keep me safe. Mary.

A phantom dagger stabbed at my heart.

Jack returned the card and the tape to the envelope.

And then we left.

The knife kept on digging into me all the way to the car.

I was ten when Dolores took me on my first holiday. Father was working away as usual, so it was only us. We left the south and headed north. Something about it, where we journeyed, was important to her, but she wouldn't say what.

It was summer; the schools were out, and my sessions with Gideon on hold. I was glad to be getting time off from her, though I didn't understand why we were travelling so far. The kids where we lived told me everywhere in the north was dark and cold and it never stopped raining. And the people there were dirty and smelly, and every other word from their mouths was an obscenity. I told Dolores it sounded as if we were heading into the jungle and I wouldn't go. But she refused to listen to my concerns.

'We'll have our own place there,' Dolores kept telling me. 'You'll see the countryside and the sea and get out of the pollution for a while.' She didn't say why we travelled three hundred miles apart from trying to convince me it was good for my health. I clutched at the scar on my knee every time she mentioned the name of the village. It had once had a thriving fishing industry but, as I soon discovered, was dying like the rest of the region.

Dolores seemed excited by the prospect, but the reality was terrible for me: a cramped house swimming in damp, with an aroma of fish impossible to remove no matter how many times I cleaned it; and she made me clean it every day.

'You must get out and experience life,' she told me. It was her daily mantra. I assumed our journey to such an alien location was her way of taking me to another world, but I explored the environment with zero enthusiasm. I missed the grey concrete, fume-filled skies, and the buzz of the city.

And Dolores didn't help; she threw me into the setting with no explanation. She stayed indoors most of the time. I think she cried behind those doors, but I never witnessed such a miracle. So I sought the experience she wanted of me.

My first encounter was the jetty's massive grey winding finger and the blokes battling the elements and the creatures beneath the waves. I don't know why, but the fishermen fascinated me. They were a small group of rough-looking men, but one remained apart from the rest, lurking at the end of the jetty in isolation.

That first day I ran past them, I was in a playful mood, singing some tune heard on the radio, not realising the song was about a woman who died from a broken heart. The men of the village ignored me or scowled at the noise I made.

'You'll scare the fish away,' they shouted at me through wind-ravaged faces and yellowed skin; but not the isolated man. He was always quiet, eyes sunk into the coarse beard covering most of his face; facial hair so overgrown, it could have housed seagulls seeking refuge from the changing climate.

As I pirouetted on my heels to return home, I noticed the gigantic bag near his legs containing a pile of dusty-looking books squashed together. That's when the unfamiliar world hooked me in because reading is the greatest love of my life.

Within a week, we would be on first-name terms, and I would have read the first book he gave me: a faded copy of *Moby Dick*. Some people may have thought it too difficult for a ten-year-old, but he didn't.

'Call me, Joe,' he said as he handed over the novel. I ran back to the house and avoided Dolores. Later, as we ate the food she'd cooked, I told her what had happened. I expected her to tell me off for talking to a stranger, for taking something from him, but she only smiled.

'Books are not real life,' she said, though she never stopped me reading.

I saw Joe again the next day, sitting at the furthest part of the jetty, his line far out into the sea. He turned to me and held out the rod.

'Would you like to fish?' he said.

Of course, I would. Anticipation rippled through me. I wanted to see the fish in the water, but despised the thought of killing them.

'Don't worry,' he said. 'I always throw them back. It's one reason this lot don't like me.' He nodded towards the other fishermen. I felt the hate seeping from them; not just for him, but for me. Why would a bunch of adults hate a ten-year-old girl?

Maybe they loathed my youth. As people get older, do they resent the young around them? 'Do with your life what I didn't do with mine,' I imagine them saying. And then they want to smite you down with words or deeds because you might have a life they never had.

It scared me to hold on to the fishing rod, my eyes drifting towards the bag full of Joe's fishing paraphernalia and sandwiches, before settling on the tower of books threatening to tumble over and sink into the ocean.

It took two minutes of us grabbing the rod together to get a catch, lifting it as the fish struggled on the line, bringing it closer. I saw the scales on the creature glistening in the fading light, smelt the aroma of the sea and breathed in that unknown life existing beneath the waves. Joe freed the fish from its bondage and gave it to me.

'Release it back into the water, child; give it the gift of life others want to deny it,' he said.

I stood, struggling to hold on to the creature, amazed and scared by its alien feel against my skin, before returning it to the dark blue waters. Life exhilarated me then. Now I understood what Dolores had tried to teach me, how she'd pushed for me to experience life and not just exist within it.

He smiled, and I ran to the house. Dolores asked me what I'd done, and I said nothing. I couldn't bear to tell her she'd been right all along.

She never took me on holiday again.

I left home at sixteen and I'd recommend it for everyone, leaving the day of my father's funeral. I'm not sure how many people attended, but I slipped from the house with a thousand pounds Dolores had hidden under the marital bed. London's streets are paved with gold, so it's said, but I discovered concrete and grass teeming with vermin and insects crawling on two legs.

But there's one positive thing I'll say about how Dolores raised me, including those sessions with Dr Gideon: it prepared me in body and mind for what waited for me. And the money helped. I rented a flat and found a spot at college. Then I was ready to explore the rest of the city, to fall into a life where pleasure and pain came with a guarantee of safety.

But safety soon becomes boring. If life isn't about taking risks, then what's the point of it? That's Dolores speaking through me. Or is it me speaking through her?

Mr X knows about taking risks; not just taking them, but seeking them out.

'You're my greatest risk,' he told me.

He took his time to balance out risk and reward before showing me his face. Missy stood with us, as always, as we left the club at four in the morning. She led me by the hand, X behind us, as we headed to the river. London was quiet; the only sound I heard was the noise of my heart thumping inside my head.

A group of homeless people peered at us as we walked, probably curious about the masks we wore. Was this part of my initiation?

'It's time you saw me as I really am,' X said. I thought he meant his face. Later, I'd know differently.

Missy went first, but I'd seen her real face before: blonde like me, wide-eyed but not so innocent. Then I followed suit. But they'd seen me before as well; only he was the enigma.

The moon shone behind him as he slipped off his mask. When he did, I realised why he kept it on around others. He came on like a back-room drug dealer: confident but shifty, glittering eyes flickering everywhere, scrutinising people as if they were barcodes, and he was a scanner checking their details. An archaic Beatles haircut covered most of his head, but I guessed it was a wig. He spoke to me for minutes, a litany of promises and rewards to come.

Every word out of his mouth was part of a larger plan focusing on selling you something or purchasing your soul for a pittance of the price.

But he hooked me. I was the fish on the line, never returning to the water.

'You're ready now,' he said, taking me by the hand. Missy held onto my other one. We left the riverside, into dark alleys and grim shadows, a ten-minute journey to an abandoned building. We walked up five floors, along a corridor, and into a room at the end. They must have been there before. Graffiti covered all the walls, the windows either broken or boarded up.

A set of chains hung from the ceiling; Missy moved to the wall and lowered them. The stink overpowered me, the decay and human waste forcing my heart to claw at my ribs.

'Is this what you desire?' Mr X said to me. Missy bit at her fingernails. Did she want me to agree or not? I recognised what he wanted. It burnt through his eyes. Dolores, and my father, and Dr Gideon, and Joe buzzed inside my head, with each of them telling me different things.

Books are not real life. This is real life.

I stepped into the chains willingly. Why wouldn't I?

I'm not sure how long the session lasted, five minutes or five hours, but I'd experienced nothing like it before. This was what Dolores had pushed me towards all my life. I may have blacked out. When I came down, there was someone else in the room with us, a boy about my age. He didn't move. The smell of fresh blood lingered everywhere, the food in my gut threatening to explode out of me.

He hung naked and pale; pale apart from the purple bruises and the red blood.

'Is he dead?' I asked.

'Not yet,' X replied. 'But soon.'

And then he set to work.

And I watched. I could have fled; no one would have stopped me. I looked into Missy's eyes and I knew that's what she wanted. Did she want me to run and save us both? Or did she need me to leave, to have all this for herself?

But I didn't run. I blacked out.

There were dreams or nightmares, none that I can remember. Dream sequences are for lazy writers.

When I woke, Missy sat opposite, staring at me. My arms ached, my legs throbbed, my skull possibly split in two.

Yet it was euphoric; I'd crossed Damascus.

'I don't know why he likes you,' she said. 'You're weak. Weak and feeble and puny and pathetic.' There was love in her voice as she spoke.

The boy and the blood had vanished.

'Where's the kid?' I said

'Cleaned up,' she said. 'X has people who look after him. He's gone to work now,' she said as she got up. 'You won't last long like this.' Then she left.

I sat there in the damp and the stink.

I couldn't give this terrible thing up. But perhaps I could make those involved pay for what they'd done.

Even if that included me.

29 CARRIE

It was seven o'clock on Saturday evening and, even though we'd promised not to go into work, here we were listening to that tape for the third time. Jack placed a hand to his face.

'My head hurts.'

I dropped the cassette into an evidence bag; it was my turn to take it to be processed.

'We should head home and think about this and Gideon's information. Hopefully, we'll have something concrete to go on when we return on Monday. And we've still got the staff at the Houses of Parliament to interview. One of them might remember seeing Mary that night.'

The dark shadows under his eyes threatened to drag him into the underworld.

'Did we get anything from Gideon, though?' He pointed at the bag in my hand. 'Are these tapes useful, or are they just a distraction?'

I placed it on the table. 'I feel like I understand more about Mary than I do with most victims we deal with. Don't you?'

He ran fingers through his hair, and I hoped he wouldn't pull a sizeable chunk out.

'Is she telling the truth, that's the question?'

And it was an important one.

'I think she is. I believe Mary had several challenges to overcome, and she gave herself a voice the only way she could; one in death she didn't have in life.'

'You're right, Jen, but if everything we've heard on these tapes is true, then you must realise she's culpable in some crimes she described.'

'I do. I didn't say this would be easy, but we have to continue.'

He grabbed his coat from the chair. 'So where do we go next?'

We strode to the door together.

'I'll drop this tape off, and then head home to make sure Abbey hasn't annoyed the neighbours too much with her guitar playing. And you'll have a well-earned rest. We'll return on Monday refreshed, sort out the Parliament staff's interviews, and then, somehow, set ourselves up to speak to Carrie Cromwell. I'm convinced she's at the heart of all this.'

We said our goodbyes, and I left him to enjoy the weekend.

I SPENT Saturday night with Abbey, eating junk food and watching junk movies. We didn't talk about the band or her music. I think she wanted to keep as much of it inside her, fearful she could lose something so important to her. For me, I didn't know how to broach the subject of her lyrics. Was she writing from her heart, from her experiences, or were those songs, in particular *Death Dance* and *The Knife*, expressions of her life? Plus, there was the switchblade and the drugs.

So, I avoided all these things as we pigged out on pizza and *Groundhog Day*, which isn't a junk movie, but a classic.

When Abbey headed upstairs, my mind returned to Mary Witney. There was one last avenue we hadn't visited in pursuit of her killer. I got my phone and dialled the number.

There was no answer. It was my turn to leave a message.

Then I finished a bottle of wine and went to bed.

THERE WAS a reply to my message waiting for me when I rose on Sunday; I read it with curious eyes and hoped it would lead to something. After breakfast, I dropped Abbey at Francine's house for a band session. She had the guitar with her. Then I drove to Greenwich for my meeting.

It was the first time I'd been to the National Maritime Museum, passing the Cutty Sark and a flock of tourists to get there. I made a mental note to return with Abbey and show her the birthplace of both Henry VIII and his daughters Mary I and Elizabeth I, hoping it would give her something else to write about. Her lyrics continued to disturb me as I strode towards the meeting.

Sitting on a bench in the grounds was the woman I'd come to see. I scanned the area looking for bodyguards or security, but there was nobody visible. I removed my jacket as I approached, as the sun turned it up a notch.

Carrie Cromwell glittered in the heat. 'I feel like Vera

Lynn every time I see you, Jennifer.' She glanced into the sky. 'And it is such a sunny day.'

I sat next to her. 'Thanks for agreeing to meet me. I was sorry to learn about your husband.'

I wasn't. He was a scumbag who wouldn't be missed by anyone but her and perhaps their daughter. As I thought that, a vast shadow came towards us. Only when the sun slipped behind a cloud did I realise it was Holly Cromwell, dragged along by the largest and darkest mutt I'd ever seen.

'Tommy was a good man,' Carrie said, and I stifled a laugh. She turned to her daughter and the massive animal. 'Come here, Holly, and bring Digby with you.'

I gripped the edge of the seat as the hellhound bounded towards me.

'Digby?'

'You know, from the movie *Digby the Biggest Dog in the World*.'

The beast stopped a foot in front of me, gasping great breaths across my face. It stank to high heaven, and I put a hand over my nose.

'I've never seen it,' I muttered through my fingers.

Holly Cromwell, a wisp of a girl, must have been far stronger than she looked and dragged the dog to one side. Her mother grinned at her.

'Say hello to Detective Inspector Flowers, Holly.'

The girl's face, so bright and cheerful a second ago, transformed into the same colour as Digby's hide in an instant. She appeared about fourteen, but her voice sounded like someone twenty years older.

'I don't like the police.'

Her mother laughed. 'Oh shoo, Holly. Go away now. Inspector Flowers and I have important business to discuss.' The teenager skulked from us, and Carrie turned to me.

'The poor girl was always around when your colleagues came to harass my dear, dear late husband.' She never stopped smiling. 'But that's all in the past. What can I do for you, Jennifer?'

Sometimes, when faced with an expert in deception, it's best to start with a lie.

'We have evidence you're controlling your husband's criminal organisation.' I let that sink in. She was unresponsive. 'And you're involved with a sadomasochistic group, providing them with people to torture.'

Her face changed from stone to unbridled joy as she burst out laughing.

'Well, Jennifer, there's a lot to unpack from that.'

'Are you denying it?' In the distance, I sensed Holly Cromwell scowling at me.

'I'll start at the beginning, as truthful as I can be for you, Inspector.' Two joggers ran by. 'It's true Tommy inherited some dubious connections from his father after the old man died.' She did not explain his death 'But he only kept them because he understood things would be worse if he didn't.'

'How so?'

'Because of his brother, Pete.' She gritted her teeth as she spoke. 'Now there's a bloke you never want to meet in a dark alley. Seeing him in broad daylight is bad enough.'

The gap between us on the bench was about two feet, but the distance, in reality, was a lifetime.

'You're saying Tommy continued his father's reign of drug trafficking, money laundering, extortion, prostitution, and murder only because it would have been worse under Pete's control?'

'I can see why they made you a detective, Inspector.'

'So what happened when Tommy got a terminal illness? You just gave his empire away?'

She laughed at me. 'Empire! My, my, Jennifer, you sound dramatic. Have you been watching too many American TV shows?' She leant closer to me, the smell of her jasmine perfume invading my senses. 'You can never trust the yanks. I mean, look at who they elect as their leaders, blokes who couldn't lead a horse to water with a map in their hands.' Her laugh scared off the birds nesting behind us. 'Still, we can hardly talk, can we?'

'You sold it off, didn't you?'

'I did. I mean, apart from the morality of it, why would I want to manage a group of desperate men scrambling around for power and money they don't know what to do with?' She was deep into a lecture. 'How much money do people need? One million, two, six, a hundred, a thousand? It's madness.'

'How much do you want, Carrie?'

She shrugged and gazed towards Holly as the kid dragged the beast from a smaller dog.

'I need enough to keep my daughter safe.' She turned back to me. 'Wouldn't you do everything you could for Abigail's safety, Jennifer?'

The sun bounced off my neck and transformed my head into a toaster.

'You leave her out of this, Cromwell.'

She appeared chastised. 'Don't take it the wrong way, Jennifer, I meant no harm. I'd never hurt a child.'

'So you say, yet you've got your people helping sadists torture and kill kids.'

She sighed. 'I've told you, Jennifer, that has nothing to do with me.'

'But you know who's involved?'

'I said I'd be honest with you, so here it is. I sold off the separate parts of Tommy's business to interested organisations. I made enough money to look after Holly and me for the rest of our lives. There's even sufficient for me to contribute to charity events, like the one I saw you at the other day.' I raised my eyebrows. 'And before you get carried away, no pun intended, that event wasn't about me selling a part of the so-called Cromwell Crime Empire via a public auction. Imagine how idiotic that would be. That was just a stupid rumour started by a mutual acquaintance of ours.'

'Ruby Vasquez?'

'The one and only.'

'How is she involved with you?'

'Didn't she tell you? I guess she spun some massive web of lies about crime gangs. Well, it's nothing like that. She's writing a book about influential London women, and I'll feature in it.' She peered at me. 'I'm surprised she hasn't included you in her list. Then again, she's already written about you in a best-selling tome, hasn't she?'

I dodged the question. 'Tell me who is helping those torturing and killing runaways.'

'Can't you guess? Who's scrambling through the city for money and control and wants to hurt me?'

I considered it. 'Your brother-in-law, Pete?'

'Bingo, Jennifer. We'll make an investigator out of you yet.'

'So you know where he is?'

'If I did, I'd tell you. He still has influential friends here and whoever is helping him in his sick new fantasy has a personal interest in it.'

As I got up to leave, Holly and her dog headed towards us. Staring into her teenage eyes, I feared her growl more than I did the hound. I ignored the kid and turned to her mother.

'London is my city, but I wasn't born here.' I glanced around Greenwich's sights, taking in the architecture, the statues, and the river beyond. The mutt was so close to me, I heard the beat of its heart. 'I'm from the north of England, but we had people there like you, Tommy and Pete. There were criminals and gangs, but you got to recognise who they were by their dogs.'

Carrie pouted her lips. 'Their dogs?'

'Yes, we recognised them by their dogs. The villains and the general scumbags always had black dogs because the coppers couldn't see them at night.'

I turned from her, but she had a last parting shot.

'We must get Holly and Abigail together one of these days, Jennifer. Maybe they could form a musical duo.'

Her words rang in my ears as I headed to the car.

Now it was Pete Cromwell I had to find.

30 MANIC MONDAY

The first thing I did at work on Monday was take Jack to one side; then I told him what had happened with Carrie Cromwell. He hunched his shoulders, and the colour drained from his face; everything but the red burning behind his eyes. I waited for him to explode, but he went to the coffee machine instead. While I observed the smoke smouldering from his ears, Constable Sutton approached me.

'I've been in touch with the Houses of Parliament, ma'am, regarding the staff on duty when Mary Witney was there.' She handed me a list. I kept one eye on Jack and scanned the paper with the other.

'Hard to believe it's been a week already.'

'Or that Friday night seems so long ago. Has Abbey recovered from it yet?'

'I think it's me who needs more time to recover.' The words on the list were a blur. 'Abbey's still living off the euphoria from it, and now she's got a guitar and had the first lesson from Inspector Monroe, there'll be no stopping her.' I tried to focus on the names, but my head hurt. I wondered if it was an accumulation of guilt, giving me a migraine. I flicked the paper in front of my eyes, but it didn't help. 'What am I looking at here, Sarah?'

'There were twenty members of staff at Parliament that Monday night. When I spoke to someone there on the phone on Friday, they agreed to send me the names and what shifts those people work this week. Half are on the day shift; the others are working until it closes tonight.'

Jack returned with a large mug of coffee for me and a Coke for him; he was transforming into a walking sugar bubble.

'This will clear your head, partner.' I wondered if he meant the guilt.

I took the drink from him. 'Have you seen this list Sarah compiled?'

He nodded. 'She showed it to me first thing. We'll split up into two teams for the interviews.'

The mug warmed my hands, and he appeared to have defrosted towards me.

'Do you want the morning or afternoon?'

I looked at the list again. The times against the employee names indicated the morning shift would already have started, while the evening one was in from two o'clock.

'Sutton and Grealish can head there now; we've got something else.'

I twisted my face to his. 'Anything good?'

He grinned at me, his previous irritation having disappeared. 'We're off to see Pete Cromwell.'

The cup slipped from my fingers and I only just caught it before it crashed onto the floor.

'What?'

He smiled at Sutton and Grealish. 'If you two will excuse us.'

Then he took me by the elbow and guided me past our desks and towards the murder boards at the back, pressing me against the photos of the murdered Daniel Hathaway in his dog costume.

'You know where Pete Cromwell is?'

Jack cracked his knuckles so loud it irritated my ears.

'I'll admit I was upset when you told me about your meeting with Carrie Cromwell, with you going off on your own without informing me again.' He breathed out. 'But I've done things without you, so I shouldn't be mad at you.'

'You're too kind.' I wished I'd put some sugar in the coffee to take away the bitterness. 'So how do you know Pete Cromwell's location?'

He puffed out his cheeks, preening like a peacock pleased with itself.

'Well, after we met with Croft over at the National Crime Agency, I think we both realised he'd kept things from us about the Cromwells. So I contacted someone inside the NCA, an old friend of mine, and called in a favour.'

'What did they say?'

He downed his Coke with a gulp and threw the can into the bin.

'Finish your coffee, and I'll tell you on the way.'

HE DROVE TO WHITECHAPEL. The Thames was on our right as we moved through Blackfriars. I was keen to quiz him about this meeting with Pete Cromwell and how he'd found one of London's most wanted when others couldn't. The first question was on my lips when I got a message on the phone; it was from Abbey, telling me she had band practice for most of the day. And she had a request for my partner.

'Abbey wants to know if she can have two lessons a week with you.'

We turned into Spitalfields.

'Sure, why not? We might have this case closed today.'

I texted a quick reply and put the mobile away.

'Tell me about Pete Cromwell, then.'

'It's probably best if he tells you himself, but what I will say is there are disagreements within the NCA about how they're handling this.'

He took us into a car park on Whitechapel Street.

'Are we going on a Ripper tour, Jack?'

He laughed. 'Something like that.' He led me into the heart of Whitechapel. 'My mate Bob at the NCA told me some interesting things about the organisation.'

We dodged a large group of tourists listening to how a psychopath murdered five women nearly a hundred and fifty years ago. I glanced at them, curious at the excitement written across their faces. I'd never understood the public interest in killers, the fascination with crime books, real and fictional, and all the TV shows, movies, and magazines surrounding it. Perhaps I was too close to the reality of it. I could empathise with wanting a distraction from everyday life's difficulties, though it's been elusive for me so far. But why not find that release in something which isn't murder, rape, or torture?

One person in the group glared at me as we walked past them; he wore a shirt with Ted Bundy's image on it. I winked at him.

'I hope there's a pub at the end of this, Jack.'

He stopped me as we reached the crossing.

'Bob told me nearly all the NCA's most significant

"high-harm" operations involve people, commodities or money transfers across international borders. Groups satisfying criminal markets, whatever they may be, are much more common than they used to be. These are businesses trying to exploit markets. He said this is why Carrie Cromwell sold off the separate parts of her husband's organisation to interested parties, not only ones based in the capital.'

'I bet Pete was pissed off.'

We watched the Ripper tour group cross the road. The Ted Bundy man avoided my gaze.

'Apparently, he wasn't happy to be cut from the operation and the profits. Unfortunately for him, according to Bob, he didn't have enough people on his side to muscle Carrie out of it. So now he wants revenge on her and those she did business with.'

'And how is he doing that?'

He nodded as the lights changed. 'You'll see when we meet him in a minute.'

Jack strode ahead, straight towards the Ten Bells pub on the corner of Commercial Street and Fournier Street. We stepped inside and to the main bar; blue tiles littered the wall while a barman wearing a Slayer shirt served cocktails to three young women. I had no idea what Pete Cromwell looked like, but I scanned the residents: two large bulldogs in black suits stood at the end of the bar, while an old bloke reading a newspaper propped up the other end. There was no one else apart from us.

'You brought me here as a joke, right, as part of the Ripper tour.'

Legend had it that Mary Kelly drank in the pub before leaving and becoming Jack the Ripper's final victim.

'Nope. Here's the man we want.'

Pete Cromwell emerged from a narrow set of stairs leading to the floor above the one we were on. He hadn't shaved in a while, long hair obscuring most of his face. Cromwell appeared to be a bloke who once had muscles; broad over the back and thick in the neck, now gone to seed. His frame drooped, and his leg dragged as he made his way to a table and sat in the corner. The two bulldogs watched him, and then us as we approached. My hand was on Jack's arm as I nodded at them.

'Security?'

'Yes. But not what you think.'

Cromwell slurped from a pint of Guinness as we sat opposite. White foam stuck to his beard as he peered at me.

'Are you Bob's mates?'

'I'm DI Monroe, and this is DI Flowers.'

Cromwell stared at me. 'I recognise you.' I waited for him to talk about the Hashtag Killer. 'My sister-in-law hates you.'

'Tell Inspector Flowers who your friends are over there, Pete,' Jack said.

He wiped at his face. 'It's only the best for me, Inspector Flowers. Those beefy lads are the finest on offer from the British security service.'

I looked at them again, recognising the vacancy behind their gaze. It was emptiness made from pure concentration on what they were there to protect: Pete Cromwell.

'Why is MI5 protecting you?'

'Didn't your partner tell you about me, Inspector?'

Jack took the glass from him.

'Get on with it, Cromwell.'

He didn't get on with it; unless he was part of the Ripper tourists' attraction.

'I wonder if Mary Kelly sat here before leaving in the arms of a butcher?'

Jack formed his hand into a fist around the pint.

'Do you think the MI5 boys would be quick enough to stop me shoving that glass into your face?'

Cromwell coughed out a laugh, his chest rising as if he was about to give birth.

'Now, there's no need for that, Inspector Monroe. Bob's been good to me, so I said I'd do him, and you, a favour. So I will.'

He twisted his neck up and something crunched along his back. Jack scowled at him.

'Get on with it.'

'I have a degenerative disease of the spine. The doctors tell me I could have had it for a while, but the effects of it, ironically, only appeared after my brother's diagnosis of cancer.' He leant towards me, and I thought his entire body would collapse into jigsaw parts. 'So, even after Tommy died, I wouldn't have been able to prevent that wife of his from destroying everything our father built.'

My lack of sympathy oozed out of me.

'I'm heartbroken. And this had nothing to do with you having no friends to help you stop Carrie selling off the business?'

He tried to shrug, but it left him grimacing in pain.

'I've got more important things to do with my life than deal with her and that weird daughter.'

I agreed with him about the girl, though I didn't tell him that.

Jack butted in. 'Pete's a supergrass now, protected by the security services because he has information on a right-wing terrorist group, one organisation Carrie sold parts of the Cromwell empire to. They're called the George Cross, and they bought into the business to fund their activities.'

Cromwell retrieved his pint from Jack.

'Everyone has to have a hobby.'

He raised the drink to me and grinned.

'What do you know about a sadomasochistic gang who give themselves names based on the alphabet?' I hoped it didn't sound as silly out loud as it did in my head.

Guinness dribbled over his lips as he spoke.

'I know of people traffickers who force women into prostitution and slavery; of cybercriminals who steal millions every year; of entrepreneurs who buy and sell weapons; of those who use children to trade drugs across county lines. I even know a gang who kills for money.' He wiped his nose on his arm. 'But I don't know of any sado-masochistic gang who give themselves names based on the alphabet.' He glanced at his security detail. 'If I did, I would have told them like I did with all the others.' He finished his drink. 'If you want to continue talking, you need to get me another pint and a packet of crisps.'

I moved the seat back and stood. 'We've got what we came for.'

I left, and Jack followed. A different Ripper tour had gathered outside the pub, listening to the gory details of Mary Kelly's murder in 1888. I dug my nails into my palms.

'Do you believe him?' Jack said.

'He looked like he has less than a month to live.' I watched the group shudder as their guide described a murderous scene from the nineteenth century. 'I don't see why he'd lie to us.'

We headed to the car. 'This leaves us back at square one, Jen.'

'Not really. Now we know Carrie Cromwell was wrong

about her brother-in-law, or she lied to me about him. This means she's still an avenue of investigation.'

'If that's the case, then who is helping Mr X clean up his crime scenes? Where are they disposing of the bodies connected to the severed hands and fingers, not to mention the victims from Mary Witney's tapes?'

Where were those bodies?

It was a twenty-five-minute drive, taking us across the river and through Brixton. Jack stared at me in the mirror.

'Why are we going to Lambeth?'

'We're off to see an old friend of yours.'

I gave him directions to outside the Herne Hill entrance to Brockwell Park. I put the police badge on the windscreen as we left the car on a set of double yellow lines. It was close to lunchtime and the only thing making more noise than my stomach was his.

'I hope you're taking me to a café.'

Groups of children ran past us as a man struggled to keep his dog from chasing them. I had a sudden image of Holly Cromwell setting her hound loose on all and sundry.

'Our friend is bringing a picnic.'

We stepped beyond the trees, the scent of fresh flowers and cut grass drifting everywhere. Jack rubbed at his guts.

'They better have a Coke.'

His addiction to sugary drinks affected his concentration. As he moved forward, I dragged him back by the arm.

'Watch out, partner.'

A small train full of adults and children missed his leg by a few feet.

'What the Hell?'

A mixture of bemusement, indignation, and hunger consumed his face.

'It's a miniature railway. Normally, it only runs on Sundays, but there's a summer special on today since the kids are off school.'

We watched the carriages trundle through the trees, and I assumed the adults were enjoying it as much as the children, especially the red-haired young woman sitting in the back. She waved at us as the train sped by. Jack clutched at his ribs.

'Isn't that Ruby Vasquez?'

'The one and only,' I said when the train stopped.

All the kids jumped off full of excitement and enthusiasm, while most adults unwrenched their bodies from the small carriages constricting them. Ruby detached herself with the expertise of a gymnast and looked at us.

'Come on. There's somewhere to sit over here.'

We followed her through the park and towards the tennis courts. Halfway there, she dropped her skull bag onto the floor and sat down. She reached into it, and I imagined those severed hands reappearing. Instead, she pulled out packs of food and threw one at each of us. Jack caught his like an expert cricketer in the field. I laughed at his scowling face.

'This is alfalfa with roast red pepper hummus? Don't you have any meat sandwiches?'

She extended her eyebrows in mock horror.

'I'm a vegan, Jack, remember?'

I got a Bloody Mary: tomatoes, black pepper, salt and

sun-dried tomato paste on olive ciabatta. I wondered if she was taking the piss. My legs creaked as I sat next to her. Jack huffed and puffed before joining us.

'You told me Carrie Cromwell was auctioning off the separate parts of her husband's crime empire, Ruby.'

She bit into her sandwich, which appeared to be avocado and nothing else. Bits of it were stuck to her teeth as she spoke.

'Yeah, I'm sorry about that. My sources got their wires crossed. She'd already sold off her criminal business before that auction.'

Jack stared at his food as if it was about to explode.

'You've improved little as a journalist, haven't you?'

Ruby pouted at him. 'We all make mistakes, Jack.' Then she smiled. 'Even you.'

'What do you know about Pete Cromwell?' I said.

She flicked a piece of avocado for the birds hovering nearby.

'I hear he's going the same way as his brother and won't be on this mortal coil for long.'

'What else do you have; anything connected to the Velvet Underground club?'

I ate half of the sandwich, surprised at how nice it tasted. My stomach stopped growling.

Ruby flashed her eyes at me.

'Pete Cromwell and the Velvet Underground? That would be a more unlikely coupling than Jack here deciding he'd like to dress in women's clothes.'

My partner devoured his food with relish.

'You'd be amazed at what I get up to when I'm not talking to criminals or fakers, Vasquez.'

She burst out laughing, spitting avocado all over the

grass and bringing a hail of pigeons down on us like a scene from Hitchcock's *The Birds.*

'I've now got this image in my head, which won't go away in a hurry.'

I finished my sandwich. 'Tell me about Pete Cromwell, Ruby. Is he connected to Daniel Hathaway's murder?'

'You think he's involved in Zed's death? But why?'

'Let's imagine there's a fetish gang in London, we'll call them the Alphabet, and they've taken things further than what happens at most nights at the Velvet Underground and places like it. For this argument, let's assume this group has killed and maimed young people, possibly runaways. They may have used some criminal contacts to procure or provide them with their victims, and then these career criminals have helped to clear up the mess afterwards. If all this is true, and Carrie Cromwell isn't involved, how likely is it to be her brother-in-law?'

Ruby crunched through her food and considered my question. Jack scowled at my side, and I was unsure if it was from what I'd said or because he liked his vegan sandwich.

'I've met Pete Cromwell before.' She threw a bit of bread to a squirrel in the trees. 'It was before his illness, not long after I left the hospital because,' she stared at me, 'well, you know why I was there. Anyway, I visited a community centre in Camden; they were throwing an event celebrating what I'd done. The place was full, mainly of women, single mothers, and people from different ethnic backgrounds. It was terrific, with a positive vibe everywhere. And then I glanced at the rear of the hall and saw him standing there with two of his goons.' Her throat croaked, and she had to cough to regain her voice. 'I didn't know who he was then, but I realised he was one of those blokes who suck all the light from anywhere he enters, a man who looks like he couldn't tell the truth to his reflection. Someone spoke to me, so I looked away, and when I turned back, they'd gone. I only found out later he was there to collect protection money from those who ran the venue.'

'Protection from what?' Jack said.

Dark shadows crisscrossed Ruby's face.

'Protection from him returning and taking some of the women into his employment.' Her voice became a near whisper. 'And he had dozens of centres like it for his collections; all under the control of his brother, Tommy.' She wiped the sweat from her head. 'So, I wouldn't put anything past Pete Cromwell, no matter how ill he appeared to be.'

We sat there for a while, enjoying the food and letting the sun caress our skin. Then we got up, and I thanked her for coming. I had something else to say to her.

'Carrie Cromwell tells me you're writing a book, and she's in it.'

'That's true, Jen. Would you like a signed copy?'

I shook my head and left, not mentioning the book she'd already written with me in it. Jack's sudden appreciation for vegan food, and the quietening of his noisy insides, hadn't erased his grumpiness.

'You believe Pete Cromwell lied to us?'

My scepticism of Pete Cromwell's words may have impacted on Jack's pride. I pondered this problem for a minute.

'Criminals always lie, you understand this, Jack.'

We were sitting in the car before he spoke again.

'Wouldn't MI5 know if Cromwell was involved with sadomasochistic killings?'

I'd barely put the seatbelt on when he revved the engine, and we left for the Houses of Parliament.

'I'd like to believe the intelligence services possess some

intelligence, but that doesn't mean I'd be surprised if they turned a blind eye to something if it allowed them a win in their bigger picture.'

'Their bigger picture being Pete Cromwell helping them catch a terrorist group?'

'Absolutely. And that's if Cromwell speaks the truth.' He put his foot down, and my body snapped into the seat. 'Someone with a brief time to live has little to lose.'

I texted Sutton as Jack drove, asking for an update on their interviews at Parliament.

'We need to speak to Cromwell away from his security guards,' Jack said.

'That won't be easy, but I agree.' I read Sutton's reply and passed on the news to Jack. 'This is what Sutton and Grealish got this morning with the Parliament staff: two of them might have seen a young woman of Mary's description outside the entrance at Portcullis House just before ten o'clock. None of the others saw anything.'

'Brilliant.' Jack puffed out hot air. 'That's more wasted time, and I bet we do little better this afternoon, either.'

I didn't argue with him. 'At least you've discovered some new food you like, so it hasn't all been a waste.'

He sulked through the journey, increasing the volume on the radio, so any conversation was fruitless. I listened to songs about an interventionist God, the end of the world, and how every day was like Sunday. Except this was Monday, one week since Mary Witney's murder; seven days of us ending up back where we started.

Jack only smiled as we got inside and approached the police check-point, then the security checkpoint, so he could wave his ID at them and get through before the public. With that completed and visitor passes around our necks, a staff member led us into a meeting room just off

Westminster Hall. We had tea and cakes while we waited for the first person to arrive.

I sat down and removed the list from my pocket.

'This'll be over soon.'

He picked up a blueberry muffin and bit into it.

'This is a nice touch.' Bits of cake dropped onto the floor. 'We wouldn't provide this level of service at the station.'

'That's because politicians receive a pay rise annually while the police get cutbacks.'

He'd scoffed three cakes before the first interviewee arrived. The interviews followed the same routine: we asked each member of staff what they were doing last week and how long their shift lasted; then if they'd noticed anything unusual while at work; finally, we showed them a copy of the old photo of Mary from her mother and questioned if they'd seen her that Monday, or knew her at all. We ran through eight interviews, making minimal notes. None of them knew anything useful, with only two of them vaguely recognising Mary as someone they might have seen around.

All the cakes had gone, and we were down to the last two on the list: Josephine Parish, a student on a placement, and Ted Valance, Communications Manager at the House of Commons. I remembered Valance giving us the brush off last time we were there.

Neither of them was at work. Valance had been off for two days, Parish for a week. We got their addresses and gave our thanks to the staff as we left. Josephine Parish lived in student accommodation near the Barbican, fifteen minutes' drive away.

'This is nicer than where I was when I studied in London,' Jack said as we walked inside the building.

He went to the reception while I checked the interior.

Apart from the blue sofa opposite the desk, everywhere was as white as a hospital corridor. Jack left the receptionist and returned to me.

'Parish rents a sixth-floor room. The receptionist rang her, but got no answer.' He showed me the key card in his hand. 'But we can get in with this. The lift is this way.'

He pointed ahead of us, and we strolled around a group of teenage girls talking about reality TV shows. They glanced at Jack and giggled as we headed to the lift. We squeezed into space barely built for two people. I pushed the button for the sixth floor and listened to the metal breathe as we rose.

'It won't be long before you lose Abbey to this world, Jen.'

'She might forego higher education now she's focused on a musical career.'

'Abbey could do both and join university to study music.'

I considered that idea as we exited the lift and went to Josephine Parish's place. Jack pressed the key against a pad next to the door, and it opened. It was a squeeze to fit both of us inside the room. It contained a bed, desk, small cupboard and bathroom. But no sign of Parish.

It didn't take long to search. We found leather clothes in the wardrobe, but they didn't stand out as anything but typical for a teenager her age. We left and went to the reception. Jack spoke to the same guy while I approached the girls from earlier; none of them knew Parish or remembered seeing her in the building. They departed as Jack returned.

'No staff have seen her for a week.'

'Could they tell you anything about her?'

'Not really; she's quiet and keeps to herself, but apparently that's not unusual here. The guy at the desk works here and at another two apartment buildings run by the same company in the city, and he said a lot of the students, especially the girls, are very insular and shy.'

Was that a potential future for Abbey? It was something else to worry about for her. We stepped outside as I spoke.

'Josephine Parish worked at the Houses of Parliament, one of the last places Mary Witney was seen alive, and hasn't been seen since Mary died. She's the same age as Mary and is a student waiting to go to university later this year, same as Mary was supposed to do. I don't think these are coincidences.'

'You think Parish might be Missy?'

'Don't you?'

'So, where is she?'

'Let's ask Ted Valance.'

32 HANGING AROUND

Ted Valance lived at the other end of the social strata compared to Josephine Parish. The flats at Cavendish Road in Colliers Wood were something the likes of Josephine and Mary Witney couldn't imagine in their wildest dreams. Jack whistled as we stood and admired the residences of Cavendish Gardens.

'How much does a Communications Manager at the House of Commons earn?'

I held the phone. 'Not this much.' I called Constable Sutton. 'Sarah, can you do a background check on Ted Valance, the Communications Manager at the House of Commons?'

We waited in the sun for her to call back.

'How do we get inside if he's not there?' Jack said.

The phone was still in my hand. 'I'm looking through the website now for Cavendish Gardens, and they have twenty-four-hour security and a concierge, so we should get into Valance's apartment if he doesn't answer the door.'

'We don't have a warrant to search the place.'

'No, but there's cause to be concerned since no one has heard from Valance for two days.'

'Do we know that?'

I shrugged. 'We'll find out when Sarah gets back to us.'

Which she did five minutes later.

'I've texted the details to you both, but I thought it would be quicker to tell you.'

'Go on.'

'Ted Valance is the only child of property developers Harvey and Samantha Valance. They're both retired, and I assume that, even though there's nothing concrete I can find on this yet, they provide their son with a healthy trust fund. Ted is thirty years old and left Oxford with a First Class degree in Politics. He's worked at the Houses of Parliament for two years. I've sent you both a photo of him.'

'Thanks, Sarah.'

As I checked the image, a uniformed security waddled over; he looked bored and out of condition. I left Jack to deal with him as I concentrated on the picture; did Ted match the description Mary gave of Mr X on that last tape? I didn't think so, since he could be anyone in the picture. I put the phone away as Jack finished with the guard.

'The concierge will show us to Valance's apartment.'

We followed the security guard up the drive. There were three buildings ahead, and he took us into the middle one where Mr Miller, the concierge, met us; a tall man whose words tumbled from his lips like grass churned from an electric lawnmower.

'Hello, Inspectors.' When I let go of his hand, I had to wipe the sweat from my fingers. 'I hope there's nothing wrong with Mr Valance. He's one of our most valued residents.'

I rubbed my palm against my leg. 'That's what we're here to find out, Mr Miller.'

He took us inside and kept on talking. 'Mr Valance was one of the first to move into the building after completion. It's a first-floor three-bedroomed flat.' The words flowed out of him. 'They are beautiful living spaces.' I guess he believed it was his job to sell one to us. 'There are Woodbury white gloss cupboards in the kitchen, all the appliances are by Zanussi, there's Novilon patchwood flooring to lounge and hall, carpeted bedrooms, and even a cycle storage facility in the basement.'

We reached the door, and Miller had the key in his fingers. As soon as he opened it, the smell hit us. I looked at Jack, who held onto Miller's arm before he could go any further inside.

'It might be best if you wait outside, Mr Miller, until we know what's happened here.'

Miller placed a hand over his face and didn't argue. Jack followed me in and closed the door. It was plush and impressive, but the stink of death was overpowering. The aroma came from the master bedroom. Everywhere was immaculate, with not a spot of dirt.

I stepped across the carpet and pushed the bedroom door open.

'Shit!' Jack peered over my shoulder at the body hanging from two hooks hammered into the ceiling.

'You should call this in, partner.' As he did, I stood on my toes to get a better look at the deceased. There was a plastic bag over Ted Valance's head. I checked for a pulse in his wrist. 'Tell the ambulance there's no rush.'

'Is it a suicide or sex game gone wrong?' Jack said.

'I'll leave that for Athena to decide.'

I moved from the body and walked to the large

wardrobe next to the bed. I did my best to ignore the smell as I searched through his clothes, picking out suits, shirts, and ties and finding a collection of bondage gear, and a box of masks at the bottom of the closet. I removed them and showed them to Jack.

'This has to be Mr X?'

'Let's not get carried away.'

We combed the rest of the flat as we waited for our colleagues. It didn't take long to find compelling evidence we were in the home of Mr X. There was a drawer full of photographs of faces exhibiting agonising pain.

Jack glanced at a few. 'Killer or not, he was one sick bastard.'

If the photos didn't convince us of his identity, the handwritten file of papers hidden behind a bookcase in the living room was the nail in the coffin; more than a hundred pages of a manifesto dedicated to the ideology of the Alphabet Group. I handed the first few to Jack.

'We weren't far off with the name.'

He glanced at them before handing them back.

'It's the ravings of a lunatic.'

'You should tell Miller the circus is coming to his town.'

He left, and I held the papers in my hand. I had no desire to read them, but I'd have to eventually, and it was that or stare at the body again while I waited. I moved towards the window, seeing a door to a balcony. The view looked out over a park of magnificent trees and summer flowers. I leant over a little, taking in the breeze to replace the stench of death. Then I read the first few paragraphs.

The Alphabet Manifesto.

Life is constructed of twenty-six particles. These particles control the universe. They control you.

Unless you control them. Then you can control everyone else.

But you need to control yourself first, control your desires.

Because if you don't, then you'll be lost.

It takes time to climb to the top of the twenty-six, and to do this, you must sacrifice others to achieve your goals.

He then listed a point-based system that allowed adherents to get to the top of this alphabet of particles, centred around how much pain you inflicted on others. I stopped reading when he talked about plucking out eyeballs and chopping off fingers. As I looked across the city, sirens and blue lights flashed their way towards me.

I returned to the apartment and the bedroom, staring at Ted Valance's body, our assumed Mr X.

There was no need for sirens now.

BACK AT THE STATION, we spent the afternoon compiling everything we had into a single report. I left it with Sutton and Grealish to check and headed home. Abbey was in the living room, strumming on the guitar when I arrived.

'When's Jack coming again?'

'And hello to you too, Daughter.'

She was a bundle of energy, struggling to keep it all in.

'Come on, Mum. You must remember a time when you were this excited?'

Her cheek made me smile. Perhaps this was the moment to broach difficult subjects. I borrowed some of Jack's tact.

'Abbey, I found a knife and drugs in your room.'

The light continued to blaze inside her eyes. I waited for the inevitable explosion, but it never came. Something unexpected occurred instead.

'I'm sorry, Mum. They're not mine. I took them from a friend so they wouldn't harm themselves.'

There was no rage or yelling because I'd gone through her stuff, no drama or accusations. All the things I'd worried about never happened. I'd focused on my perceived negatives of her behaviour: joining a band, writing those lyrics, hiding the knife and drugs, and blown them up into the worse outcome I could imagine. I should have concentrated on the positives this had brought for Abbey. I looked at her and knew she told the truth.

'Are they Francine's?'

She nodded. 'Yeah. She's been struggling, you know, because of her condition, and I was worried she'd do something stupid.'

I didn't tell her we all do stupid things.

'How is she?'

Her smile transformed into a huge joyous grin, which made me feel ten feet tall.

'She's a lot better. Getting the band together was what did it. She's got a positive to focus on. And she's learning to play the drums.'

'That's great, Abbey.'

'And some of our fans say bald women are sexy.'

Now I was worried again, but it was a conversation for another time. My phone vibrated with a new message. It was something else to add to her joy.

'Jack says he'll come over to give you a lesson tomorrow night, but there's one condition.'

'What?'

'You must make him burger and fries again.' I'd need to start an exercise regime at this rate.

'Tell him it's a deal.' She high-fived me. 'But what's to eat tonight?'

'Chinese or Indian?'

She pondered the question for a second. 'Indian.'

So I walked around the corner to our local Indian restaurant. It also gave me an excuse to get alcohol from Tesco.

After the food, we watched *Spinal Tap* as educational training for Abbey. She was still in a good mood when she went to bed. I was doing okay, helped by half a bottle of wine.

Then I got the text message.

TUESDAY MORNING, Jack and I delivered our findings to Detective Chief Inspector Merson and Chief Superintendent Cane. I'd taken a seat while Jack stood to speak. I was happy to let him lead. He started with the autopsy report for Ted Valance.

'Athena reckons it's death by misadventure. She can't rule out suicide but, considering what we know about Valance's lifestyle, it's more likely to have been an act of auto erotica gone wrong.'

The Prophet stared straight at him. 'Does she give a time of death?'

'She says probably sometime on Sunday evening.'

'So he could have been at that fetish club on Thursday night and killed Daniel Hathaway?'

'Yes, ma'am.'

Merson added her two cents. 'It appears as if this

Alphabet group he mentions in his manifesto was a figment of his imagination or something he used to intimidate teenagers into doing what he wanted. He murdered Mary Witney because, going by what she said on those tapes, she threatened to expose him. And he likely did the same with Josephine Parish. He murdered Hathaway to silence him.'

They had it all nicely tied up in a bow with two murders solved.

Only it wasn't, and they weren't. I didn't get up when I spoke.

'If Athena can't tell if Valance's death was suicide or an accident, then it could easily have been murder.'

Merson rolled her eyes at me, which was an unpleasant expression.

'There's no evidence for that, Inspector.'

'Just like there's no evidence Valance killed either Mary Witney or Daniel Hathaway.'

'But he had a motive for those murders, don't you agree, Jennifer?' said Cane.

'For Mary, maybe, if we believe what's on the tapes. There's no concrete connection between Valance and Hathaway.'

'Oh, come on, Inspector. The two of them partook in this... this fetish world, and one was called X, and the other was Z. That's connections straight away.' Merson was enjoying this.

'They'd laugh you out of court with that.'

She grinned like one of those fortune-teller dummies you find at the seaside.

'Yes, but we don't have to go to a court with this, do we?'

She enjoyed tying knots out of the ether.

'What about Josephine Parish? We don't know where she is.'

'Valance obviously learnt from his murder of Witney and hid the other girl's body.' She couldn't even say her name.

'What about the severed fingers and hands? Who do they belong to?'

Merson looked like a kettle ready to boil over.

I watched my superior officers stare down at me. The incidentals didn't matter to them now. They could close two cases at once and get their success rate increased for this month's figures.

The Prophet threw me a bone I couldn't catch.

'Do you have any fresh leads, Jennifer?'

I thought about the message on my phone. I'd read it without reply so far. Was it worth telling them about it? No, it wouldn't make a blind bit of difference.

'No, I haven't.'

'Then let's wrap this up, shall we?'

I got up and left with Jack.

'Do you agree with what they said?'

He shrugged. 'Where else can we go with this? Valance is dead, and even you think he was our Mr X. If someone has been murdering runaways and hiding their bodies, we'll never find them.'

'What about Carrie and Pete Cromwell?'

'They were distractions, nothing more. Look where the information came from about them.'

'Ruby Vasquez?'

'Exactly. Her motives are never pure, are they? It wouldn't surprise me if she planned all of that to include it in this book she's writing.'

'There's something wrong about all this.'

We stepped into the Murder Room, where Sutton and Grealish stood dismantling the evidence boards.

'What aren't you telling me?' Jack said.

I got my phone and showed him the message.

Come and see me. I've something important to tell you. Come alone.

'This is from Dolores Witney?' I nodded. 'Are you going to visit her?'

'What do you think?'

'That's up to you, Jen.' He looked over his shoulder as Merson walked past outside. 'But this investigation is over now.'

He sat at his desk and finished up his notes, and I did the same; then I texted Dolores Witney. Her reply was instant.

Come at four o'clock.

I confirmed my agreement. Then I told Jack.

'Abbey will have the food ready for six. I'll return then. After, if you're up for it, you can give her that guitar lesson. How does that sound?'

'Perfect, partner.'

I spent the rest of the day brooding, drinking tea, and eating snacks bad for me.

Then I set off to see Dolores Witney.

It would be one mother to another.

33 LET IT BLEED

Music blared from the cassette player when I entered, the Rolling Stones singing about the *Midnight Rambler*. Dolores sat on the bed, cross-legged, surrounded by tapes and paperbacks. She lifted her head to me.

'It's amazing what you can do without leaving your room these days.' She picked up a novel by Ian Rankin. 'If the internet had existed when my mother was a child, I believe I might not have been born.'

'Why am I here, Dolores?'

Next to her leg lay a cassette of the *Goon Show*. 'Do you watch TV shows with canned laughter? Did you realise most of the people you hear laughing are dead, probably for fifty years or more, because that's how old the recorded laughs are?'

'Tell me, Dolores.'

'You should sit down, Jennifer. This might take a while.'

I took the chair behind me. It was hard and uncomfortable on my back as if designed for torture.

'You've been busy since my last visit.'

The tapes were an eclectic collection from the sixties, seventies, and the eighties. I guess the recording industry had moved onto CDs by the time it got to the nineties. As well as the Rankin novel, she'd accumulated quite an assortment of crime novelists to read: Lee Child, Patricia Cornwell, Linwood Barclay, Lawrence Block, Raymond Chandler, and Val McDermid. The non-fiction books were all about serial killers. She dropped the Rankin and grabbed a tattered copy of *Beyond Belief: The Moors Murderers: The Story of Ian Brady and Myra Hindley*.

'My mother, God bless her soul wherever she is, was born in 1966.' She gazed at a spot on the wall behind me. 'People always talk about how great things were in the sixties, with the Beatles and the Stones, England winning the World Cup, the Sumner of Love, yadda yadda yadda.' She returned her focus to me. 'And yet my mother, a decade after her birth, became obsessed by killers of children.' She pointed to the famous photo of Hindley on the cover. 'She used to write to them both and show me the letters.' She put the book on the bed. 'I wonder where the replies are now. I could sell them on eBay. Not that I need the money.'

'Why are you telling me this, Dolores?'

Her eyes sparkled. 'Well, you're a bit of an expert on serial killers yourself, aren't you, Jennifer?'

'No.'

She reached behind her and got a book I'd always avoided.

'This is fascinating.' She held it towards me. 'Have you read it?' Then she laughed. 'No, of course not. Why would you? You know what it's about: *The Killer and Me* by Ruby Vasquez.'

'Should I get the author to sign it for you?'

Dolores clasped the volume to her breast like a mother

with a new baby. 'That would be fantastic. You should read it, Jennifer. There's some fascinating stuff in it about the sister she never realised she had, the girl who died in her mother's womb.' Her eyes narrowed, and her voice lowered. 'It rekindled memories I'd tried to bury deep inside me, but that's never a good thing, is it?'

'Memories?'

She placed the book on her leg. 'I brought you here so you could learn about Mary, and you can't do that when there are so many secrets hidden from you.'

'Do you know who killed your daughter?'

Her eyes were sparkling pools of water, shimmering as the light hit them, with a promise of veiled knowledge beneath those dark orbs.

'Which daughter do you mean, Jennifer?'

My spine creaked against the hard wood of the chair. 'You had more than one?'

'I did. Grace died before Mary was born.'

'What happened to her?'

'Do you want to hear a story?'

'Will talking about it help you?' I recognised the hurt in her eyes; not just the pain of losing a child, but also of burying her feelings for so long.

'I took my first psychology class in school, and it piqued my interest in the subject. My second was during college, and my third and fourth. I then diverged into sociology before I met my future husband. My pregnancy halted any idea of a career or further academic progress.'

'What happened to Grace?'

She tried to shake the pain from her head, but it only increased the shadows consuming her face.

'The clinical term for it is Sudden Infant Death Syndrome, also known as cot death. It took Grace from me at six months old. My husband hated me; friends and neighbours shunned or suspected me. Everyone believed I was evil; I'd killed Grace and got away with it or was negligent in her death. Some mother I was. Eighteen months later, I fell pregnant again. It's amazing how alcohol can erase a man's anger for sixty seconds while fuelling him for a lifetime of resentment and hate.'

'It can't have been easy for you.' I didn't have to imagine the fear she must have gone through at the thought of losing another child.

'During the pregnancy with Mary, I had to ensure I wasn't as ill as some people claimed. So I bought a pocket version of the *DSM-IV-TR* guidebook. Do you know what that is?'

I shook my head. 'No.'

'It's the *Diagnostic and Statistical Manual of Mental Disorders*, fourth edition. At one point, I'd self-diagnosed myself with twenty serious disorders, until I put the diagnoses into perspective. Everyone has a little crazy in them. Many people exhibit characteristics in the DSM. The concern is when the behaviour becomes extreme and dictates our lives, sabotaging our ability to work or interact with others.'

As she spoke, I remembered all the things Mary had mentioned about Dolores on those tapes.

'Your husband was no help to you?'

She guffawed. 'Only by not being there.' She cradled a Jack Reacher book in her fingers. 'I used to take the DSM with me everywhere, so I could diagnose those I knew, or who I encountered in shops, or at the movies, or just playing with their kids in the park. And then I started diagnosing those I watched on the TV, celebrities and the like, until I focused on politicians and high-flying business people. It's no wonder the world is screwed when you see who the masses put into power regularly. If you vote for clowns, don't be surprised when the circus turns up.'

'This can't have been healthy for you, Dolores.'

She stuck out her lips like a pufferfish.

'It kept me busy; leading me into interesting paths and corridors, and I met some fascinating people and rekindled relationships with old school friends.'

'Like Dr Gideon.'

Dolores laughed. 'Helen's family had plenty of money and lived in a sizeable house on the hill. She took me there once, only once, and showed me this room where her parents kept huge tanks of tropical fish. I started calling her Helen of Koi. She went off me after that.' Her eyes lit up with the memory of it. 'But these journeys into the mind led me to one irrefutable proof. Would you like to know what?'

'Why not?'

'Normal is a setting on your washing machine.'

We laughed together this time. 'That must be why mine keeps devouring my daughter's socks.'

The music finished, and she hooked out a book about animal Serial Killers.

'Did you know there was a Killer Whale in North America who killed three people over two decades?'

'I think I've seen that film.'

'If you made this into a movie, no one would believe it.'

'Like those sharks caught in a tornado.'

'Exactly. Once upon a time in Sealand, a Canadian water park lived a Killer Whale named Tilikum. Tilikum was eleven years old and weighed 12,000 pounds. Everyone loved him, both staff and the people who turned up in droves to watch him perform.

'That is until he dragged a female grad student underwater one day after she fell into his tank. Tilikum blocked the panicked woman from exiting and tossed her body around with his two female tank mates. The girl died. But since this was his first offence, Sealand chalked the killing up to a terrible accident and didn't hold Tilikum accountable.

'Sealand eventually went out of business, and they moved Tilikum to SeaWorld in Orlando. He won over that community as well with his tricks and his charm and seemed every bit the fun-loving performer he was before. Then, in 1999, a twenty-seven-year-old homeless man sneaked in after-hours to visit his favourite whale.

'By the time the park opened the following morning, the homeless man lay dead and naked on the whale's back; almost as if posed that way. But Tilikum brought in so much money for the owners, the death of a homeless man changed nothing and another eleven years passed without incident. Then, in front of a packed crowd of five thousand people, Tilikum snatched his trainer off of dry land and kept the poor woman underwater until she drowned.'

She gazed at me and waited for a response.

'Is this why you got me here, Dolores, to show that killers come in all shapes and sizes, including whales?'

'No, that's not it. But isn't the world strange? Don't you think after two mysterious deaths, they would have kept Tilikum away from the public? And then you realise how much money was involved and that human greed is the mental illness which triumphs over all.'

'Are you saying it was greed which killed Mary?'

She ignored the question and replaced the tape in the cassette with *Station to Station* by Bowie. I'd forgotten how good the album was. She gazed at the machine.

'The title track takes me far away, to better places than this.'

'You can leave here anytime you want.'

The frown stretched across her face.

'Why would I do that? It's much safer in here.'

'Safer from what?'

Her grimace exploded into a burst of laughter.

'Safer from everyone, Inspector Flowers. The outside world is full of psychopaths and the deranged. You must admit the propensity for violence is hard-wired into most, and for some, it only takes the slightest of pushes to send them over the edge. Modern society is a bubbling cauldron of anxiety, ready to explode.' She picked up a book about the Yorkshire Ripper. 'It's much safer in here.'

'Studies have shown only about one per cent of the population are classed as psychopaths.'

She dug into her stack of books and pulled out a large volume: an encyclopaedia of mental health disorders.

'Studies can be wrong; as can the experts. The public has grown tired of them. They require something more spontaneous, someone more spontaneous: like me.'

'Is this why you sent Mary to see Dr Gideon, even though your daughter was only seven?'

Darkness crossed her face. 'That was a mistake, and I realise that. The whole experience stigmatised Mary from that point onwards.'

'I've spoken to Dr Gideon recently. She said Mary's only problem was you.'

Her eyes bulged. 'I tried to prepare her for the dangers of the world. Wouldn't you do the same for your daughter, Jennifer?'

'I'm not here to talk about my family, Dolores.'

I was ready to give up on her. There was nothing she

could tell me which would help in catching Mary's killer. I watched her rifle through the books and tapes surrounding her and made to leave.

'No, you're here to catch Mary's murderer. But you'll never do that, Inspector. That's why I brought you here. There's something you have to know.'

I stood at the exit. 'What's that?'

She smiled like a circus clown. 'Mary isn't dead, Inspector. She visited me yesterday.'

I sighed. 'I don't need to listen to any more of your delusions, Dolores. I promise I'll find your daughter's killer.'

I had one foot out of the door when her voice froze me on the spot.

'Don't you want the tape she left me?'

I turned as she searched through her cassettes. She pushed aside the first Public Image album and dropped a punk collection onto the floor before finding what she wanted; Dolores lifted it from the mass and offered it to me. It had a painted cover of a man lying dead in the desert while a vulture picked at his rotting flesh.

'I've heard that album before. It's not their best work.'

It was *Give Em Enough Rope* by the Clash. It made me picture Mr X hanging from his roof.

'Look inside, Jennifer. You might get a big surprise.'

I took it and opened the case. It wasn't the Clash. Written on it were the words TAPE 5.

I stared at her. 'Have you listened to it?'

She got off the bed, scattering books and tapes everywhere.

'My daughter is alive, Jennifer, but I'm dead to her.'

Her eyes were black, her face a mess of trembling flesh as she pushed past me and into the corridor. I hesitated for a second, and then stopped the Bowie album. I removed it from the cassette player and replaced it with what she had given me. I played both sides, fast-forwarding and then going back. Dolores never returned in the thirty minutes it took me to find out the tape was blank. I took it and left, blinded by the whiteness of the corridors. I slipped it into my pocket and headed to the reception.

'Has Dolores Witney had any visitors since my last visit?'

The receptionist looked at me through tired eyes and searched her memory.

'No, she hasn't.'

'Do you have a system for logging patient visitors?'

'No, we don't. This is a facility for voluntary residents, not a prison.'

I bit my tongue and turned away from her, the tape burning a hole in my pocket.

34 THE KILLING MOON

Abbey was frying onions when I got home.

'Great timing, Mum.'

She had her phone connected to the Bluetooth speakers, was listening to something familiar.

'Isn't this Echo and the Bunnymen?'

'*The Killing Moon*. An oldie for you and Jack.'

'I thought you'd be into modern music.'

She shook salt and pepper over the raw meat.

'Nah. Most of it is rubbish. This is my Spotify playlist of eighties post-punk.'

Once again, she surprised me. 'Is Jack here?'

'He's in the living room, on his second can of Coke already.'

She slid three giant burgers into the pan as bits of garlic oil spat out of it. The tape seemed heavy in my pocket. In this new age of honesty between us, I needed to clear something up.

'Abbey, you didn't start your band last week, did you?'

She pushed the onions around and avoided my gaze.

'No. We've been together a month.'

'Why didn't you tell me?'

She flipped the burgers over.

'I thought you'd disapprove.' Now she looked at me. 'I couldn't distract you from work. How did you know?'

I got a beer from the fridge.

'That's why I'm a detective, love.'

I left her and went to Jack. He was relaxing on the sofa, watching TV.

'Valance is all over the news, Jen. However, there's been no mention of Witney and Hathaway yet. How did it go with Dolores?'

I plopped the bottle onto the table and removed the tape from my pocket, dropping my jacket over the chair.

'She said Mary visited her and gave her this.'

He took it from me. 'Have you listened to it?'

'I did, on that cassette player Dolores has. It's blank on both sides.'

He twisted his lips into an uncomfortable position.

'She's delusional if she thinks Mary's alive.'

'That's what the staff told me in the hospital.' I got my phone and searched for the message Dolores left me. 'But listen to this.'

He put his empty can onto the table and leant forward. *This Charming Man* by The Smiths drifted from the kitchen.

'What am I listening for?'

I stood and closed the living room door, cutting off Morrissey's warbling before muting the TV. I played the message again.

'Don't you think she sounds like the voice on the other four tapes?'

Jack scrunched up his face. 'She does, but they're mother and daughter, so that's not a surprise.'

'What if they're not, though?'

'What if they're not what? You're confusing me now.'

'What if the person on the tapes isn't Mary, but Dolores pretending to be Mary? What if she's been playing with us all along? She's only a voluntary resident at that hospital, so might have been coming and going at will with none of the staff knowing.'

Jack glanced at me, his mouth pursed but slightly open and loose. His eyes fixed on mine, a puzzled expression on his face as he juggled the tape in his hand.

'Dolores has her problems, but why would she do that?'

I repeated what Dolores had told me about baby Grace.

'That's terrible, but it doesn't explain why she'd make these recordings, pretend to be her daughter, and then hide them around the city.'

'I didn't say it made any sense. But a lot of what we know about Dolores, what we heard on the tapes, makes little sense either.'

He scratched at his head. 'What would her motivation have been? Maybe she's unhinged enough to sever fingers and hands, but to kill her daughter, and in such a violent way, seems extreme.'

'Remember, Jack, this is a woman whose entire life has been about pursuing some crusade proclaiming we are nothing without extreme experiences; perhaps she finally completed the most extreme action. All of this could be her way of telling the world she'd fulfilled what must be the most disturbing experience of them all.'

He still didn't look convinced. 'You think she told you the truth about the cot death of her first child?'

I knew she did because I recognised the pain in her eyes and voice from what I went through and my forced abortion. Jack knew nothing of that, and neither did Abbey, and

I wouldn't mention it now. Maybe one day I'd tell them both, but this wasn't it.

'She wasn't lying, Jack, but it will be easy to check when we return to the station. There'll be a record of it somewhere.'

'The food is ready,' Abbey shouted from the kitchen. 'Come and get it.'

We followed her command as Julian Cope begged the world to shut its mouth. I got beers for Jack and me and pushed all thoughts of dead babies from my mind. Then the three of us devoured the burgers while we argued the merits of one band over another: The Beatles over The Stones, The Pistols over The Clash, The Velvet Underground over The Doors. We didn't mention the case, though listening to *Venus in Furs* reminded me of Sarah and that club.

'I'll clean up,' I said when the last of the food had disappeared and the two of them were discussing the merits of Kate Bush over PJ Harvey. Jack put his empty bottle on the side.

'I've set the amp and the guitar up in the garage to save the nerves of your neighbours.'

'Hey!' Abbey shouted at him before heading outside.

'Thanks again for all of this, partner.'

'You're welcome. As long as you two are okay.' I told him about the knife and drugs being Francine's. 'She's a good kid, Jen.' He patted me on the shoulder as I thrust my hands into the sink. 'She takes after her mother.'

He left as Elizabeth Fraser started singing in that made-up language of hers, and my fingers bristled under the warm water. Mothers and daughters; how fraught were their relationships? I scrubbed the last of the grease from the frying pan as *Dog Eat Dog* by Adam and the Ants came onto the playlist.

I dried my hands while the image of Daniel Hathaway's blood pooling on the floor flashed across my eyes, his head lolling to one side while wearing that dog outfit.

Was there a connection between Hathaway and Valance? Where was the evidence Hathaway was involved in a fetish lifestyle? There was none where he lived with his mother, no examples of clothes, no websites or photos or videos on his computer. Would a man who wore a dog suit to a sex club have no fetish items at his house?

Only idiots ignore the truth.

I dropped the towel onto the floor.

He would if he had more than one residence. Mary Witney stayed in two locations, so why couldn't he? I left the cloth and grabbed my phone. I rang the number for the Murder Room; Sutton answered.

'Sarah, can you text me that list we got from the Prometheus organisation connected to Daniel Hathaway?'

I received it a minute later. The wall next to the garage thumped to the same rhythm as my head. I checked the names twice. Most were bookmakers or gambling sites, one was a charity, but the name which interested me was in the middle of the text: Medusa Apartments.

They had a website as impressive as the photos of the flats. They even put Valance's place to shame. I rang the number on the site, but got no reply. Abbey and Jack returned, grinning like Tweedledum and Tweedledee.

'Look at this, Mum,' she pushed her phone into my face. 'Jack showed me how to play *Anarchy in the UK.*'

'It sounded like it.' I took the phone and stared at the image. It was Abbey, but older, with a punk rock hairstyle. 'What's this?'

'I've got an app which lets you age photos and mess around with the hair and stuff.'

I returned it to her.

'If I send you a picture of someone, can you change their age in it about four or five years and do me copies with different hair colours: red, black, and white?'

'Easy peasy, Mum.'

While she did that, I dragged Jack into the living room and told him about Medusa Apartments.

'If Hathaway had any incriminating evidence against Valance or anyone else, that's where it would be.'

'Why there, Jen?'

'Because it's owned by the same Prometheus organisation he made small payments to every month. His BDSM gear must be somewhere since it wasn't at his mother's house, and I'm betting it's in one of the Medusa Apartments.'

'We should go now.'

I grabbed my car keys, telling Abbey I'd be out for a bit.

'That's okay. I'll watch *The Great Rock-and-roll Swindle* on the computer. I sent you those photos.'

It was a short drive to get to Canary Wharf. It was a location once viewed as where people travelled to work, but not to live. This had changed recently, as residential developments had popped up left, right and centre. Now there were flats, with some penthouses and riverside expansions boasting views across the city. There was a mix of modern townhouses, a few surviving Victorian terraced houses, Edwardian cottage estate-type homes, and former council flats.

Medusa Apartments weren't hard to find; in a group of swanky glass skyscrapers, theirs was the showiest. And the giant Medusa logo wasn't difficult to spot.

'Imagine how much it costs to live here,' Jack said as we got out of the car.

'More than we'll ever make in two lifetimes, partner.'

As we walked in, the security guard looked like he wanted to be anywhere else but there. His face dropped another few flights when we showed him our identification.

'Do you have a Daniel Hathaway living here?' Jack said.

It was an instant reply. 'No, Inspector.'

'How do you know? You didn't even check.'

'We have a prominent resident clientele here. The staff has every name memorised.'

I got my phone and tried a different tack.

'Do you recognise anyone in these photos?'

I showed him the ones Abbey had manipulated for me. He stopped on the one with the long dark hair.

'That's Mr Wolf's sister. I think she's called Amelia.'

So much for memorising every name.

'Who is Mr Wolf?'

'Tobias Wolf. He has a penthouse suite. He's a hedge fund manager. Impeccable credentials.'

'Do you have a key for the suite?'

'We keep spare keys for all the flats in case of emergencies.'

Jack leant over the desk towards him.

'Give us Wolf's key, then. This is a murder investigation.'

The guard bent below the counter and rifled through something we couldn't see. He got up with the key.

'You need a code for the lift.'

We didn't have to ask for that as he slipped it to Jack on a piece of paper while I took the key.

'What are you expecting?' Jack said as we went up.

The door opened for the penthouse suites.

'Answers.'

The corridor heaved with art deco vases full of

colourful flowers which smelt of the summer, and art nouveau prints on the wall. We walked to Wolf's suite, and I put the key in the entrance. I pushed it open, and Jack followed me in. We didn't have any time to admire the decor before I saw the gun pointed at me.

I had to admit, Abbey had done a near-perfect job using that app on the photograph Dolores Witney gave us. The girl stood there, pistol aimed forward in her best Bonnie Parker impersonation. Jack was flummoxed, so I did the talking.

'Everyone thinks you're dead, Mary.'

35 REVELATIONS

Mary Witney didn't lower the weapon.

'That's no thanks to your boss.'

The traces of the girl she'd been lingered in her face, but as she inched forward, it was easy to see her mother in her steely gaze and penetrating eyes. Her arm never wavered. The gun pointed straight at me as I spoke.

'Mr X is dead, Mary. You don't need to do his dirty work now.'

A tiny grin illuminated her lips. 'Why should I believe you?' Her voice was like the low roll of thunder and unmistakeably the one from the tapes we'd found.

'I'm Detective Inspector Flowers, and this is Detective Inspector Monroe. Would you like to see our identification?'

She steadied her arm, with the gun pointed at me. How does an eighteen-year-old girl get a pistol in London? She nodded at Jack.

'You, show me your warrant card and do it slowly. Any funny business and she gets it.'

She sounded like one of the Kray Twins. This was the only time I wished my media celebrity profile would work.

Jack did as she asked. Mary gazed at his ID but didn't lower the gun.

'Valance still could have sent you. There are loads of bent coppers around. I've met more than my fair share, usually with them getting a truncheon up the arse. And I bet Valance has plenty of connections in the police, what with him working at the Houses of Parliament. You privileged bastards always stick together.'

I tried to appear as calm as possible, slipping into my best negotiating voice.

'Ted Valance is dead, Mary. So is Daniel Hathaway. We followed the trail here from the recordings you left.'

Her eyes, which had been scrutinising us since we walked through the door, widened.

'You found my tapes? When I didn't have X's true identity, I created them to expose him if anything happened to me.'

'And that's how we discovered you here, because of them. You're safe, Mary; Valance is dead. You can put the gun down.'

But she didn't. She looked straight at me, and I think she realised I recognised the truth; a truth which only came to me when Abbey manipulated that photo.

'You broke in here; I don't know who you are, so I'm justified in shooting you.'

'That's your mother speaking, kid,' Jack said. It seemed to disturb Mary, her voice trembling along with the weapon.

'You saw Dolores in that hospital she's hiding in?'

I tried to appease her. 'She's worried about you, Mary. You can put the gun down. We're not here to hurt you. We'll take you to see her if you want.'

She thrust her free hand into her mouth and bit at the nails.

'My mother has never cared about me beyond the results of her social experiments.' Her eyes sparkled as the pistol trembled in her fingers. 'You could be more of her fakes, more of her games meant to mess with my head. I should shoot you and get it over with.' She squeezed on the trigger. 'You broke in.'

I took a deep breath. 'Why did you kill Josephine Parish, Mary?'

Her hand wavered a little, the confidence drifting from her eyes.

'Me? No, it was Valance who murdered Jo. And he would have killed me next if Daniel hadn't let me stay here.'

'Is that why you executed Daniel so he wouldn't tell anyone your location?'

When she laughed, her face changed from an eighteen-year-old's that of to someone much older, a person who'd experienced more than a teenager ever should.

'You're making things up now, Inspector. Valance killed them both, and I hid from him while I decided what to do.'

'Josephine Parish was Missy. What were you doing at the Houses of Parliament the night she died?' Jack said.

Her arm trembled. If she squeezed the trigger by mistake, one of us would die.

'Once I understood how vile X was, I realised I had to expose him, for our safety as much as anyone else's. Jo knew where he worked, but she wouldn't tell me. So I followed her. I saw her, but not him. Then she noticed me and ran. It was a game we sometimes played. I chased her from a distance across the bridge, hiding in the crowds at the tourist attractions, but she always spotted me. But then I lost her near the London Dungeon.' Tears formed in her eyes. 'That bastard smashed her head in, just like he said he would.'

'Where did the severed fingers and hands come from?' I said.

'Valance got Jo a job in a funeral home. Jo told me she'd had this fetish for body parts since she was a young girl. At the undertakers, she'd cut off the fingers or the hands once the bodies were ready for burial or cremation. She only took from the ones in closed caskets.'

I played along with her. 'What happened to Jo, Mary?'

'Valance grabbed her and smashed her head in.' Her voice shook. 'He crushed her skull into the wall. I watched him do it and couldn't do anything about it. So I ran away and hid.'

'Why did everyone think it was you?' Jack said.

She twisted her foot on the carpet. Her arm had to be hurting.

'Three months ago, I found her in the squat after one of her sessions with X. He'd broken two of her teeth. We used to swap identities all the time, playing jokes on shop staff and the like, and she used mine to get her teeth fixed. I guess they x-rayed them and kept a record, thinking she was me.'

'Why didn't you go to the police after you knew Jo had been murdered and misidentified as you?'

She laughed again. 'I've learnt not to trust those in authority, especially the coppers.'

'You should put the gun down now.'

'No. I don't think so.'

In that instant, she resembled her mother in every way.

'Valance couldn't have killed Jo,' I said. 'We have witnesses who saw him at Parliament when she left on that Monday night. Nobody chased her. She stopped at the tourist spots because she was in no danger. That's until she got to the dungeon and you pulled her into the shadows. You waited for her, and you murdered her, Mary.'

She nearly dropped the gun in surprise.

'Me? Jo was my best mate. Why would I kill her?'

'I'm not sure. At a guess, I'd say it was like you said, some game you always played, perhaps rougher than what the others did, maybe more sexual, and then it got out of hand. Possibly the first blow was an accident, but then you smashed your friend into nothing. Did you know then you would let her have your identity? As Jo lay dead on the floor, did you realise Valance wouldn't be looking for you after that? Or was it all part of the plan, to kill her in such a way everyone would think it was you?'

She waved the gun in my face.

'You're as crazy as Dolores, Inspector.'

'And then you murdered Hathaway at the club. I bet if we check the Velveteen app on your phone, it will show you were there that night.' I wasn't sure who was the more surprised at my words, her or Jack. 'Did he discover you'd killed Jo? Perhaps you bragged about it to him. Or maybe he was just sick of you, or scared of you, and he threatened to tell the world you were alive. Or at least tell Ruby Vasquez for a price.' I glanced across the room and saw the kitchen door open. 'Is the murder weapon here? If we go back to Hathaway's body, how much of your DNA will we find on it? Maybe there are bits of you on those hands you dropped into Ruby's bag.'

'You've no proof of this.'

Jack took one step forward.

'You're wrong, kid. Now we know you're alive and we know what to look for, I'd guess we'll find your DNA all over both bodies.'

'Especially on the tape we found under Jo's fingernails.'

'Tape?'

Her arm wobbled; Jack moved, and so did I. My hand touched hers as she fired the gun. The bullet missed Jack by inches and flew into a copy of the *Venus de Milo* beside him; it shattered, with body parts flying everywhere. I bent Mary's fingers to the side. She dropped the weapon and screamed. I pinned her to the floor, and Jack cuffed Mary's hands behind her back. She seethed as he kept her there, and I called the station.

Scene of Crime Officers and a Forensic team were picking the place apart within thirty minutes. Mary Witney was read her rights and taken away, spewing a mouthful of obscenities all the way.

'She's lost that calm demeanour she had on those tapes,' Jack said.

'That's the greatest irony. Mary made those recordings to expose Valance, but if she hadn't, we probably never would have found her.'

Athena Temple strode into the apartment wearing a tracksuit top and bottom. Jack scratched his chin.

'Were you jogging?'

'Don't tell anyone, but I'm not here in an official capacity. I only live around the corner, and when I heard you'd brought someone back from the dead, I had to come. It's not every day you get to meet Lazarus, especially when they're a teenage girl.'

'Did you see her?'

'I did as they took her out. She didn't appear happy to be born again.'

'Do you remember the tape you found under the fingernails of the first victim?' She nodded. 'When you check Mary's DNA, I bet you'll find it matches that on the tape.' I watched the officers work through the room. 'If we get lucky, we might discover the knife that killed Daniel Hathaway in this flat.'

We left our colleagues to do their jobs.

'When did you suspect Mary was still alive?' Jack said as we got outside.

'Dolores convinced me, only I didn't realise it at the time. When you and Abbey were in the garage for the guitar lesson, I thought about what she mentioned about losing her first child, Grace. Her words echoed in my head, the image of her face fixed in my brain. I understood she had told the truth then. And she had the same look when she said Mary visited her yesterday. Once I believed she was alive, I only had to work out where she was.'

'You said if Mary hadn't made those tapes, we probably wouldn't have found her, and I agree with you, but if she didn't see Dolores in the hospital, you never would have been on to her. So, when she had the perfect alibi of being presumed dead, why did Mary visit her mother?'

We reached the car and got in.

'Perhaps Mary had one last thing to prove to Dolores. To show she'd lived through the ultimate experience.' I put my seatbelt on. 'Or maybe it was simpler than that.'

'How?'

'Never underestimate the connection between a mother and her daughter.'

I dropped him off at his flat and went home. Abbey was singing along to PJ Harvey on YouTube when I got there.

'I've got great news, Mum.'

'What's that, love.'

'We've got our second gig this Saturday.' She bounced up and down like it was Christmas and her birthday rolled into one. I took out my mobile.

'I've got good news for you, Abs.'

She stopped jumping. 'What?'

'I know just the journalist to come along and give you a glowing review.'

The only thing brighter than Abbey's smile in the room was the light flashing on the answering machine for the phone.

THANK YOU!

Thank you, dear reader for purchasing this book.

If you enjoyed reading about Inspector Jen Flowers her story continues in these books:

The Detective Jen Flowers series
Book one: The Hashtag Killer
Book two: Serial Killer
Book three: Night Killer
Book four: The Killer Inside Them

Bette Davis Eyes: Detective Flowers Short Story

Many thanks to my wonderful wife for all her support and patience.

Night Killer edited by Alison Jack.

Extra special thanks to Karina Gallagher for being a dedicated reader of my work.

Cover design by James, GoOnWrite.com

ABOUT THE AUTHOR

Andrew French lives amongst faded seaside glamour on the North East coast of England. He likes gin and cats but not together, new music and old movies, curry and ice cream. Slow bike rides and long walks to the pub are his usual exercise, as well as flicking through the pages of good books and the memoirs of bad people.

Find out more at www.andrewsfrench.com

Facebook:

https://www.facebook.com/A-S-French-Author-150145625006018

Twitter:

www.twitter.com/andrewfrench100

Instagram:

www.instagram.com/andrewfrench100

And replies to all his email at mail@andrewsfrench.com

If you have the time, please leave a review at Amazon or Goodreads

Thank you!